1

CW00501471

Nellies Lodge

Nev White

Nellies Lodge

No part of this book may be reproduced stored in a retrieval system or transmitted by any means .without the written permission of the author

ISBN 9798647725257

This a work of fact/fiction names characters places and incidences either are the product of the authors `s imagination or are used fictitiously and any resemblance to any actual persons living or dead .events or locals s are entirely coincidently.

Print information on the back page.

Because of the dynamic nature of the Internet any web addresses or links contained in this book may have changed since publication and may no longer be valid.

.The views expressed in this work are solely those of the author and does not necessarily reflect the views of the publisher and the publisher hereby disclaims any responsibility for them.

Other books in the granddad series by the author Nev White

Paint me a picture granddad   Tell me a story granddad, Make, me laugh granddad,   Will of Austun, Oosterbeek, My boy Blink, Begg Steel and Burrow, More than a Vignette, The Will, Blame , Laura Verona, Adventures of Wee Willie Douglas, Mary Keyes of Leeuwarden All available at Amazon in Kindle and soft cover Neville White books   (Amazon)

Acknowledgement

Preface

Chapters

Chapter 1 Bathtub and Black Water --------------------11

Chapter 2 I Had Grandparents Too --------------------19

Chapter 3 Mr Davis What Is It ?---------------------------28

Chapter 4 Finding Ernest ---------------------------------35

Chapter 5 Riots and Unrest --------------------------------42

Chapter 6 Thugs of Security ------------------------------55

Chapter 7 Trespassers Will Be Prosecuted ------------62

Chapter 8 Cider at Christmas -----------------------------71

Chapter 9   Goodbye Mom --------------------------------78

Chapter10 Crime and Punishment ----------------------86

Chapter11 It`s Christmas -----------------------------------93

Chapter12 A Cold and Bruising Winter --------------101

Chapter13 Your Ways Don`t Work ------------------ 108

Chapter14 It`s Spring Again ------------------------- --115

Chapter15 The Journey Men ----------------------------122

Chapter16   Going Away ----------------------------------128

Chapter17 It`s Help Rather Than Hinderance -------135

Chapter18 Leave the Law to Others ------------------ 144

Chapter19 Hang Them High-----------------------------151

Chapter20 A Decade of Prosperity ---------------------159

Chapter21 There`s Always Price to Pay --------------165

Chapter22 Nelly Focus More on Us -------------------172

Chapter23 Sir I Was Hungry ----------------------------179

Chapter24 Magistrates to be Judged ----------------- 186

Chapter25 You Will Comply --------------------------- -194

Chapter26 Work Shops and Shop Workers -------- 203

Chapter27 This no Place for a Soldier-----------------210

Chapter 28 Soldiers of Fortune---------------------- -218

Chapter 29 Geoffrey Was to Young-------------------224

Chapter30 The Trial -------------------------------------232

Chapter 31 Why Should I Think That -----------------239

Chapter 32 You Put Years on Me ---------------------249

Chapter 33 A Changing Society --------------------- 254

Chapter 34 We Are at War ----------------------------261

Chapter 35 Farewell Cheerio and Goodluck -------269

Chapter 36 Letter for Nelly ---------------------------276

Chapter 37 The War In testifies ----------------------283

Chapter 38 My Broken Heart ----------------------- -290

Chapter 39 End of Hostilities ------------------------297

Chapter 40 I Never Refuse Help---------------------303

Chapter 41 Bluebell Violets and Lilacs -----------312

Chapter 42 Any Question---------------------------319

Chapter 43 Storm Clouds are Gathering --------325

Chapter 44 A Show of Unity ----------------------333

Chapter 45 A Miner Problem---------------------340

Chapter 46 Believe it or Not-------------------- -344

Chapter 47 Sheffield is Burning -----------------351

Chapter 48 Nelly you Worry Me-----------------356

Chapter 49 No Longer a Minor Problem--------362

Chapter 50 What it Means to Me---------------369

Chapter 51 My God I Have Tried----------------376

Chapter 52 In Time of War--------------------- 382

Acknowledgements

I am forever grateful to old friends I meet who constantly remind me of our young adventures stories that have contributed to our memories of Nellies Lodge that was a real place on an estate at the edge of coal fields of South Yorkshire that are too have long gone.

It is noticeable during sale of the estate only Nellies Lodge was demolished, and rubble removed as against other cottages that were sold off and refurbished by the purchasers.

For those who don`t know in passing the site to were Nellies lodge stood are reminded It was Nellies Lodge a lady always dressed in a grey selling her wares and telling fascinating stories of what was.

Today many believe and acknowledge the ghost of Nelly the grey lady that finds its presence in the area of her past abode and the church she frequented ,the stories so fascinating that other areas having a similar church seem to claim they too have the ghost of the grey lady but there was only one Nelly Lodge.

Preface

This is a story of fact/fiction of memories of an old lady and the stories she would tell from her cottage garden as many would ponder and listen in passing on their way to church.

It is with these memories of old Nelly old Nelly Lodge who was 94 when I was 7 or 8 years old that was in 1942 ,her husband Albert Lodge a craftsman a self - taught carpenter furniture maker tool maker and stonemason as he maintained the estate walls and houses at strategic areas that stood at the perimeter of the large estate.

Nellies cottage was like a keep house that gave access to the estate with long winding stone cart tracks to the heart of the village and to the church that was built in 1180.

The old stone house that her and her husband Albert lived in appeared old as the church and like many others that were built around the estate.

Nelly Lodge would sit in her flowered garden dressed all in grey and from her rocking chair would love to sell her wares and tell passers bye her memoires until her surroundings became industrialised .

She would shed a tear in knowing how the landscape has altered and so diminished from beautiful panoramic views of wonderful field`s forestry and wild- life and of seasonal fruit and nuts.

Her heartbreak of losing 3 sons in the great war and the loss of her beautiful environment prompts her to vow that she would never leave her abode but if she does someday, she will return if only in spirit.

This is a story told by Nelly of her life and memories, her cottage has long gone but her memories live on for at the area in passing people say ``This place was and still is known has Nellies Lodge and haunted so, mind what you say and how you go, and beware of the grey lady the ghost of Nelly Lodge.

Chapter 1

Bathtub and Black water

As I would play in the garden waiting for Dad coming home from the local coal mine looking all black and dirty with a pit helmet on and a water bottle and, snap tin strapped to his belt in the years of 1941 -3 .

With Mom standing at the garden gate like a good many wives waiting to greet their menfolk with many wearing clean aprons as if there was a competition of which looks best but relieved to see their husbands home and safe as there were many pit accidents as the work was dangerous but necessary during a time of world war.

Frank you ask and know many things but for me I remember Dad who would bath in a tin tub and Mom would scrub his back in front of a good fire, afterwards when a thick black jelly like tub of water had been washed down the drain and Dad refreshed he would walk me along a short distance to the estate that was free to walk through along the lime stone paths and woodlands of trees of many species and wild life in abundance all complementing to the beauty of the small farming village and the church that was built in 1180 and still stands and frequented today.

Approaching the estate from the north side entrance Frank you may remember of two stone pillars that would at one time hang a gate and there stood Nellies cottage of lime stone with its grey smoke bellowing out from a high chimney that blanketed the area with a sweet smell of burning pine wood.

In early spring the garden to the lodge ,Nellies Lodge would be daffodils that would follow on from the carpet of snowdrops and an odd early tulip showing and contributing to the colourful cottage garden, with many rose bushes budding and preparing for a new colourful life .

Albert , Nellies husband would appear and acknowledge passes bye with his clay pipe ejecting smoke that almost equal to that of the cottage chimney, there was a war on, but Albert always had a smoke, it was much later when people learnt that he smoked herbs and dried vegetation gathered from various parts of the estate .

Albert and Nelly were well in their 90`s and seemed to have adopted well to much shortage of food and materials that the world war was creating.

Nelly in her grey dress and apron and laced up black boots as if her mother had handed them down through the early Victorian era would be seen hanging rabbits on her washing line no more than four at a time and skins of others hanging further on all treated to hurry along the drying process of the skins and a sample of their end product could be seen by Albert wearing a hat of rabbit fur .

One time it was fashion for woman to wear a fox fur around their necks but the fashion moved on but rabbit fur was always in demand as many things were in a time of a world war ,but at Nellies Lodge it was if you want something than place your order for all seasons of the year plenty could be found from flowers to fruit from vegetables to meat as we today get excited for a barbeque in the hight of summer but it was a regular thing all year round to eat outside not in festivities but in situations one found themselves in ,with fruit nuts fungi`s and vegetables growing in abundance throughout the year on the estate.

It is at Nellies Lodge that people would either hurry on or stop for a chat with Nelly as she would on a nice day sit in her rocking chair at her cottage entrance and acknowledge passers-by who would more often than not admire her hand made objects and of course her seasonal produce as she displayed on two long self-made tables much more than what she and her husband Albert could grow or produce but no one would ask questions to where they were obtained in a time of need .

Eggs from many hens running loose in and around the cottage 2 or 3 pigs penned ,and pigeon`s in a loft or coop but the attractive and most interesting to see was the pheasants in their beautiful attire of feathers of plenty as the land around the lodge was filled with a pleasant atmosphere of life and an abundance of social interaction to all who walked on by.

Frank I was only young don`t know if I was old enough for school when Dad would walk me through the estate until I was old enough to go with friend`s mates and pals and this is a time when I could take all in what Nelly would say about her long sometimes troubled life, and that of what her parents told her when she too was young around about 1858-60 and old enough to understand.

For me Frank I do remember Dad and my walks with him at an exceedingly early age.

During this period Dad would hold my hand until the Italian war prisoners passed who were being taken to an exercise area in the estate or further on to a hall occupied by the army ,there was no trouble it was as if they were pleased for not being engaged in combat as they seemed to be a happy lot, sometimes woman would offer them bits of comfort as the convoy would halt periodically while many locals would say if any damage be done by enemy bombers the Italian prisoners are here to clear the mess up for the coal fields had to keep production going to assist the war effort.

Many things were said about the Italians , but they never knew where they were as there was no sign posts or any indication where they were no lights a few sky search lights at night and air raid wardens on the ground with the home guard making their presence felt.

Frank it was mainly at weekends during light hours, when people would go for short walks like me with Dad or church goers who would be greeted by Nelly at entrance to the estate it is here Frank the story unfolds for those with time to spend would be seated down in her garden to be taken back in time as she recalls her times of troubles and woe from the time her parents and grandparents bestowed upon her ,so Frank listen up as, her cottage should have been accredited with being a listed building as it was built many centuries ago but sadly no records exist only the place that was, and the ghost of Nelly.

Now I am going into more rhetoric of what Nelly did and said as she greeted many into her life story this is the life of Nelly ,Nelly Lodge a grand old lady and Frank she told me many things about the church many things I never knew like the old walnut tree with stone steps standing at the foot of the tree for lord and master to give judgement to wrong doers on a Sunday and there were plenty as they would hand down harsh penalties to them then lord and master would enter the church and pray to God.

Punishment was cruel and harsh as many would live in the forests and have no abode and gang up to protect one another for the law was what lord and master devised and implemented ,the common people had no say and because it was the masters who provided necessary funds for buildings and of the church that's why many times the clergy would not interfere with masters ruling from the enclosure acts and of the terrible introduction of the corn laws in a time of the feudal system that many still found themselves entrapped in.

Frank for what she told me many years ago before she was placed into Gods custody I recorded it from the time she listened to her Grandparents ,stories from latter quarter of 19th century when there was no coal fields but many crofts and carr`s a word hardly used today meaning a swampy area or low land subject to flooding but in abundance of wild life and the willows that grew there provided much pleasure to the making of furniture and walking sticks the willow skin was good for belts straps and ties and further on was the river with trout aplenty .

Nelly cried a little when she mentioned the wonderful views she had from the high ground of her cottage, wonderful scenes of fields and crofts with narrow cart tracks and horse drawn carriages and carts being driven through the massive rows of beech trees that created avenues of beauty ,she would say her ancestors created the beauty whilst the present destroy it.

They had no running water electricity or gas and would try and avoid the fire going out in fear of not securing a light off someone else`s fire let alone never knowing what time it was for if it was light outside you went to work if it was dark you went to sleep.

Work was plenty but harsh and laborious with the whole estate standing on a limestone bed as the estate has 4 quarries and a small pond (1 quarry filled in with house hold rubbish) that was created when building the estate and a few miles away is the North road and nearer is the York road that travellers would call and refresh and rest up as they do today.

Frank, she took my hand and said,`` now you listen good for I am telling you the way it was, and I will never leave this place ``Frank she frightened me to say `if not in person it will be in spirit` I laughed as she lifted a crucifix from her apron pocket kissed it smiled and said come around tomorrow as I will tell you how it was.

Surely, you don`t believe all she told you.

Frank I had no reason to disbelieve her, like you at your age you tell me many things of when we were young knowing it to be true yet many disbelieve you as you have no proof only word of mouth ,Frank the older we get the less we are appreciated in word and deed as we only have memories ,so don`t be offended if they doubt you for if you know it to be the truth that's all that matters .

Frank you laugh when I mention Nellies ghost.

Nelly the grey lady?

Yes, you may laugh but when last did you go to the church or visit the site of Nellies Lodge? You expect to be believed when you dwell on the past to the younger generations .

Well, I have her life story from the time she was born in 1855 as told by her and why was the lodge demolished when other buildings on the estate remained ? The lodge was as old as the estate itself and probably older than the church.

Frank it all started one Sunday I was about 8 when I was near the lodge when a massive thunder storm broke out, I rushed for shelter under the great beech trees Nellie saw me and beckoned me inside the cottage and reminded me not to shelter under trees in fear of being struck by lightning.

Inside the cottage was nothing like the outside that of hen`s geese a couple of sheep and pig`s in a sty and rabbits in abundance you name it and Nelly had it but inside it was a most comforting abode one could visualise of woven tapestries wool rugs home -made furniture from oak and beech and many small items made from willow and in a corner stood a loom that she said was very old and still in working order.

When the storm abated ,she gave me half a dozen eggs and said go now for mister meaning her husband Albert has a cold and has to go to bed and wishes not for me to catch it.

I hurried home and told Mom.

Do you know what Frank? Mom filled a bucket of coal and took it to Nelly she then stoked her fire up and got Nelly to help her to put her husband Albert to bed after rubbing goose fat on his chest and quoting he should see a doctor.

That was the beginning of a friendship and Nelly took to me as if I was one of her own for she told Mom that I reminded her of Geoffrey her youngest son who perished along with his other brothers in the great war.

As for Albert I never saw him again and Nelly never knew my name I think she never wanted to.

It was soon after that Nelly wished to tell me her life story ,me a lad of about 8 or 9 .

Chapter 2

I Had Grandparents Too

Nelly one of 7 children born in or around 1850 -52 or there abouts she said I only know what I am told and remember from people who loved idle gossip and rumours that my parents were shipped off to some other land so I am told but that`s not true as many enter into silly talk who could neither read or write I often had to remind them not believe such silly nonsense.

I remember Mom up to the time I was about in my teens who was a screamer for greater rights for women this must be around 1862 my Dad was already in prison for poaching and threatened to be shipped out to some foreign land by the lord and master who was also the magistrate and according to Dad that was not true as false accusations were many from the lord and master`s advisors or agents.

I remember there being a gathering on a Sunday near the walnut tree or the hanging tree as many called it ,we were made to watch some judgements being made I thought I saw Dad but was pushed down to the floor, Mom screamed and helped me up by then there was no more to see as people were dispersing Mom I asked where is Dad ?

Nelly, she said ,``he has gone ``

I cried and cried ,disappointments were regular ,and pain and suffering became a normal thing every day of the week ,Mom ,I asked how are we going to manage?

Will we have to leave the cottage? No Nelly it` s your Grandparents who own the cottage and we live with them and as long as they do not annoy the lord and masters, we will be alright. for what they say punishment has be served and that ends the matter.

Mom is dad dead ? Nelly he has to go away a while, but he will be back when I don't know I, learnt later Dad was supposed to be transported away from England many argued that the practice had been stopped and rumours were plentiful but there was a growing influence of women organising a league to defend and promote a greater say in social and domestic matters and a right to vote but for Dad I remember when he appeared in the door -way holding two rabbits and a rifle, he looked like a stranger not the Dad I knew because of his thick long black beard and attire of self-made clothes . he loved me and said look after your Mom then had lengthy discussions with my bothers only to disappear again.

Doris my older sister went into nursing at the age of 17 but was never seen again word arrived to say she had died in fever somewhere in India and another sister Sally went off with some textile merchant and Harold died in flu my remaining brother` s all 3 of them having three year between them and much like Dad adventures and of a roguish nature and standing for no nonsense as I was pleased to know that Dad was not far away but were, that was kept from me as I was reminded not to tell or speak of him to anyone.

Mom would say Nelly come take my hand and off we would go across the fields of many daisies buttercups and cowslips to a spot to were mushrooms grow and next to no time we had a basket full and had them sold before we got home I carried the herbs Mom called them herbs it seemed a collection of many odd types of plants and weeds that gave treatment to various types of illnesses.

My schooling I had none, there was only fee paying schools designed for the rich so I was dyslexic like a good many more, but were I and many more lacked in education we excelled in intelligence as I argued education is not intelligence and far from it.

By now Mom secured a job on the estate has the milk women or maid milking the cows I don`t know where all the milk went but some of it contributed well to our resources and later Mom secured her own cow and kept a good distance from the lords and masters sometimes someone would call at weekends to check on the standard of our living and if found fault would try and fine Mom a few pence on her rent but Granddad would interject I don`t know what was said but Granddad and my brothers eye balled the collector until he had thoughts of wanting his underwear changing and would waiver any inspection.

Granddad would roar in laughter and say he doesn`t know his rounds or who is who on the estate and when he doe`s he will wish he never had taken the job for his predecessor was found hanged at Creepy Hollow it was recorded as suicide with many agreeing with a wry smile and wholeheartedly agreeing , but what he was looking for is anything suspicious to report back to his lordship, as Grandad would say we all know their game and it`s keep clear of them and tell them nothing.

Granddad I would say can I help you today ? He would look at me as he worked with timber in a somewhat small sawmill as carts of timber beech and oak were brought to him his tools he used I failed to understand but he was always gainfully employed with arms of much thickness and muscles admired by many standing 6 foot 2 with a gravel voice that many who would approach him would show respect even the lords and master`s appreciated him but that was not mutual for he would spit, into his pile of saw dust and saw ``yea someday`` I never knew what he meant but his feelings of the lords and master`s was not pleasant to listen to, I learnt the local language fast of words I now know to be crude and un social able but acceptable as normal at the time.

When horse shafts required repairing or making, along with many more wooden implements It was always the lords and masters that came to Granddad with fussy demands to meet the sale of such things to sell to their neighbouring friends ,Granddad was not a wheelwright or a blacksmith he was an artisan of providing the necessary needs of the day in wood and where would we be without wood Granddad would often say.

Nelly he said,`` you learn fast it shows and you will benefit from it when you grow up`` I laughed as I carved small objects from offcuts of timber and soon progressed to making smoking pipes hand rails cloth hangers animal snares and traps and children`s toy s for Christmas, there was little waste even the saw dust I sold for a few pence unbeknown to Granddad .

One day he reprimanded me when he learnt of my little enterprise but congratulated me on my initiative and financial drive ,the lords and masters were never the wiser ,so much for their education as they could speak well and use words I had never heard before and failed to understand so I argued what` s the point of learning a language if one fails to understand whilst we the common people have our own language and we were many but not allowed to muster together in holding meetings or show any dissent that prompted us to promote further additions to the local accepted vocabulary.

Granddad instructed me to burn off any waist wood from his small mill ,I did and created much charcoal that I used for drawing and marking and depicting various signs that became acknowledged to the villages of what we were meaning to say in signs ,it was another innervation to my cottage industry ,I was becoming known at an early age, the word of Nelly was becoming well known and the lords and master`s where anxious to know more of my cottage industry.

My brothers 3 of them were always close bye and would maintain contact to those who lived in the forests and had no regular abode and on the main highway to York that saw many travellers my brothers would give escort or sell to many eager travellers wishing to purchase and refresh in water and bread that was always in demand as they marshalled their area of profitable sales and if anyone would trespass upon their pitch they would feel their wrath, how at times they managed it I often wondered for I thought they were employed on the estate to lord and master.

My thoughts often wondered to think Dad was nearby and hiding in the forests for we seemed not to want for much not like a good many who suffered terribly from harsh rules from their employers ,unrest was becoming widespread and people were uprising against officialdom ,my brothers too who seemed to be in constant trouble and under threat of being flogged and ousted from the estate but Mom was having none of that of lords and masters dictating their self-made laws that she had not contributed to, she would scream, their laws not our laws or state laws but laws made by them to suit them as there was no such thing as civil law common law criminal law or statue law it was one law their law so obey it or suffer.

My Granddad was the orator of many grumbles and complaints that all seemed to go unanswered as the gentry would be in church on Sundays thanking their God for allowing them to flog and punish any farm hands as if it was their right but Granddad feared none of them as he would take his horse and trap amongst the villages at weekends and preach the gospel as he was a firm believer in the Methodist movement now growing in strength amongst the farming communities

We that is Mom and my 3 brothers were living in fear of being made homeless by Granddad and his preaching and believes ,for he was much against the poverty and mistreatment of many. The lords and master`s saw Granddad were becoming known as the voice of the people and argued for change as many liked to hear ,but Mom was worried sick and fear we will become homeless .

Granddad was hailed in front of lord and master and his son, a somewhat dominant and bullish character with a bravado streak of a self -confidence when he has done nothing to warrant his position, I was waiting outside of the room and could hear everything being said .

Sir Davis wanted to know why Granddad was a Methodist and not a member of the local church and why he preaches from a horse and trap and have no church of his own and reminded Granddad that congregating amongst many is unlawful let alone inciting people to break the law.

Granddad paused then raised his voice and said Mr Davis I worked for your father a fair and good man with people queuing up to work for him, he and I fitted the glass coloured windows in the church you frequent and something to marvel at ,we buried many and prayed over them in the church grounds because we had no vicar we gave shelter to those in need and gave work to many, your father wanted to open a hospital a few miles away and often on a Sunday afternoon ride around the estate enquiring about peoples welfare and judged people fairly in his position as a magistrate you sir are self-appointed and pass judgment on one`s appearance and of their dyslectic position more than judge their reasons .

Mister Davis Sir you have allowed your staff to mistreat your employees you have lost much respect of many and that is why many tasks on the estate have become neglected.

Ernest his bullish son shouted you lie and thieve off the estate, what is required is discipline harsh discipline that will make them wake up and put more effort into their work.

Granddad paused a long pause then said,`` boy you don`t know one end of a fork from the other you would do well to hold your tongue because much of this is of your doing`` you are in fear and frightened to ride through the estate on your own as you have robbed your father yes you ,and beaten younger children when out playing for you cannot stand anyone enjoying themselves ,so take heed and change your ways as you will be judged not only by God but by many who are employed by your father, and release the money you have been robbing off your father by selling farm produce to travellers to fuel your gambling.

Mister Davis Sir much of your troubles are looking you in your face as you are unaware of what your son Ernest here does behind your back .

No ,I don`t believe you ,and call me Sir he demanded,

Then Sir you fail to believe a man of God Granddad roared back ,and when I and your workforce have respect Mister Sir we will show it and the way I look to God is between him and me for my church is with me wherever I go and Mister Davis Sir change is coming fast ,and I would like to think you are ready for it for without a happy workforce you will struggle ,so hear me good and get amongst them and show them you care like your father did .

Now what is it you wish to talk to me about that you wish for me to resolve for there is a problem for you would have not sent for me ?

Father don`t listen to him screamed Ernest and kick him out and out of his house, send him packing

Ernest Granddad said, he cannot and would not if he could, ``would you Mister Davis?``

Sir I have tried to inform you of the feelings of your labour force and would like to help you but whilst you allow your son to interfere, I shudder to think of what the outcome will be ,``good day Sir``

Chapter 3

Mr Davis Sir, What Is It

That following morning there was a loud knock at the door as Mom had gone to milk and Granddad was preparing to go to his workshop ,answer the door Nelly he demanded, and there stood Sir Mr Davis, Granddad I shouted it`s his lordship ,Granddad appearance was of anxiety knowing something to be wrong ,what is it Sir he growled?

We are looking for Ernest as two of his escorts dressed forward and entered the cottage Granddad held his thick walking stick ready for any trouble as he confronted the two escorts to say ``I have not invited you in so stay were you are, Nelly he said bring Sir a chair, Will ,have you seen Ernest for he has not been seen all night through?

Sir you call me Will and that is first time you have done so, your father called me Will but you although I taught you to hunt and guided you well and learning of the land and the wild life and saw to your safety you never called me Will as you got into a habit of saying ``ha you`` when wanting to talk to someone until you got a smack across your face off your father.

Will no lessons now for we can`t find Ernest , well what`s these two guys doing with you they should be looking for him, Will we have searched many places and failed to find him and feel there is a lack of concern ,Mr Davis we go and talk to people and seek for him , thank you Will I knew you would help ,right then tell these two here to mount up and ride the estate and look for him and get others to help and not to bully the crofters as we go and call upon them.

But, Sir would you be prepared to enter the forests or go down Abbes Walk towards St Helens church and talk to whoever is there for I think you may learn more there than what you will from people around here ? Will its dangerous to ride out there, not with me Sir and if you believe that then, that is the place to go as I have no squabble with them ,and neither have you.

To get there we take a short cut through the forest, Will I can`t enter the forest its full of all types of characters ,Sir you should know for you put them there and many there are good people who were mistreated when seeking a living, for what would you do if you were them?

Will don`t talk to me like that and remember who I am, Sir when did you last ask for help from your subjects? Sir your subjects were and are constantly asking for help from you and get none, only condemnation of their station in life so why should they help you ? But they will if they can because they have the intelligence to know what pain one can suffer when in need.

These are people who lack education and are subjects to your mistreatment yet contributed well to your standard of life yet you when requiring help come running with escorts as if you are prepared to use force for I saw them armed so I suggest you alone follow me unarmed .

No never who do you think you are addressing ?

Sir I cannot help you with an attitude like you have ,you either accept my suggestions or seek help elsewhere .

I shall call my escort`s and have you flogged for your insolence, Sir if your escorts enter my abode you will be responsible for what may happen, ``dam you man`` ,you are encouraging me to threaten you with force Sir I am offering help but all you offer is physical force something that is in bred in you from your Mother`s side of family certainly not your fathers.

Sir send your escorts away with instructions not to use force in making enquiries meantime we ride to Abbes Walk across the fields to the church that was built before the one here and suffered during the time of the Catholic dominance.

Sir come if you have confidence in me, if not, I cannot help you.

Arriving at the fresh water well on Abbes Walk we were joined by 3 armed men that took offence to our dismounting for water ,one approached me to say you cannot have water less you pay us ,I said, we do not come to ague or fight we come to seek Ernest the master`s son`` can you help us``?

A small pistol was pointing at my head mister if you don`t ride on or pay I will shoot, I mounted to ride away when I heard a voice say drop your guns, Sir screamed to say its Jack ,It sure is and I heard you at home as I was in the back of the cottage and ran across the fields ahead of you in fear they may be trouble .Sir shouted behind you Jack as he turned and smashed his hand gun across the man`s head he dropped and cried in fear of having a bullet in his head then Jack my Dad turned to the other men and said who do you work for?

He then noticed a purse hanging from the man`s waist he slashed it off him with his knife opened it and found it contained many coins and suggested it to be from sales to travellers along the York road from the area he claimed it to be for locals only ,and you are not locals he snapped so I take all your monies and shoes as you get away from here before I take your life too, the men disappeared quickly across the fields towards York road and not seen again.

Sir looked surprised and shouted you supposed to be in New Zealand or prison anywhere but here Dad turned to Sir and said your rules and judgements that you inherited are no longer valid they are null and void, for there is change social and domestic change as people are drifting into towns and seeking industrial work and farm work is changing too for new methods in farming is threatening ones labour, Sir screamed you were adjudged guilty of stealing and hunting on the estate .

Sir, who says so? I was tried and judged by you by the word of mouth by some creeping idiot you employ whom is no longer with you to back up his evidence ,now I wonder what happened to him ? Furthermore Sir you penalised my wife as she was put in the so called work house or some place to serve time of her punishment so Sir I suggest you go and bring her back and compensate her for time lost from her family and if it was not for my father here what would have happened to my children? And now you call upon men of the forest to help you Sir you can go to hell for around here was a Catholic presence in the 16th century where many was put to death either by hangings or burning to promote the English churches and you are very much in a dangerous area.

Sir the common people are crying out for change and you live in fear of it, well you better get used to it as you will be thinking of raising your men to succumbed the threat, Sir I strongly advise you not to do such a thing .It`s Jack ah I remember you ,yes Sir Davis that`s good to know as you will be seeing much more of me.

Will your son Jack seems confident in himself ,Sir I`m old and care less what you think but can tell you all the searchers you have employed are wasting their time, and if we encounter any mistreatment amongst people and your workforce then you could have a war on your hands so I suggest you quickly think about organising a panel or body to discuss grievances amongst the work force.

Where is my Son? Sir where is my Wife? When my wife is returned maybe we can help you ,now I only need to whistle and you could be surrounded with men who could not give a dam about you or your son and if you get the soldiers out to hunt them down you carry the responsibility for it is not force that is required it is dialogue now I will let my father talk to you .

Mr Davis Sir I am old and seen plenty and could have warned you but you do not listen like your father, who contributed well to the growth and prosperity of the estate I have withheld many things from you not as if I had a duty to tell you but lacked confidence in telling you for your ears are full of your sons misguided stories.

Then Jack can ride with me and bring his wife home ? No Sir I will not for she has been home for some time and if you took more notice of what happens in the estate you would know she has been milking your cows for several weeks, I went personally to bring her home from that hell hole she was in ,I had to pay 2 pounds and half a crown for her freedom Sir you owe me that although it appears there is much coinage in this purse ,further more Sir I suggest you pay my father better for what you get in selling his work to dealers for I know what you get so pay father more or he comes up here to work alongside the blacksmith.

How dare you blackmail me? How dare you Sir demand, Sir you`ve robbed us for years and we are not blackmailing you we are negotiating a fairer deal now come and follow us into the village here and learn to bury a long feud you have had with the Catholics as we locate your son.

Jack your father could have told me all what you have said ,your father indeed you address me not quote me I am his father and my name is Will and you know it and my father and his father go back many years hundreds of years to this estate that they helped to create and because of their contribution the cottage I have was given to us for services rendered and who do you think built the walls and road ways?

You go to church with your eyes shut look around inside and you will see much work done by my ancestors who were stone masons and built the very house you live in ,it was through wars that many of my ancestors perished almost wiped out our families, in creating this estate helped to restore our families again ,and from there we progressed yet right to present time Sir you are in fear of change from crofters and those in the carr as they are seeking a more suitable life.

Sir I am an old man and have said what is to be said now we seek your son as I have protected mine and united him with his wife who is unwell from the sufferings received from the hell hole you prescribed and you want my help knowing I am a person to turn to as I am a man of God, you would do well to look to yours for a guidance as he will judge you the same as anyone else, not matter what you think.

Chapter 4

The Finding of Ernest

Will, you seem to know your way around here, Sir I have many friends and my son Jack too who seems to think your son Ernest could be in that house over there gambling and with his girl -friend, Sir you are safe with us as I go and make enquiries .

Sir you ask for Ernest , wish I knew where he is for he owes me £25 and much more to others around here he left to go home and get more money with his girlfriend the fool for she was setting him up for she is married to Dilly Swanson a well- known thieve around here.

Sir I know you, sorry Sir I never noticed you, but your son was here many times and gambled heavily but left with Dilly and entered the forest for a short cut home about an hour ago ,

Thank you for your help, Sir we ride into the forest, but I warn you that we may meet many men to whom you think may be somewhere else, but no harm will come your way whilst you are with me ,Jack I hope you are right Sir I am as many eyes are now upon us ,and you call me Jack now you are in need .

Sir, stop right there, as my father and me will go into that area as I think there is something wrong here .

It`s Ernest hanging from a tree .

Sir, sorry we have found Ernest, Sir he is dead hanging from a tree come we we`ll show you.

There was much silence as Sir watched us cut him down, Sir said a prayer over him whilst we could see many forest dwellers creeping slowly forward in the undergrowth I signalled to Dad to be prepared as we raised our guns as two men appeared Jack, one shouted what the hell are you doing here with Sir Harry?

Now he knows our whereabouts ,men he came looking for his son and found him look here we want the person who is responsible for this ,Jack, Sir here is responsible for us being here and once sentenced me to death because I killed a deer and we are joined by many men who feel Sir should hang so drop your weapons.

You Will have set us up and have called the soldiers out? ,No he has not my father is here to help Sir Harry and negotiate for your return to the estate, Will he lies for as soon as we return we will be arrested and probably hang from the hanging tree near the church for time and time again they have violated the very principles of life of decent men and now many here are seeking vengeance.

Men you know me it is because of my Dad here who wishes through negotiation to try and improve your way of life and to achieve that we must have trust .

Jack the first opportunity he has he will hang us.

Sir what is it ? Jack let me speak, men I come here to seek my son and found him murdered and I seek who is responsible as you would do if that was your son ,roars of anger echoed through the forest as many shouted you killed my son and you broke up many homes as people here are seeking ways to survive so we hang you too ,then It was you who hanged my son ? No Dilly Swanson did that not us.

Yes , I killed your son and we are going to hang you too, then who are you? I am Dilly Swanson who has suffered from your judgement and flogged numerous times so vengeance is mine ,Jack drew his gun Dilly he said ,stay right there ,listen men if you seek vengeance here then the place will be surrounded with soldiers and you will be hunted down caught and hanged so what good would that do to your families that me and few more have been supporting in your absence ,here ask my 90 year old Dad and still rides a horse and many of you pray with him as he brings you food so think long and hard for your families sake .

You Dilly have committed murder and will be judged accordingly.

Like hell I will as he drew his gun and pointed it at Sir Harry, a shot rang out and Dilly dropped and died in much pain, jack walked over to him as he replaced his gun and said a short prayer over him, Dad you have killed him, Jack he would have killed Sir Harry Davis and many more if given the chance ,I looked at the gathering of men who were in need of care and attention as Dad said ``men you can come home now and all charges will be dropped``

Sir Davis do you guarantee the safety of these men in returning to their homes and taking up their employ again? Will you have my word Sir do you agree that they appoint a spoke person and a representative or councillor to join the team of magistrates.

Will, I can`t do that for they are required to be property owners and have some financial capital ,true so you provide property by giving permission for houses to be built and reward workers better wages for many are leaving you to join new industries that are speedily providing much work .

Will let me speak to them, Men come back home with me and return to your families and we will see what can be done ,Sir someone shouted ,we have a few scores to settle with some of your lap dogs so you will have to move them on for their own safety as there are many scores to settle .

Men listen to me ,I don`t wish to know that so don`t let me hear such things so get your things together and come home with me, Jack someone said we look to you to help us, Men I will serve you so come follow our horses and sing your way home so your kin folk will hear you but those who do not come home I cannot do anymore to help you .

Songs broke out and echoed across the meadows as people appeared from their cottages and women folk ran across the meadows to greet their love ones it was a day of happiness except for Sir Harry Davis who rode with his son across his horses back head bowed and in sorrow many noticed and quickly moved from an happiness occasion to a sorry full position and followed

Sir from behind his horse with heads bowed and all in silence.

At the cemetery next day prayers were said, and much respect shown as a hand carved cross was laid at the foot of the head stone that was hurriedly prepared from men who were stonemasons before seeking sanctuary in the forests .

Jack I am looking to you to help me to get this estate noticed again from a few years of neglect, Sir Harry you must show respects to your subjects for you cannot no longer stand in judgements over your employee`s you cannot device laws to suit yourself that the governments are responsible for, you cannot do the things that your forefathers did.

Sir we will cooperate with you to bring this estate back to a happy place as we see many acres of land being taken over for industry and we want to be part of the economic growth ,for now many lime stone paths that weave their way through the carr and crofts are being improved with tar and gravel ,and deforestation is being carried out at a speed that seems a shame to see our beautiful landscape disappearing, Sir I don`t like it but have to accept it as progress and not have any distorted thoughts as it is a necessary factor for growth and development.

Sir your estate is self -sufficient for all the rented cottages and land that provides capital as you have little expenditure now ,for everything you have has been secured financially many years ago as you now own everything apart from the church but do owned the burial site so I suggest you spend some money and improve your surroundings in relaying the road ways in and around people`s houses and spruce up the estate for you have lots to be proud of .

Sir you can if you wish sell off or rent off much of the land to be farmed by someone else and have less responsibility Jack I was thinking of an estate agent for someone to overlook the estate and take the responsibility off me .

Sir ,I know why, because you are planning to get married again.

Jack there is much to do here, and I want men who I can trust .

Sir you have many you cannot trust they have misguided you and robbed many crofters, and down at the carr there lies many stories of people disappearing not to be seen again and further on at the blacksmiths many stollen horses appear for shoeing now roads are becoming solidified and some of those horses are yours and at the butchers there appears sheep I recognise to be yours.

Sir many of your employ know that but not likely to help you when you gave them no help , you have people working for you who robbed you blind and put the onus onto others to take the blame so I suggest you ride with me to the crofters not in your present attire but in clothes suitable for everyday use and not in your carriage but on your horse do not appear aloof or we will not get any cooperation and whatever you do remember if you accuse anyone think first for we are not looking for trouble we are seeking evidence before we accuse .

Sir, many steal because they are in hunger as I want you to see for yourself the poverty some crofters are living in, we go not to accuse but to see what can be done and to reduce the thieving and then we find those who we think is cheating on you for Sir some of these thieves are in your employ for when did you last count your sheep in the fields close to the crofter`s dwellings?

Chapter 5

Riots and Unrest

Jack again you take me into a dangerous place Sir, the place is safe it`s the people who we wish to talk to and those can be dangerous as they are in need of help so do not show any form of aggression hide that whip and keep your gun hidden away Sir we ride this way as we have a view of all around us and over there I see a group of crofters .

I dismounted as a young boy came to hold the reigns of my horse I reached into my saddle bag and gave him a small loaf of bread he looked jubilant as his father approached me ``,what do you want he demanded`` I want a bundle of willow sticks any for sale? I know you its Jack so what brings you here ? I want some willow ,no Jack that`s not why you are here, you want more ,so what is it ?

This in Sir Harry Davis from the estate he is looking for a good shepherd to tend sheep by day and night ,and able to do some fencing off some land ,and how old is your boy here ? He will be 10 soon why ? Well, Sir here requires someone to keep the water buckets full ready for when needed as water arrives from the spring. So, ``are you interested?`

Jack, I know you and you want some information so, what is it ? I want you to tell me who has been thieving off the estate not apples and pears or nuts when in season but sheep hen`s eggs and most of all horses .

Why come to me for its not me? I know that ,Jack I cannot help you and to be a shepherd would be like committing suicide ,then you don`t want the job ? No Jack but the boy can help you out to be a water boy, fine but we ride on to make further enquiries as Sir Harry intend to put a stop to this thieving .

Jack, I want a job and so does many around here ,many are hungry and desperate and frightened to go to sleep in case of being robbed from little they do have, and many have nothing to rob from.

Market days at your place were great occasions people with happy faces and much to offer and barter with , but sadly those days are gone as many people have nothing to offer anymore.

People are packing up and going into the towns or other areas to seek work as many factories are offering security in wages and employment ,whereas here deforestation is becoming a concern for people here are being chased out to make way for development and many times without compensation .

Jack go with caution as there are many bad people around here so keep your gun at ready and Sir no harm will come your way not whilst you are with Jack and Sir do not look for names as that means nothing as people do not use their true names as they move on when things get a little too uncomfortable.

Many have stopped using the York road as you Jack recognise many who use that route they now go by the old North road ,Sir we here know many things but I cannot help you ,as you never helped us ,all the people get is punishment and that is not a cure to the many problems here ,is that it?`` Sir it is all I can offer.

Come Jack show me further into the croft for I intend to find out as my interest grows and they know who I am and as the magistrate I see many running for cover as they fear me ,Jack they should not perceive me as they do , Sir that is what you have created with your harsh penalties for I warned you but you failed to listen and now you have a self -made problem that requires addressing quickly.

Jack I am the magistrate and expect people to abide by the law ,Sir there you go again ,what law is that? For the law is designed to suit you and people like you not the crofters or anyone else these people cannot read or write and sometimes fail to understand in what you say ,Sir we go home now and come back tomorrow as they will now know of our presence and intentions.

No, I want things settling now not tomorrow, Sir don`t be a fool come we go home Sir, I know of these people do not aggravate them for some have only their lives to think about and for what it is worth they care little, Sir listen to me ,

Then why have you brought me here ?

Sir you now know where the troubles lay or are ,so let them sweat a little for in the house when I gave the boy some bread there were men peeping through the curtains I saw them so the crofter we talked to was shielding them and dare not say anything different to what he did say, but I have a hunch that his boy will come tonight to see his duties as a water carrier and because of that we may learn more ,so Sir this way if you please.

Jack you confuse me ,you are very much like your father Sir go home and I will see you tonight .

Later the boy came and said there are 3 men as leaders and hold their meetings in his Dads house and will be there tomorrow at midday and Dad asks for me to stay the night with you on the estate for safety as night falls quickly around here and thinks there could be trouble amongst the crofters, Dad fears there could fighting .Mister Jack will my Dad be alright ? I knelt down to him to say ``young man he is not your Dad he only pretended be ,so what does your mother want ?

`` Mister he told me to say that, yes I thought so, mister my Mom wants me to tell you about some men who are causing trouble`` Mister, they use that house you were at this morning to hide stolen goods and if any one refuses they will tell of them in holding illegal meetings and be thrown out of the house, one was a stonemason on this estate but they got him into trouble so he left ,is his name Peter? Yes, Sir then I know of him.

I informed Sir Harry Davis who mustered his men to bring to justice whoever is responsible for thieving off the estate Jack, he said I am going to hang then when we get them back here.as I pleaded not to go and let me sort it and find reasons why .

Morning broke as Sir had arranged for the constabulary policemen to assist him and myself but I refused to be part of it, eventually we were not required as the police went and arrested them but not without a fight 2 were shot dead 2 wounded in their legs and Peter was unhurt along with a few who surrendered , back at the estate Sir was jubilant to say they could all hang for I am holding court.

No sir you cannot do that you cannot prefer charges and sit in judgement, I can, and I will they stole two horses 2 sheep and God knows what else Sir it is not for God to know but the witnesses if any ,and proof in man-made laws, Jack you are too smart ,for if I do not sit in judgement I know who will and he will have them strung up if only to frighten others.

Sir they have not been tried and you are sentencing them before hearing their case and defence, Jack you are far too soft with people they must abide by the law and to hang to deter others from doing such things Nelly what is it?

Its Granddad I can`t wake him come quick we rushed home with many around his bed side it was too late he had gone aged 90 the oldest man for miles around, leaving the cottage and all his shackles to family.

The funeral was arranged for a church service with many there unbeknown to me who had travelled afar and mainly common people who packed the church and gave more condolences as many said he was our friend and saviour a man of the people and because of that we have erected a headstone well carved with masons fine tools depicting a tribute in words of such a good man to know.

Sir Davis said his piece and went his way whilst many came back to the cottage to join in the wake and update me with any regional changes and developments particularly that of the farming communities and still witnessing hardship in working the land but as they show their respect it was daughter Nelly doing the honours in passing and providing refreshment to our visitors for her mother was sick in fever from the time she was in confinement from the place she was sent too by Sir Harry Davis who claims it was other magistrates that voted her to be punished.

Nelly I had no proof to know any different as we had to accept the outcome as I paid for your Mothers release Nelly it is times like this that I dwell on and try to sort many things out .and now your mother is sick wife and you have Nelly and sons to care for but your troubles are little as you can look after yourselves.

It`s that young men are showing interest in Nelly as she is doing the job her mother was doing that of milking the cows Sir Davis is none the wiser and even today a villager is doing the milking for Nelly could not do it on a day like today and Sir Davis is none the wiser or interested in individuals who slave their time away all he is bothered about is physical and financial matters but not individual effort as he overlooks many things..

Two days had elapsed when I thought of calling on Dads workshop and to continue with plans with Sir Harry Davis to talk to the crofters again, and try and eliminate the thieving from the estate and see how the police have dealt with the troubles and when the trails will take place .

Sir good morning , have you secured a shepherd yet and how is the boy shaping up? No shepherd yet and the boy is fine as for those thieves they are in prison awaiting sentence along with some of the others, then you have had them in court? No, there was no need for that ,as 3 were hanged who were insolent.

``You`ve done what?`` Sir you blabbering fool ,you have committed murder these were not the thieves of your cattle Sir it was only a short while ago we buried your son as the villages rallied around you in support of your loss ,I take you into the crofters and you became disillusioned with what you saw. Sir those men in the crofter`s house were men holding a meeting to formulate a policy in and how they could promote their places of work they call it ``a union meeting`` illegal but soon to be recognised.

Sir they were discussing how and means they could improve all around them and protect their employ and promote growth so what was said at their trail ? No trail well there was a short one just to pass sentence.

Sir I pity you for what you have done as their will be much unsocial and domestic unrest.

Jack I have had enough of you defending these idle uncouth rabble and any more of your defiance of my actions I shall have you flogged and I have men here who will do it when they come back from the crofters

.Sir, they were not stealing your live -stock ,but were holding an illegal meeting.

Sir you have hanged the wrong men.

What are your men doing with the crofters ? None of your dam business ,then I shall ride and find out, no you will not ,and I shall have your gun ,for you are under arrest for aiding the crofters in organising unlawful meetings and gatherings with intent to cause unrest.

Sir, who is going to stop me? 2 men appeared with guns at ready, men take him and put him in the cell we will deal with him when the others are brought in.

Jack I am not a blabbering fool, as I intend to have respect and civil order.

Then Sir I suggest you earn it as you roundup your cattle particularly the sheep that was seen hoofing it down York Road and if or when you retrieve them if you do how do you know they are yours as you can be or your men can be accused of rustling cattle and arrested.

Sir do to me as you feel but the populist are in revolt and whilst your cows stand un-milked your livestock scattered all over the place whilst your horses have gone for a run without riders and your barns are under threat of being fired.

I thought as I was thrown into an old prison room that, Sir is sick with his power that is quickly demising as he dislikes change no more than some of his workforce and is annoyed that the cottage we own and area adjacent to it was given to the ancestors of the family soon after the Church was built in 1180 , King Henry of England and France marvelled at the project and for the stonemasons effort the King bestowed the property upon them with Prince Richard in attendance who became King Richard much before the Magna Charter was signed.

Now crofters are seeing change all around them and dislike it in having to move out and abandon some of their local habits and customs.

We own the small woodland opposite our cottage with its massive beech trees and space for leisure activities that we allow crofters to come up from their low land and hold markets days and festivities there to Sirs displeasure as there is nothing he can do about it only send his escorts in to try and cause unrest but their days are numbered .

My thought`s pained me has I held onto the jail bars whilst Sir and his men attempted to round up their scattered live - stock but I was quickly diverted from my thoughts as Nelly appeared at my cell door dangling the keys, we ran across the fields to the crofters who were in a riotous mood but welcomed us as friends and wished to know what to do.

I cannot entice you to riot but can help you with negotiations of a better social standing Mr you`re wasting our time as we march on Sir Harry to demand release of our men folk I looked hard at the women as Nelly whispered Dad they have not heard what Sir Harry has done for the they are not allowed on the estate.

What`s your name Dad asked Rose Hardwick ,then it is you who is demonstrating for more justice for women ,Jack we know your wife is unwell so we have sent someone from here to tend to her ,young Nelly here told us for you could not be found so Jack what is going on ?

Rose Hardwick you have changed Jack last time you saw me was about 5 years ago since then I have done many things Jack help these people here to get their men folk back.

Rose who is your husband? I have no husband I had one and glad to be rid he was a swine and was jailed somewhere down south but escaped and joined the merchant navy and the ship was sank off Bay of Biscay with no survivors, so I heard.

Tell me about Sid Smith one- time a hostler for Sir Harry Davis and others ,Rose he is dead hung yesterday by the authority along with Tom Oats and Nick Moon ,Nick Moon you say well he was only a boy my God what are things coming to?

Rose whatever you do be careful, for Sir Harry Davis will be hiring many men to check this area out and the people here.

Jack what do you expect us to do stand by whilst woman`s men folk are murdered ? I thought you would have done something for what he did to your wife ,Rose ,he claims it was not him, Jack he lies for I served time with your wife and escaped and probably still wanted under the name of Beth Bell .

Jack I`m going to kill that swine ,hold on , Rose be careful what you say in front of many ,Jack come inside and bring Nelly with you now here have some tea with me for I have some lovey lamb stew boiling.

Jack listen to me carefully there is plans afoot to kill Sir Harry Davis now I tell you this because you are one of us and respected around here and we know you are backing the fight for union recognition and the abolishment of many ant-social laws and for education to be state controlled and available for all children.

Rose all is true but we have a long way to go as liberalism is growing fast and fighting hard against the ruling classes who wish for only the educated to rule the masses and have one rule for them and one rule for the masses but the masses are beginning to learn and want more of the nation`s wealth and prepared to fight for it .

Rose things are changing except the severity of judgements as we ought to look at reasons why people break the law and its social effects and address that, Jack we know the reasons.

Jack, we have no say and look towards people like you to help us and Nelly I`ve seen young men looking at you, Rose I`m far too busy for boy friends with our workshops in wine making and health products from the herbs I gather not to mention gathering of seasonal fruit and fungi but could do with help now Mom is unwell.

Then Nelly my Alice can help you, and I have a boy who I take care of, he was left orphaned his dad worked on the estate but was murdered by poachers and his mom died in fever what`s his name? Albert Lodge he was only one year old when I took him in and told him about his parents about 6 months ago he said thank you but I will always look upon you has my Mom he can be water boy for Sir Davis.

Nelly ,can find Alice some work, Dad if you say so, but the boy ,what`s his name again ?Albert but answers to Al, Jack he`s a good boy and very clever, then we can find him work too but let him carry on as water boy for now ,how old is he? He is about same age as your Nelly and Alice is about a year older and Nelly she can ,operate a spinning wheel.

I know you have one and she can make items from rabbits fur like gloves and hats ,Rose bring her tomorrow with a few bundles of willow whips for replanting and a good bundle of cuttings as long as your leg, thank you Jack and you Nelly you`ll not be sorry.

Rose it's the present problem that I come here for ,Jack I know what to do and so do people around here, Rose be careful Sir Davis has armed men at his disposal and will not hesitate to fire upon you and the force of the law is behind him, well what would you do for something has to be done?

Rose the women around here look to you for leadership so I will talk to them if you can muster them together this time tomorrow and wish not for you to do anything until then , I have some ideas until then take care come Nelly we must get back before dark .

Chapter 6

Thugs of Security

Sir Davis are you looking for me for I have lodged a complaint about you for illegally holding me in captivity so expect some peeler`s (police) to come knocking.

Jack it was for your own good I did it to protect you, Sir it is not I who requires protection as I can ride freely amongst the people and so can Nelly here and what are these two men doing at the your door way ?

Sir are you if fear for your father never was because he was a lovely man a man of the people along with your Granddad ,so my father told me they were responsible for assisting the crofters to settle here.

Sir remove your lap dogs from my shoulder, unless you want a riot on your hands for if I fail to show myself within half an hour then the crofters will assume, I am in danger.

Don`t you come here threatening me, Sir I`m not threatening anyone I am here to clarify a few things one being did you send my wife to the home for wayward women and did you announce death sentence on those men that hanged a few days go ?

Also are you responsible for men like these standing beside me to go amongst the crofters and seek out any meetings being held to form trade unions or to form groups to show dissent as you have distributed many leaflets amongst the people which is waste of time as many can`t read and to that you condemn them to say it`s their fault.

Sir Davis if any of these men standing by my side insomuch as lay a finger on me than I am not responsible of what may happen, Sir you have no family no wife no children now Ernest has gone and for some unknown reason you are turning on the common people the very people who you rely on ,for these men standing by my side are of little use to you when it comes to farming so who is going to harvest the crops milk the cows and plough the land and feed the livestock and speak for you when you are accused of murder so, dismiss them as I wish to talk to you in private.

Don`t look at me as if I am armed for if I wanted to kill you I could have done it long ago ,now send these two here out or I go on my way and leave you to sort out your own mess for these here cannot do it .

Nelly go now and tell the crofters I am alright and that I will be along shortly , go on Jack I am listening ,first of all if you ever again turn against me I will not be responsible for what may happen from the crofters ,

Placing me under arrest and throwing me into some hellhole Sir you are a magistrate and do not have the powers to do such things years ago yes but not now ,you are not the law you are a person to sit in judgement not on your own premises but in courts designed for such purposes you are not the peeler`s (police) and neither are your lap dogs who commit crimes amongst the crofters and get away with it right under your very nose and you ignore it by that you as a magistrate are neglecting your position and encouraging crime and, who appointed you a magistrate ?

I will tell you it was your property and wealth and who built your house and who created your wealth ,for you were not considered on your education or intelligence for if you were you would never be a magistrate .

Now Sir ,you are to be questioned about these hangings and false arrest of others ,Sir you do not have the power of arrest or have the legal power to announce the death sentence Sir times are changing and you in authority must change ,unfortunately you have failed to, and now face charges of murder because you are ill advised from these hippos you have around you something your father never had for he never required it.

Sir you have committed murder your responsibilities do not allow you such powers and shortly the peelers (police) will be here to arrest you.

They cannot do that I am the law around here Sir stop it, for you are not the law you do not make the law you are part of it and subject to it like everyone else .

I have called upon you to tell you to expect to be arrested if that being so your work force will not support you and your estate will be neglected .

Jack you are threatening me ,no Sir I am warning you for some of your workforce have left and found temporally shelter in the forest again which is all right this time of year but come winter ,well we wait and see.

Well what can I do ? Now sir we talking, Sir I`ve lost a lot of time its neglecting my work in trying to bring harmony between you and the crofters and the crofters are not your responsibility and in just losing Dad and my wife is very sick I have plenty to do without all this hassle ,now what the hell are you playing at ?

Something is wrong and I intend to find out .

Jack I`m being blackmailed ,What, to commit murder? I didn`t do that it was Walt Higgins and Olly Cloud who out voted me in my recommendations ,and you are right I do not have the power, but Walt Higgins has the power over me in authority and financial standing ,Sir you glorified in telling me that they were hanged as you boasted about your station in life.

Jack, I had to for those men who were present here are eyes and ears for Walt Higgins and Olly Cloud and they are ruining me .and now trying to pin murder charges on me or pay up , No Sir if you are not responsible for murder it must be something else so what is it?

Come Sir you can trust me as I will think of something and these hippos here, try and avoid them, Sir keep them away from here with 2 very fat thugs hanging about here puts the whole place under threat ,I call them hippos for it seems appropriate, Sir I will be here after darkness so tell me everything then and what I want you to do now is create a scene here and throw me out for these hippos will then form a wrong impression and I`ll see you night .

Jack these are dangerous men and I wish not for you to be involved Sir I shall decide that after tonight now trust me for these last few weeks you have not been the man I know, right then here goes.

Get out of here or I shall have you flogged and if I see you again I`ll hang you now clear off as the two hippos burst in ok, ok, I shouted and I`m going as I mounted to ride home .

At home I told Nelly I want you to get another young person as well as Roses girl and find them work and sell your product`s at the cottage gate, you sort it out in what you pay them Dad don`t you think I`m a bit too young for that ? Nelly I was working at your age, don`t you want to do it ? Shall I get someone else? No Dad I will manage, but what about Granddads place? Nelly ,I have someone in mind.

Who my brothers ? Nelly, I have something different for them well Ben wants to a preacher a Methodist vicar, but we talk about that some other time.

Nelly, get the crofters to keep you well stocked in willow the best time to cut last year`s growth of willow is in early spring and autumn so during that period collect and stack it in bundles in a neat stack at the bottom or edge of the garden for when required and Nelly I`m giving you £3 to start with spend it wisely and always have some capital for wages and expenses.

What about Mom ? I have someone looking after her ,Nelly don`t let me down or bother me with problems and learn to sort things out yourself and if you find someone you can trust then treat them with respect . Thanks Dad.

Now you go to the crofters and find your team and take this message ? Tell Rose I am sorting thinks out and not to do anything yet ,but if Sir Harry`s men come calling do not be frightened to defend yourself but let no one see you.

At 8 tonight I want Rose and two more women of her choice to come to Sir Harry Davis house along with the men who have been holding meetings in organising a union, and tell her no harm will come their way tell her to trust me , Dad shall I go now ?

Nelly have you got a boy- friend down there for I saw you getting much attention Dad many know me because I helped Granddad to clean out that very large hut that's down there for his Methodist meeting`s so what will happen to that ? Nelly its yours for a church amongst the crofters Nelly you are popular so get them to help you, your brother Ben will be away a while studying and when he comes home, he will have a church .

Nelly you are popular and liked, so honour your Granddad and form your Methodist church as you are required to put method into what you do. No dad it will be Bens church no Nelly it will be the peoples church.

Dad what`s the meeting about tonight ?

Nelly there is trouble about and I am going to resolve it as crime and punishment requires addressing if people around here wish to live a decent life,

Dad people here look to you for help, why ?

Nelly it is a long story and someday I`ll tell you.

Chapter 7

Trespassers Will Be Prosecuted

Nelly your brothers Matt Wilf and Ben are thinking of going into farm management to a school at Cirencester in Gloucestershire the place where judge Jeffries hanged many farm workers for, well whatever, but along with their own funds I can manage tuition fees and accommodation but I want Sir Davis to contribute, Dad he is annoyed with you ,no Nelly he will soon be pleased with me.

Nelly get someone from the crofters to milk Sir Davises cows and get one to help you to do the sales pitch on York road full time, you use that hut that once was used for cattle shelter now get many hands to help you to position it at the fork of the roads across Abbes Walk for that field is mine as Fred the fruit man gave me when he emigrated well I gave him a penny for it, but if things don`t turn out right for him he can come back and find accommodation on the land we bought off him.

Nelly make it a trading post with stables but at this stage of development I suggest you do not leave any stock their overnight Dad, where are you getting the money from ?

`Hooray` you have the sense to know the value of money I am not funding you there except for providing the means Nelly you have much stock so get your friends to help you right here at home and at the junction off Abbes Walk .

Dad what are you going to do ? Nelly. I think ,no I believe Sir Davis will want my services to run the estate.

Then Dad ask him now for he is here and on his own

Sir good morning come inside, Nelly you have a few tasks to do so away with you ,Sir what is it? Jack, I hear your wife is unwell Sir many say you are to blame for that ,no Jack many say many things to discredit me but that is untrue and may I see her.

Sir Davis I heard that many blame you for putting me away but it was not you for I learnt it was that evil man called Duffy , and so it was, now I have arranged a doctor to come and see you ,it`s alright I will see to any expenses so rest you well.

Jack ,do you have time to talk ? Sir ,I was coming to you remember ,but I want them to know I am talking to you ,Sir have some elder wine and tell me all.

Jack I will ,but coming to you through the estate I saw many crofters so I rode like hell to get here Sir they would not have harmed you and they are there to protect your property and livestock and the crops for I have asked them to do it and that you will feed them and pay them it`s alright Sir don`t get alarmed and hear me out.

The purse I took off the fools at the spring at Abbes Walk contained £30 yes a lot of money and were it came from I shudder to think and no way of knowing so Sir I will compensate the crofters for assisting me in my task of which I am about to tell you.

Sir what you know of what is happening on the estate is little you don`t even know who is milking your cows feeding your hens pigs and horses let alone who is working the fields and maintaining water supply and who is thieving your winter store of hay and straw.

Jack what are talking about ? Sir have some wine, Sir you quickly recognise the poor who thieve as their need is great because of hunger, but if the rich thieve there seems a blanket of silence or a pile of excuses and free from prosecutions.

I can give you examples but what`s the point?

Jack it is Magistrate Duffy who is blackmailing me ,I know it is and George Mudd who is stealing your livestock to sell on at various markets but it is Duffy, Jack you know,`` how do you know?``

Sir this has been going on for some time and you were showing contempt towards me and the crofters, you were becoming arrogant and unsocial and many people were leaving your employ as I sensed something was wrong.

Sir 2 years ago you had a tradesman traveller or somebody that travels the country selling their wares he had many guns with him that he had stolen from the armoury at York, you bought some off Duffy not knowing them to be stolen Duffy then arrested the tradesman and you held him over night .

Next morning, he was found in his cell dead shot in the temple ,Duffy came with another man to take the body away to the mortuary it never arrived they told some that it is was buried not far from here.

All the evidence points to you ,Duffy has a witness ,and some of your clothing was found there and a gun and fingerprints a new innovation that the police have adopted but not reliable, and Duffy paid others to say they saw you shoot the traveller.

Sir, am I right? Jack there is little more to it but yes that is about it, everything points to me I was set up and have no defence and if this came out I would be ruined Sir if this carries on much longer you will be ruined he want`s your estate and what do you mean there`s more to it ?

I want to know all here and now, Jack he tried to get at you for he wants your place too he thought of getting your wife away he could then put pressure on in order you would move out but sees you have many friends in the crofters and backed off .

Sir thank you for telling me ,Jack I didn`t know which way to turn and still don`t ``will you help me?``

Excuse me there`s someone at the door Rose, come in and the doctor Sir I have nicked your carriage to bring the doctor here for he has no transport and your cows are milked and I have nicked a few apples whilst a few men I know have chased away a few intruders for who they were we never asked as they ran like hell one with a pitch fork in his back side whilst others danced and skipped away from the shot from your shot gun and Jack I`ve brought you a rabbit.

Doctor go through,

Sir hope you don`t mind as some of my woman friends have tided your, much neglected kitchen up ,Sir you are so untidy tttut ,how the devil did you get into my property ? With the key from under the door mat ,how did you know it was there ? Sir we have no work and little money but have a lot of time on our hands as we become more alert in what is happening around us .

Sir don`t worry we are not there to rob you ,but to help you, and your house is now clean and tidy the people are not there to rob you although I have told them to take a few potatoes and a turnip each, Sir I am responsible for that as I have appointed 2 men good and true to marshal your property in your absence.

Who gave you the authority to do such a thing? Jack here why is there something wrong? Jack please explain ,what`s going on? Sir, Rose here will explain for she is teasing you but what she is saying is true your property is safe.

Rose tell Sir the time you knew Duffy Sir I wanted to kill that swine Rose please address Sir with what you told me and not of what you should or would have liked to do ,Jack it`s alright let her go on in her own words.

Sir there is no body buried by Duffy at the place he claims for the body was buried in the unknown area of this church and nothing was said ,it was never reported or buried away from here, I know the spot and I told Jack of the spot, we have been there and dug down and the body ,``that right Jack?``

Sir much of guns were sold off to traders and how do I know? Sir Duffy was a bit sweet on me and a heavy drinker and like many men talk freely to woman if they think they are getting what they want Sir your troubles are over .

No Rose I don`t think so, for he will hunt you down and me when he gets to known what you have said .Sir I doubt it ,Rose he is a clever man and will use the law to wriggle out of it and has men who will lie for him. Sir he cannot threat or blackmail you anymore.

Rose ,you could be first on his list when he finds out what you have done.

Sir I have Jack here to speak for me, ``that right Jack?``

Sir Davis ,Duffy is dead found early this morning drowned in a lake whilst out fishing.

Jack, oh I don`t know what to say, `` Sir you are the magistrate I think you will find something to say when confronted with the evidence.

Then who were the men that Rose chased away earlier this morning ? I don`t know probably thieves pinching your turnips and potatoes

Doctor ,what is it ? Jack, she has a cancer of the breast and requires further treatment in hospital, Jack a year, doctor, thank you.

Jack I`m really sorry Sir Davis thank you, but I think she knows and tells me not to worry and carry on as I do so Sir I will report to you tomorrow and get this estate back on its feet as interest of it is as much has yours as it is of mine.

Sir, yes Rose come I`ll drive you home Rose I have got my own horse no Sir I have sent the doctor away on it do not get alarmed you will get it back.

Rose I want a good house keeper and as you know where I keep the house keys I thought it would save me time in telling you to where they are Sir ,when you get home you will be surprised and happy in what the cleaners have done Sir, no Rose call me Harry , Sir ,Harry Davis Rose tomorrow we ride to the crofters and look at suitable land for the present site they dwell on is not suitable for dwellings.

Rose what did you go to prison for? 6 weeks no I mean reason, I was protesting against harsh treatment and greater rights for woman and we want the vote and social change from these draconian laws, and I threw a spud at Duffy well he said I did.it ought to have been a brick.

Rose in time you will get change but not yet, but change is coming as I see in my role has magistrate my powers are diminishing as new roles are created and steam driven engines and the advent of new industries are driving workers from the land ,farm workers are witnessing change as new machinery is introduced.

Sir, er Harry do you think the growing of fruit will change ? I don`t know why, because I do like your apples, Rose there are many and I want some pickers and you can have as many has your pockets will carry

Sir, with apples about 7 or 8 inches in diameter I`m not likely to get many in my pockets ,true Rose very true.

Sir er, Harry do you have any apples good for cider making ? Yes, but the practise has been neglected for a couple of years Sir-Harry we`ll not go into that or reasons why, but we shall have cider for Christmas.

Sir I nearly forgot to tell you those people who we chased off the estate this morning were thieving your straw and hay for their upkeep of horses, a few were caught and received a beating .Rose I don't wish to know, Sir they thought they were doing you a favour, indeed they were and the less I know of your or other people`s actions in matters like that will give me much comfort.

Rose what`s all this about woman organising for better rights and having illegal meetings ? Sir I would not put it that way as it appears, we are breaking the law in which we have no intentions of doing.

Sir the law is a discriminating cloud blanketing our human rights and many should listen to what is being said right across Europe not only from us woman but men too as the right of man is growing in strength to promote a cause of creating a better social and financial station in life.

Rose you must obey the law Sir, there are good laws and bad laws true, then you Sir,`` do something about it for the good of the people and society then and only then will you win support of the people as you can do little without their support.

Sir, law and punishment requires an overhaul as many laws are outdated, we the common people are not against the fact we have it we are against how it is implemented.

Rose you are not common people, you are valued people so get this word of common out of your mind and have your peaceful meetings if you must but I wish to know your agenda not to hinder you but to help and guide you and Rose I shall expect to see a few more in the church on Sunday .God bless you Sir, Rose it`s Harry.

Chapter 8

Cider at Christmas

Nelly here comes Sir ,Sir Rose tells me its Harry I know but its custom and practise and politeness to call him Sir Dad Albert is helping me working in Grandads workshop and things are really racing ahead with demand for some factory owners are bringing their repairs to us and for Albert to put right but Albert is only in his teens Dad he is good at his work so can he have a lad to help him.

No, no, he is only a lad himself but Dad he has a lot of work on, Nelly he shall have an apprentice for 5 years and Albert will be offered further work on the estate in training others in work as it becomes an ongoing business then he can have someone yes on a 2 week trial then we see.

Nelly we are invited to Sir`s Christmas dinner, Dad it`s Harry ,Nelly how things have changed in these last few months its almost unbelievable and I am more than pleased with Albert in the workshop for I thought he would have become a blacksmith for there is plenty to do there ,he had thoughts of it and knows the craft but sees more in furniture demand and a better future in it.

That is true but that is not the only reason he is here is it Rose ? Rose bring him for tea at weekend for I would like to know more about him Dad you know much about him you knew his Dad who worked on the estate and did those ,metal gates and chains let alone seeing to the horses shoes that was not Alberts Dad, It was Dad Rose told me and Albert was left alone when he was one year old well I remember Joe Lodge yes I would see him going to church on Sundays yes Nelly I remember him a very intelligent man and he was good in working with wood .

Dad ,Alberts Dad was shot dead by poachers who he confronted stealing Deer from the estate ,Dad you now and I know that you know all about him. Rose that is the truth as some would say different if it meant avoiding the blame.

Rose I wish not for you to hide things from me so bring Albert for tea on Sunday Dad you know of him ,Rose I`ve known some time that he`s sweet on you now away with you go and earn some money for you`ll need it if you`re planning for the future ,steady on Dad he is just a friend yea your Mom said that to her parents many years ago .

Dad I see a change in Mom and it concerns me Nelly I know ,all we can do is keep her happy and give her our loving care and I am thankful for what Alice Rose`s daughter does for us, Dad so is Sir Harry for what Rose does for him, yes I now but your Mom has to go into hospital now and I am in fear of the outcome Dad don`t upset yourself .

Nelly you have brothers a sister and could be here at Christmas with her fella and fancy frills and posh talk so embarrassing to listen to but your brothers are doing fine at Cirencester but, you Nelly are the one who has given me least problem`s and had the least from family in help as you have sorted things out yourself and clouted a few fellas who dare make fun of you.

You have cared about your Mother much more than others Dad don`t condemn them has they have their life to live and organise, Dad I will not desert you if that is what you are thinking of besides I love it around here and wish to make it even better ,Dad I am not going anywhere and I do like Albert a lot, because he is much like ,what I am looking for .

Firstly it`s this estate all of it and the cottages that surround it, and everyone who works within it and Dad Rose has been talking a lot lately and Sir Harry Davis should be clapping his hands upon what she is doing.

Nelly ,they are to marry in Spring, and I don`t blame him for he has a good woman something that has been lacking in his life for a long time.

Dad I know many crofters will turn out and offer them their best wishes because I see many happy faces when I go amongst them and no bad words said against Sir Harry but they are sorry to learn he has sold all his sheep .

No more sheep Nelly but, more agriculture land for potatoes swedes carrots and peas and a swede like vegetable called `mangal` perhaps s because they are crushed or mashed up and mixed with chaff for winter feed to the bullocks that will be in their encloser yards till spring.

Dad I didn`t know Grandad had an apple crushing machine Nelly he made wine until some government official came down on him it made little difference but he stopped making it when the demand fell off it was a bad time around here it was not cider they wanted it was water and that became very precious around here, many died that year of 62 and if truth be known many were buried anywhere apart from the church cemetery because they had little or no money.

Nelly set your sales pitch up do as you please ,well Dad there are now glass bottles made not to explode when opening and I was thinking about making fruit drinks as this estate provides much fruit like strawberries brambles gooseberries elderberries beside other wines that Mom used to make from vegetables and meadow flowers

Nelly you are not asking me for I know you have made a start Dad, at the sales pitch near Abbes Walk the roads are getting very busy with travellers and many like to stop for refreshment so I thought ,Nelly you`re always thinking so get on with it for if there`s money to be made then exploit it but be careful with those exploding bottles.

Dad Mr Codd the bottle maker has inserted a small marble in the neck of the bottle that allows slow release of gases that protects the bottle from exploding ,Nelly how do you know that? Because I have ordered several dozen after being tested. Nelly anymore secrets?

Dad what are you doing? You seem to be sending people to me who wants work as if I know what is required on the estate that's your job ,you are the estate manager for Sir Harry not me ,I don`t work for him anymore I`m not on his payroll, Nelly I want you to be aware who does work on the estate Dad, why should I care it`s none of my business?

Nelly ,people pass your place when going for an interview ,I want you to be aware in who is , that`s, fine Dad but those that do work on the state give them an identity tag as we get many poachers and thieves sometimes we don`t know who is who ,may do that Nelly but I like what they do they set the traps and I go along and claim the catch long before they have any chance of retrieving it and they know what to expect if caught that is why Nelly we have much game for lunch sometimes some people approach me with trout to exchange for game but for now I leave poachers alone for this estate is overrun with wild life.

What I wish to know, will there be any wine ready for Christmas ? Dad I might just manage it for Albert is helping me and he seems to know what it`s all about that`s why sometimes I have been late in arriving home we have been putting wine down to ferment.

Nelly your excuses are much better than mine when I was you're age Dad there`s nothing going on that I wouldn`t want you to know as we are preparing for Christmas and Dad I want you to call on us and just see what we have done in such a short time, some young lads and lasses have been helping us and happy to receive a few apples and a handful of nuts

Nelly those apples and walnuts nuts are Sir Harry`s not yours true Dad so I`ve bought some off him and he gets paid when I do, and on Sunday from our brewing we will be selling fruit and nuts well, the children will and

Rose has found me a trust worthy woman to manage my sales pitch up at Abbes Walk and Tommy Brown will be with her he once helped you when felling those trees that Granddad used to make furniture with he burnt off all the timber waste.

Nelly who is this coming. Its Flora Mr Jack you are required at the house ,why, what for ? Mr Jack come quick, Flora what is it ? It`s Mrs ,Dad ,there is something wrong, Nelly your Mom has died, the doctor is there and awaits you Dad thought she was in hospital ,she was supposed to have gone there.

Why should I ask such questions as Mom laid there with crucifix held tightly on her chest? Her hair neat and tidy for people to see her neat and tidy as I recall now her saying goodbye my love and give us a hug which I thought no more of it but know now of what it meant.

Nelly she only said other day look after our Nelly for she deserves some one good ,and I like Albert her boyfriend, and I knew his folks when they first came here in setting up a blacksmiths shop and Jack you knew his Dad for he sold off the blacksmith business and came to work on the estate Joe Lodge as you would say we have a lodger working on the estate ,that's not him for Rose is his Mother, true Jack so she is but not biologically yes, I do remember him.

Dad oh Dad it was only yesterday when she said the best friend one can have is their mother and when she`s gone all has gone.

Dad I feel empty and lost Dad hold me ,Nelly cry if you must, here cry on my shoulder Dad ,I love you, I know and I love you too Nelly, your mom was suffering as there is little cure for cancer maybe in a few year`s they may know more but for now, Dad we have company its Rose .

Jack we are sorry, but people here want to help you and if anything you want doing they will do it ,Rose make then all a drink of tea ,sure and Flora and Alice here will take care of things for you.

How do I let the boys know and Nelly don`t you go and desert me?

Dad, I don`t know about them but I`m here to stay for these people are my kind of people but for now Dad just sit back rest and have this pot of tea.

Chapter 9

Good, bye Mom

A day to remember as many stood in silence in black many who remembered the difficult and harsh times as Mom would open her garden up and feed many who would be in hunger, they never asked or begged they were invited along with their children and to bring their own bowls plates or whatever holds a good ladle of rabbit stew .

A sad day as Mom is put to rest in a church cemetery that will embrace Mom as it did her parents and many more and will go on doing so to the good people of this parish for there is nothing wrong with people it is the circumstances they find them self`s in that causes much anger and turmoil, not everyone but most people who seek pleasure rather than pain for pain will come eventually to everyone as I view the gathering more of pity of what can be done to improve the crofters and those that find shelter in the carr.

I looked at Dad with a tear in his eyes he took my arm within his and said Nelly it`s down to you now, you take up the reigns and forge ahead with your plans before these so called industrialists start to rip this country side apart because for what I hear it`s going happen.

Dad you should not be concerning yourself about things like that on a day like today, true Nelly but I feel all has gone I have nothing to look forward to it is all behind me the memories are sweet joyful and happy but the future is untold uncertain and unavoidable but because of that I am not going to hurry or rush to the pearly gates to heaven nor attempt to journey to hell for I have work here unfinished and to accomplish that I must seek ways and means to address the tasks.

Nelly what is done is done we must learn and live with our sometimes trouble lives in a changing world ,come Dad we have a wake laid on at home Flora Alice and Rose have arranged many things .

At home Dad was not so disturbed as I thought he would be as he acknowledged many and very talkative and pleased to see many friends who shown their respects as men folk talked openly about wars in the Empire and young men joining up to see the world and seek a more decent life than working hard on the farms or in the much in demand industries .

Dad listened intensely to their rhetoric only to say look I am a Methodist like my father and have inherited his mode of preaching`s and his horse and trap and we shall have a church soon very near the carr , I don`t advocate you to neglect your church here or any other English places of worship but feel sometimes it's a comfort to bring the church to you .

Jack we are talking about people joining the army to settle problems abroad with many troubles in the Empire ,Dad braised himself looked hard at the men present and said I was talking about change here not of sons going off to war and to be proud to wear the uniform and defend the commonwealth, my friends do not build their ego up as many will not come back .

as I hear it ,fight for king and country as many don`t know we have a King or Queen or anything else beyond were they live.

Jack you condemn people fighting for the defence of our country ,no I don`t condemn anyone as they are doing good and fighting very hard to protect and improve our common wealth as it is so unfair as it should be more evenly distributed amongst the common people who help to create it , now do any of you advocate we take up arms to secure it.

No, I thought not and so you should not ,gentlemen your country is not under threat but constantly your wages and employment are let alone your places to where you live .

The, Church bless you when you come into this much troubled world. and when you leave it. but when old enough the state wants you to take up arms to defend your country no different now as it was when I was a lad.

Many stately houses and halls are decorated with war trophies whilst the common people have extraordinarily little to show for their efforts some may have been fobbed off with a medal or two and a warm handshake .

Gentlemen I see much here that requires, but what can be done without education ? Very little, gentlemen we must press for education for all not just a few and support the argument for change if it be for the better and that is what is being echoed throughout the country as we see the growth of woman`s league and trade unions and industry.

The growth of railways a massive introduction to transport from the overcrowded canals and the movement of labour is projecting many changes to our locality .

My friends it is not wrong to pursue a peaceful progression to improve your life before the good Lord takes it away, so I will fight and protect the rights of man as those who apply economics and theories to defend their arguments we the people will applaud their interests and present our considerations to achieve it and that is known has a union of consensus.

Dad whatever are you talking about these people don`t wish to know all that, Nelly your Dad talks sense, yes Bill but he is in sadness, Nelly I can speak for myself and what I say is true or will be true you just wait and see so Nelly hand around some of your homemade wine but do not make beer on these premises or enter into drinking alcohol.

Albert is here Mr er ,Albert you call me Jack not Jim as some do, so put your hand in mine, Jack I have made some furniture for our church near the carr, a table a chair and some benches and a stand for your reading material, Albert it`s your church and anyone else who wish to use it ,Jack that is why Nelly and I were sometimes late home for we wish to make good use of the light hours whilst we could as the chestnuts are falling a sure sign of autumn setting in.

It ,was a good wake if ever there was one as Dad took it well he is at his best when people are around him I could say he loves people as people love him but what concerns me is that some people may try and take advantage of him and his generosity Dad I said don`t let these people take an advantage of you for you are very kind, he smiled and said Nelly do not think like that, as it will make you a doubting and a suspecting person hardly the right words but you know what I mean, he smiled and loved me in to say Nelly that will not happen, and you just see, you don`t alter.

Now about Albert here, Dad don`t embarrass him ,Albert, you see you take care of my Nelly for you will not find a better woman apart from your mother so, when are you ?

Dad stop it ,well Nelly I have plans for him so, Nelly go on and get married to him before someone else comes along and Albert your adopted Mom is pleased with you and she too wants you to marry ,well thanks Dad.

Nelly you can have a double wedding in spring when his Mom marries Sir Harry ,it will look good to see Mom and Son marry in the same church at the same time and there`s not many can say that.

Dad stop it , Nelly it`s all down to you with decisions plans and everything else for I intend to take a back seat I`m fine with game keeping the estate but running a home is different so Nelly it` s yours for if and when ,Dad what about you? Nelly I shall not interfere with your life as I was thinking of the cottage at the east end of the estate .

Dad Sir Harry has promised it us and you can`t leave here.

Nelly, I`m making plans and statements and all the time , you let me go on knowing full well plans are made and wait to I see your mother young man, Dad they were going to speak to you but not to day Dad have your wake and then we will take care of things, and don`t worry things will be fine.

No, I`m not worried but concerned for Albert here can read and write yet there was no school for you, I knew of a feepaying school and you never went there it concerns me to know how you learnt.

Jack it is written seek and you will find so I knew of that fee paying school so I went along and created a hide away in the nearby bushes near the window of lessons and could hear everything going on, at first it was a bit difficult but gradually I learnt and learnt fast for I had to in case I was found out someone nearly caught me so I pretended to be cleaning the windows ,this went on for a full term and by then I had the basics so I went on to further education the following year unbeknown to them, and during the weekends I talked to the fee paying boys and exchanged notes and gleaned much off them unbeknown to their fee paid education as I quizzed them whilst playing marbles with them.

Jack it was not an education as more of intelligence as I had the intelligence to secure an education as I saw from the sometimes cold of the hide away in the

Rhododendrons but what I could not hear was written on the blackboard as I learnt to lip read too.

Jack how appreciated I am of the affluent and well to do, as they will never know how I in silence argued the points of History English and Maths for all the students did was to accept all that was said to them as I was going home seeking answers and alternatives in particularly that of history.

Jack here we have massive resources in forestry agricultural and farming now I here prospectors are scanning the land for coal I now that some coal has been had in what they call open cast but these people are talking about drilling deep down and send men down to get it.

Albert that will not be for a good my years ,perhaps you are right but I have seen strangers walking the land carrying all kinds of tools as if they are measuring distances and seen men with their high hats and dove tailed coats showing great interest as they all seem to nod in agreement Jack what is it they could be doing with many instruments ?

Albert you`ve said it for it is becoming known that coal is to be extracted from deep down and some land will have to go as I hear many stories about what will happen to the crofters and what kind of compensation can they expect and to where to live?

It will give work to many but sadly disrupt many lives to achieve it ,and Albert I anticipate trouble physical violence as opposition to it is growing and some have already been warned about their threatening behaviour as the magistrate` s like Sir Harry have been briefed .

Sir Harry understands the crofters plight for he would not like it to happen on his estate but has to act within the law yes there is trouble even now before the first sod is lifted God knows what future holds for the crofters, but that's not here for some time as the prospectors move on to other areas to explore.

Jack, we have a murderer amongst us for down by creepy hollow a man has been found hanging from a tree, many claim it to be murder that is why Sir Harry had to hurry from the funeral,

Chapter 10

Crime and Punishment

Dad tell me about Creepy Hollow, Nelly just a dip in the road that was created by quarrying for lime stone during the building of roads within the estate a dip and a twist of road with over hanging trees that gives a spooky feeling during foggy and dark nights but at the time of excavation they hit the jackpot in finding a never ending supply of spring water that was so precious and fresh that the estate had to restrict hoarders, thieves, merchants ,and opportunist and livestock from trespassing upon their heaven sent fortune.

Nelly I have told you the story many times and yes it has taken a few lives for to find a man hanging was horrible to see but over many years it has taken many lives for many fought over water as it was at that time on the estate who stationed guards over it, unrest broke out and several guards feared for their lives and refused to man it, fighting often brock out and some claimed the rights that caused a spate of deaths after dark by people unknown because of denying them access to water.

On some wintery days Nelly many would try and avoid the area but the killings stopped when the crofters found fresh water in the carr ,some tried to claim the rights to that area too and some suffered because of it and again some people disappeared not to be seen again but the area was common land and the troubles eased off as the crofters banded together to act in unity and from that their community grew to such an extent that their cottage industries expanded and provided a much better life.

At that time the crofters enjoyed a period growth and many sheep were to be seen in the valley beyond the carr the growth and prosperity in a cottage industry promoted the idea of centralisation of firstly small factories then as demand grew so did the producing factories .

The producing factories required raw materials of hides and skins of various animals and squirrel and fox fur was constantly in demand it was a time of progress as lime quarries expanded and contributed well to the crofters agriculture development and that of the building industry and road making.

Wool was an important factor and in constant demand has many crofters had spinning wheels but it was a time of development and the growth of factories was beginning to take effect upon the crofters cottage industries mode of life and much dissent and disturbance once again raised its ugly head as many would go about smashing the factories spinning wheels.

Here on the estate it was not only alive of much wild life and fruits of the forest but that of trespass of poachers day and night because of the demand from the factories as the rewards were great for example the price of 1 caught squirrel would keep a family in food sometimes for a week.

We would lay hidden at night and see and catch many poachers kitted out with snares traps and nets and the more experience poachers carried guns and when they thought they were being apprehended would not hesitate to fire not to wound but to kill for if caught there punishment was harsh and severe sometimes resulting in death.

Dad not much has changed, Nelly it was people like me and your Granddad that changed many things here we stopped or argued for change from people being hanged or transported to other side of the world for poaching or even thieving off traders to feed their families.

Nelly there are people here who still poach you know that, and they carry guns and prepared to fire them although when caught the penalties are no were near as those of their fathers for now their greatest penalty is loss of earnings .

The public view these offences of poaching as nothing serious and laugh in jubilation and think how foolish the poacher is in being caught, magistrates usually landowners still take a serious view ,but their powers are limited much to their annoyance.

Dad I don`t believe it for I know of people who have been dragged through the courts and suffered terrible at the hands of the magistrates, Dad there is a growing problem of the crofters who are complaining of harsh punishments for they know if they have to go through the criminal courts it`s a death sentence.

Dad you now and I know that nothing has changed only you are much older and less active amongst the people as long has you have a pipe of tobacco and a bite to eat that's all you seem bothered about ,Dad you don`t get far these days and fail to see much in what is happening here on the estate and that of the crofters.

Nelly I know what`s going on and hangings are many just because I am a friend of Sir Harry do not view me as history I know all about the crofters and industrialists and their way of life but here on the estate not much changes all what will change will be the land scape and I may not be here to see it geographically domestically industrial and commerce will prove to be a great asset to all involved but there will be a price to pay in life and the environment.

Dad since Mom went you have done a lot of memorising and anticipating the future .Dad try and get out more for we know you are sadly missing Mom and the past is tormenting you .

Nelly if it was not for you I don`t know what I would have done for you have been a great help, your brothers at Cirencester missed the funeral through no fault of their own but that sister of yours well we all know that she is not like us anymore. Dad they will be coming home from Cirencester in the summer I have a letter from them and they are doing well they will be here for a two week break then go back until Christmas then home for good ,you mean they will be here for Christmas, Dad we will have a good Christmas you just wait and see.

Dad what will they do after Cirencester ? Hopefully pay me back, Dad be serious Nelly I will see what I can do for there are great changes in farming and the demand for more produce growers and less sheep and I do like the idea of the cooperative movement in what they advocate known as the Rochdale Pioneers but I don`t think there will be a problem with either of them for they are intelligent and have the education and Sir Harry has many times enquired about them and I think Sir Harry will know something of interest better than me but Nelly you`ve made my day.

Then Dad get yourself out of that chair put your mug of tea down get your gun and go get us a rabbit or two, Nelly I don`t shoot rabbits I snare them or wait for others to snare them for me, for I know where they go I just let them do the work for me and if they see me they run like the devil across the fields ,Dad what would you do if you caught them ?

Nelly I only act if there is any violence and when there is I back off and let them run away but next time I see them and have Sam Waters with me we take then into custody because of their violent nature but mainly I give a warning and use a bit of common sense because that is all they have through no fault of their own what`s that Dad? Common sense

Nelly times are changing and crime and punishment is no were near has bad as when I was boy but it is till painful, Dad someone was hanged down in Cirencester for stealing some bread ,Nelly in the 18th century many were hanged sometimes on the same rope.

Dad it is in this letter as they say the law and punishment towards the farm labourers is very harsh and there is rioting and many hangings because of it ,so Dad don`t lecture me in crime and punishment as you are no longer active amongst people around here and I am, so Dad get back to it and get that horse and cart out and go amongst the people and preach to them on Sunday and see what we have done to the hut that is now a Methodist church.

Dad life goes on you have to carry on for we all miss Mom but life is about people living people and whilst we are part of it we have to do what is right to one another ,so Dad there is much to do to try and eliminate bad laws and unjust punishment.

For Dad this Is not you as you know and I know there is still much to be done in improving one`s station in life and it`s not by harsh laws and severe punishment as that will nothing to promote the interests of the crofters.

Then, tell me Nelly what can be done?

Dad I am in search of it.

Dad Ben says in his letter he may go on and study law, Nelly he is studying agriculture yes Dad and many farmers want representing in deals and agreements for far too often deals have been broken you know that as people want less of crime and punishment and more of agreements that stand good in a court of law. I, thought he was going to be, a vicar Nelly, I thought Geoffrey was

Dad people are restless for change and the group or party of liberalism is growing fast to the disappointment of the Wigs and ruling classes.

Chapter 11

It`s Christmas

It is Christmas time and turkeys geese pheasants fowls ducks and pigs were in desperation in wishing that Christmas was over as they viewed me with contempt and displayed an arrogant attitude towards me for no matter how I tried to look friendly they refused my presence, I think it was the thick stick that Dad used to place over my feathered friends neck on the ground with the stick entrapping their head and neck then pull their body quickly and it`s all over as we look and prepare for Christmas.

I could see I was not popular as silence fell over their place of residence but as soon as I rattled the grain bucket and the smell of Mangal`s and chaff the place became a riotous scene of activity except the hens who are well behaved as I gather their eggs In abundance,

The bullocks bumped and shoved their heavy bodies to be first to their mangers whereas my feathered friends large and fat with yellow beaks pushed and forged their attention into the bucket as I noted their destination and life expectancy .

Rabbits were pleased to see me as were the ferrets that I netted from poachers who did a runner but the ferrets seemed restless with each other and trouble - some so I gave them plenty of space in their hut as they seem to desperate to be free.

Dad shouted me who had a cart load of holly freshly cut Nelly I have customers coming and some market traders who make various displays with it and I like to sell to the crofters for there`s no holly down were they live but some are not in want for they seem well supplied.

Dad it`s not so much about the holly but more of livestock so if we don`t reduce our stock soon someone may do it for us before they trespass upon Sir Harry`s stock, true Nelly and we have demand from market traders so we better get started.

Dad I catch them and you do it, no Nelly for Albert is here you see to those mince pies Dad ,I have no meat ready for the pies you have I have brought you some meat all mixed up and ready but don`t ask me what`s in it as there is a bit of all sorts of minced meat in.

Dad Ben Matt and Wilf should be here soon and I can`t wait to see them for I have missed them and learnt to defend myself as they taught me a lot in how to fight back and Dad I do hope schooling has not spoilt them for they were good to have around.

Nelly we go tomorrow to Sir Harry at about 11 because there maybe a few tasks want doing Dad nothing wants doing for they have a lot of help for I have asked Rose and she seems fine with some people from the village are helping her and her daughter, really they have lots of help and on boxing day there is a hunt organised you should enjoy that for the place is over run with fox`s so Dad get me one for I want a neck wrap.

Dad, there is a few other farmers joining the Christmas dinner with us as Sir has invited the Masons and the

Johnsons so the large banqueting room will be decorated out that`s not been used since his dad was alive .

Nelly you`re telling me there was a time when I was telling you these things.

Dad look they are here now Ben Matt and Wilf as I ran to greet them in wrapping my arms around each one in a welcoming embrace my how you have grown I said just look at you all three of you ,Dad ran to them with open arms embraced them in his loving way as any good father would.

Matt Dad said, the coachman is waiting as he has unloaded your luggage and with a generous tip from Matt he was on his way along the avenue of giant beech trees and a somewhat rocky road of lime stone chippings as children ran behind the coach in excitement of not seeing such a turnout of fine horses and a carriage made for comfort travel, and painted in shiny black with a trim of gold paint heading for safer travel to the old roman road with Dad shouting at the youngsters from trying to hitch a lift at the rear unbeknown to the coach driver.

Dad how are you baring up ? We never received the message of Mom until it was too late, and we are sorry because of it but we are here for a while then we go back the carriage is booked for our return .

Then my boys you must enjoy yourselves whilst you are here ,Dad we have worked hard, and we have good results as we have secured our pass marks, we go back to receive our awards but have to do two weeks of practical work nothing serious but part of the programme.

Some part of our practical work is market trading and we keep a good percentage in what we earn, Matt never mind about that you` re here and will be thinking in what you are going to do when finished schooling.

Dad I`m going to be a property and estate agent at Harrogate in North Yorkshire I have secured the position Wilf have you anything sorted? Yes, Dad chief hosteler at the racecourse and you Matt, I`m staying here with you working for Sir Harry as sales and estate accountant `what`` what`s; that supposed to mean?

Good lord you have kept this back to surprise me, well congratulations what a Christmas present I am overjoyed I don`t know what to say for you have really pleased me, Dad we would n t wish to disappoint you nor miss the wedding.

What wedding oops, Matt I have not told Dad it was supposed to be another surprise, sorry Nelly.

Nelly are you to marry? Well you are only; only what Dad for I really don`t know how old I am but you should know better than me so when was I born? Well let`s see, Dad you don`t have to count on your fingers ,well I don`t know you must be about 18 now Dad, if what you told me I am 18.

What are you 3 laughing at ?

Nelly tell him ,not another secret Dad, I don`t know If it`s right or correct but the vicar seems happy with it that we that's Albert and me along with Sir Harry and Rose are to be married to morrow Christmas day a double wedding and you think I am going into our kitchen and stand and make mince pies you are mistaken so girls come forward.

Alice Mary and Flora meet my brothers and you Dad take them inside and show them their rooms, I thought I heard some movement indoors Dad there is a meal laid on for you all so let the girls take you inside and I will see you tomorrow for Albert will soon be here for lunch with you and will stay with you until tomorrow as Dad you are giving me away, Nelly if you don`t get going I`ll chase you away with this broom so clear off and Nelly come here and give us a love ,you darling of a daughter and you lot can stop laughing.

I trembled a little and shred a few tears as I danced through the rose garden and on my way to know what such a loving Dad I have.

The church bells rang loud and clear as many packed the church with all good wishes and to witness the happy event that brings joy and happy thoughts in a 10 to 15 minute ceremony and after to see many casting their best wishes as we are guided into the banqueting hall to feast upon our much prepared Christmas dinner.

Turkey of plenty as we are waited upon as I thought how fortunate the geese pigs and fowl are for a while as I was distracted from my off track thoughts to congratulations and speech`s from both supporting sides that I seemed blind to but not deaf to for it`s a day to remember as speech after speech echoed through the great hall .

Suddenly I felt I was expected to speak why I don`t know as it seemed a man`s responsibility maybe through custom and practise and thought if that be the case then it`s about time we woman did something different .

I stood up too much surprise as silence fell as I looked around me to see eyes of much expectancy to thank them for all they say and wish for us.

It is with much pleasure I thank you as my husband and I will be living amongst you as we both know this estate that goes back to the Norman Conquest and seen many changes, We love it and intend to see it maintain its beauty and accessible to all whilst development takes place all around us with the growth of industries and that of the crofters.

Things are changing fast, and I welcome it as the populist are increasing and we must welcome it as we are living longer and demand for our products is increasing too and so is the political scene as we that is my husband and I intend to work towards improving ones station in life along with maintaining this beautiful estate for all to enjoy and Sir Harry knows that and when telling of it he said don`t tell me but tell them on your wedding day as you will be partly responsible for it.

I replied good for the paddock will hold feasts exhibitions markets and livestock sales.

Merry Christmas everyone and thank you.

Dad thank you ,Nelly take your responsibilities with pride as this estate will be here no matter what changes take place and the church will embrace these new communities into its parish and Dad I know you are a Methodist and have a place of worship amongst the crofters but have no vicar as yet, yes you have preachers but no vicar so do not be offended by us marrying in the all saints a church of England .

Nelly that does not bother me and neither him that watches over you, for your information you were born right here in 1847 September 9th and its December 1865 and how do I remember it?

On the great beech tree over hanging our garden you will find inserted all your birthdays and many other things ,then Dad you look like getting your knife out again, no Nelly they are burnt on with a hot iron.

Now Mrs Nelly Lodge where is that husband of yours Dad that sounds good, I like it , ``hmm Mrs Nelly Lodge.`` but Nelly you surprised a few with your speech ,Dad what annoys me is lack of information to the masses ,main news comes from the ale houses and usually distorted so partly through that I support the woman`s league to pursue a path of non- violence to secure more rights for women.

Nelly good for you but you should n t be thinking about things like that when you are just married Dad I am so happy Nelly you have a good man in Albert and I`m pleased for you so here is a present from me to you on this happy occasion,

Dad its Moms rings, thanks Dad.

Nelly take heed for what you think and do in your women`s league for you can easily make enemies as well has friends, as it is the laws that require addressing.

Chapter 12

A Cold and Bruising Winter

February and cold with logs piled high near rear entrance to the house door and covered in night fall of snow and icicles hanging dangerously from the house roof gutter that a little warmth from near the chimney allows a thaw until the water runs towards the gutter and freezes depicting a dangerous situation of watch you head.

Further on down the small hill the crofters are blanketed in clouds of smoke of burning beech wood as many people hurry on bye with wrappings of little clothing on to comfort them, some so desperate and hungry they turn to crime and that accounts for the loss of some of our livestock.

Albert has a continuous fire glowing all the day through with men stopping from their snaring for a warm, then go back to check their traps Albert laughed in telling me Nelly he said,`` I perhaps should n t tell you this but that is what they are doing`` ,but I cannot say poaching is done on the estate for some could go into the forest which is not part of the estate but if it was I don`t know what I would do as some leave me a rabbit or two.

Albert I said, you are responsible to the estate it is our duty to report all what you see ,true Nelly but if I don`t see anything for I`m not going to make false statements and get some crofters punished on hearsay and punishment is severe and harsh for Sir Harry has not let up on his judgements and in harsh times like his too.

Nelly the snow is 18 inches deep and I can see footprints leading to many areas of wildlife activity but who`s they are I can`t say nor refuse a rabbit or two but Nelly this is not what I want to say for I was hesitant to tell you for its sad and sickening to say but you are here now and have come here to tell me something too, so you first .

Albert ,there is rioting amongst the crofters and some lives are in danger because many people are hungry and homeless those with money get drunk at the tavern than boast in a drunken manner and because they have money they chastise the less well- off and fighting breaks out there are 3 dead from fighting and 1 has been found frozen to death in the snow.

Rose from the hall with her daughter has gone to them with a basket of food and to see what the Peelers (police) are doing but I know there are some voluntary groups there giving assistance and that's good for we have been discussing such things in our meetings but here again we are at risk in holding meetings or organising group meetings.

Albert do you require anyone with you for security in case you have some angry visitor`s? Good lord no I have an apprentice here but no in -fact many keep me well informed but I didn`t know about the rioting Albert did you recognise any poachers ? No ,but I doubt if I would tell you If I did, for these are difficult times for the crofters.

Albert don`t be stupid it`s your duty ,no Nelly I know were my duty lies, Albert I admire you for that , good but those people are not from around here as we have found horse tracks in the snow leading to York road and beyond ,and the crofters problems are from those visitors in the night 4 horse men with carts who came riding to rob and ride off with all they could carry and Sir Harry has organised a party to hunt them down but they could be well away by now.

Albert Since early this morning there has been a presence of police ,2 carriage load s of them with 2 magistrates dishing out punishments and Sir Harry is amongst them there are many skirmishes and much dissent as many are made to stand in the cold with arms wrapped around their bodies and stamping their feet to keep warm as many are much in need of clothing someone tried to run away but was struck down heavily and killed.

Albert there is blood shed amongst the crofters as the white of the snow turns to red as children stand screaming and crying as their moms and dads fight the peril of hunger and cold whilst at the same time trying to defend what little they have and argue their cause to little avail as many are taken away.

Albert on the magistrate`s nod of approval punishment is dealt in a madness cruel and unforgiving way in enforcing the law with physical force and I hope dad is safe with his rabbit stew and bread at his chapel whilst many seek sanctuary there.

Nelly, last night or early this morning there were disturbances near the paddock near the church as people around there went to find out what it was, the people saw horsemen ride away leaving a trail of blood in the snow and much more was found this morning .

People there had difficulty in seeing who it was in the dark and a blizzard was blowing, and it became dangerous in not knowing who it was.

Nelly we found 2 men lying in the snow dead and that's what I was going to tell you ,Nelly it`s not the locals around here for these dead men were bought here from the water place down at Abbes Walk and I do know there is unrest at the village too.

We know this because at first light Nick and I from Sir Harry`s stables rode out to there and found lots of blood about the area and in the wood further on we found many people in distress who claimed they had been attacked and pointed to 2 men hanging from a tree and just said they`ll think twice before they do that again.

Nelly the blood we found was animal`s blood and learnt some livestock had been stolen from there during the night ,but why were they on the estate during the night?

We learnt from some forest dwellers that they were rustlers with two carts to carry off the sheep thy came here but not knowing we had no sheep and attempted to steal the pigs and it was the noise from the pigs that alarmed the residence.

Two men came to me later as I have said right here at my workshop one had blood on his coat and it was obvious to me that they had been in search for some time and looking cold and hungry, they appeared friendly maybe because I had my pistol ready but they wanted horses so I enquired how they got here ,we walked as our horses were stolen and who did it is around here we have chased them from the village near Abbes Walk spring, then I said follow their tracks in the snow but seemed not bothered about that as they found comfort around the large fire I had going.

Who are you I enquired, we work for the magistrate beyond Abbes walk Mr Philips who knows Sir Harry, then we heard screams as someone came running and breathless struggled to say there`s rioting by the crofters and police and magistrates Sir Harry and Mr Philips are there he then ran off, the two men just said to me thank you and cocked their guns and ran towards the crofters about a mile away that surprised me to find they were armed.

Albert you said you knew nothing about any rioting and trouble amongst the crofters, Nelly I wanted to know what you had to say ,Albert you knew something was wrong for you left early this morning it was still dark all you said was `` I have a lot to do today``

Albert what`s going on? Nelly there`s people going around smashing up new introduction of farm machinery because its putting then out of work and they are prepared for violence and because of that these travellers get to know when they are to strike then take the opportunity to go and get what they can whilst the magistrates and police are deployed elsewhere and this is the case here.

Unfortunately, many crofters get involved and punished severely as lives are lost and the travellers here are apprehended and will probably hang too, Nelly we are surrounded in violence and killings and as usual Creepy Hollow seems to be the place.

Albert, it`s because the spring of clear water is there as people go for water and have grievances with one another Nelly, we can`t move the spring.

Albert no fooling because there`s going to be much to answer for and I wonder what Dad knows and Rose, I know this Nelly that some have genuine arguments and some are agitator`s to fuel their own interests and too many are out of work and these times are dangerous and unsafe as the killings go on.

Nelly if we are to stay here and seek a good life ,things will have to change as there are many death`s and many don`t get buried in the cemetery so where do the penniless bury their dead?

Albert I don`t know but Dad might as he is here now and Rose too, Nelly it was awful and Sir Harrys court will be busy all day tomorrow as there will be hangings and burials as this estate offers much help only for outsiders to come here and try and discredit us.

Nelly if you have any ideas on how to promote and improve things here and amongst the crofters then come tonight for Sir Harry is holding a meeting at 7 and your Dad will be there Albert I am here and it`s me who has organised it ,but it should be these magistrates not me as they get paid I for it I don`t, they should be looking for peaceful ways and answers into this ongoing problem of hunger and strife.

I have given sanctuary In the Methodist church as many staggered in from the cold frozen and hungry a pitiful state ,but not has pitiful as those outside who are beaten and coerced into submission because they are hungry and misled into believing what is said from agitators.

Chapter 13

Your Ways Don`t Work

Sir Harry we cannot carry on like this as daily I see poverty and strife as we had a good table at Christmas and ate in one meal more than what crofters eat in a week .

Jack I could agree but some seem to be doing well from our wildlife and you know that, and I have the responsibility in seeing the law is obeyed.

Sir that's not true your responsibility is to sit in judgement it is the police who encourage the law not to be broken by their presence, Sir we have spoken about this before and making no headway as the police presence and your presence only act when trouble breaks out, Sir we require like most places throughout this land for police to be ever present and for it to be paid through a rateable tax for these new factories are bursting at seams with great profits as they pay poor wages and you Sir would never miss the money if you had to contribute to that course too.

Sir there should be an overhaul of our domestic and social life for the poor man`s house does nothing to eliminate the problems and what I hear is that it`s much worse in the south of England as my father`s sons can tell you as many hang for petty offences and if this carries on as it is we shall have a civil war only what is holding it back is the growth of industries and growing demand for wool and introduction of ergonomics steam and invention of mechanisation.

Jack I am expected to act as the law allows me for the goodness of all, I am not responsible for their social standing or places of work my job is too a judge their behaviour in breaking the law. Sir we must ask ,``why do people break the law`` Sir you judge the circumstances .Jack ,I don t have to do that, all I am required to do is listen to the evidence then pass sentence ,it is the accused who should be asking themselves that.

Sir what does one do to become a magistrate? Jack, I own much land around here I have more than enough wealth to warrant my position then, Sir you are area magistrate to protect your financial and social self - interest. Jack, I protect all the peoples interests that is why many are punished for not adhering to it ,for law must be upheld for the goodness of all.

Sir who makes the law ?Jack you are becoming all questions and annoying me for we are here to discuss the recent troubles and what further action to take for our prisons are full and the hangman is fully employed,

Sir I suggested and called this meeting and thought I would chair it ,you Sir agreed for it to be here on your premises with Mr Johnson from Abbes Walk ,now I don`t know of what he thinks as yet for he wishes to talk after me as I wish this meeting to be orderly so Sir with respects if you wish to carry on in your recommendations and suggestions good but what you do say is not what necessarily will be done for Sir you are not the law as you say, so with all due respects I expect to hear in what can be done to reduce the social and domestic problems for people living in our parish .

Jack, have you taken leave of your senses ? ``Who do you think you are talking to?`` I am responsible for this parish and shall have order and respect and to do that the whip will be used and if that fail`s we shall have more hangings and that's all I intend to say so all of you remember were you are in my house.

Mr Johnson ,thank you Jack, Sir you come across the fields to our water spring on Abbes Walk although you have found one that is used for communal purposes at Creepy Hollow and that`s good for the majority of people in order to pursue a good communal life as we act that is me and you Sir Harry to provide the greatest happiness for the majority and how we do it, well Sir we get paid for what we do and I think you are failing ,for you can and must do your job better in order the majority can enjoy life better .

Our task as magistrates is to search and study in what can we do to promote the greatest good, for flogging and prisons and hangings does nothing to support my thoughts ,Sir Harry I am not in support of your intentions and acts upon the villages for we must seek other ways and society expects us to do that for this Parish and mine.

Your parish Sir have had a poor administration for far too long Sir you know it and I know it and so does a few more that this Parish was unrepresented as you had magistrates who only thought of themselves so Harry come off your high horse and remember what people did for you when you were being black mailed yes Harry everybody knows about that so show some respect towards them.

It is, help that these people require, and you and I can help and Harry don`t you let me hear you talk again like that or do you still have problems ? In which I think you have .

Harry you have a lovely wife and you are more settled now but you still have problems and this is not the place to discuss them but we will sort it so if you haven` t anything constructive to add than let Jack proceed.

Thank you Mr Johnson, Now hear me good for Sir Harry here has had his life threatened that`s why he is so angry, Rose and me have few ideas so we leave it at that for now ,for we are here to seek ways and means to stop this rioting and killings and why us ?

We are looked upon as the answer to many of their problems and I do believe because we are charitable and property holders and I have a church amongst them a Methodist church no preacher as yet but that does not mean you neglect the church here or anywhere else as they are places of worship and of meetings congregations and hopefully a place of reconciliations.

Enough said about that as I am to express my thoughts about this awful situation that is more work will be available through Albert here who intends to expand into carriage making and contracted work from the millowners as you Sir Harry will draw a list of does an don`ts within factory places of work and the sale of land or renting of it.

The land reformation acts that many of us find outdated are under discussions to be amended as deforestation is making rapid progress and the movement of labour is vastly creating demand for all kind of things accommodation food clothing lots of things and here on the land farmers are investing in better machinery to meet the growing demand,

What`s that got to do with the present problems you may ask ? At present we do not know who is who ,you are given a name and that`s it and nobody gives a hoot who you are except people like you Sir Harry or Mr Johnson well things are changing as you will be told to register when born and when you die ,the state is taking more interest in you as it should we are subjects of the state as we help to make the state thus where would the state be without us?

Now about fairness for what is fair to one is not necessary fair to another, so it is what is fair to the majority for the greatest good as what was said previously.

So I suggest like me you go amongst the majority and see what you can do for the greatest good for I was amongst them as I gave comfort in the church whilst they appreciated me so what does that call for ?

It calls for groups of people to come together to discuss and form a policy to create the greatest good and at the moment it`s against the law ,I ask who`s law ? Whilst parliamentarians sit and scorn at the poor Sir`s we must endeavour to eliminate dissent and promote happiness and if you are against me then I shall go it alone.

A moment of silence as Rose turned to Sir Harry she said we have work to do but your personal problems are in the past as we that is Jack and Mr Johnson and I have sorted it but never again must you be so daft as to listen to unrepresented lawmakers who are only concerned about enriching themselves by exploiting the poor but having said that it does not make it right for the poor to rob the rich as same laws apply to all.

Jack, did you have to mention my problems ? Rose has just done so. Sir Harry we all know of your problems and you neglect them as you have done with the people in the crofts now my sons will soon be going back to Cirencester and seen much here that they shake their heads in sorrow as many are fighting over land rights whereas many kill for the land that does not belong to them.

Sir from the Mill and up the hill is fine and claimed, and from the avenue of beech trees up to the estate that was once enclosed is yours and all at top of the rise that runs down to the crofters and there it stops.

Sir with the growth of industries and demand for land we are having strangers here who are claiming to be landowners and selling land to unsuspecting purchases then disappear not to be seen again.

Much fighting occurs from the taverns when some find out they have been robbed in buying the land and those found hanged in Creepy Hollow were two of them who falsely sold land

Sir some of these people are not to be seen again and the purchasers are angry and in despair this is causing much unrest so Sir I suggest land can only be sold by agents known by you and must be a solicitor or a man of the judiciary to confirm a genuine sale .

Jack is that your Idea ? No Sir it is Bens my son now preparing to go back to Cirencester, well it's a good idea as would circular posters to that effect but many can`t read, true Sir but you can speak and Sir like a good many things you or who- ever does it charge for writing up legal documents and for correspondence and documents to be secured away if requested this is not new but a practise sometimes ignored.

Jack that`s not new, Sir it is for new communities and settlers and let them elect a spokesperson then we will know what`s going on long before trouble erupts into a riot ,

Jack your sons have done you proud Sir they hate to think we up here had a George Jeffries the hanging judge of Cirencester Jack that was 18th century than Sir you know of him ? I do than ,Sir there are lessons to be learnt.

Mr Johnson thank you for coming and two of my men will escort you home to Abbes springs, Harry Sir that`s not necessary for I have an happy community who will be waiting for me near Nelly`s Sales pitch on York road so good day to you all.

You Sir Harry those that threaten you, Rose and I have sorted it as they will not threaten you again.

Chapter 14

Its Spring Again

Jack, I wonder if you would speak to me as you do, if you were less dependent in having your own property ? Sir if that was the case you would n t call me Jack it would be `` ah you`` as your father would box your ears for using such disrespect Sir if you expect respect than you must show it.

Sir you have an over fed body that a weight loss would do you good rather contributing to it for it fails to suit you as you look un -healthy , so are you ailing from something Sir?

Jack it has been this long dark winter of lighted lanterns and candles of long dark nights ,hoping our livestock will be here when we wake up next morning, but now we are entering into spring and lighter nights are approaching as people are acknowledging each other as spring is in the air.

Sir my boys are back and ready to take up their duties and Sir I know and you do that this estate could do with someone to take control of sales expenditure income and investment ,Sir you have done great things and made yourself ill at times and that`s not been fair to Rose but my boy Matt will sort things out for you.

Jack your boys are men now and perhaps you are right why should I have the problem ? Then Sir start right now for my boys are full of exciting and progressive ideas and Matt will see you tomorrow.

Jack its spring and time to catch up with things like mending these damaged fences and walls that thieving villages caused , Jack I know you take great interest in the estate and because your cottage is at the entrance of it but you involve yourself far too much it`s not your concern I know you promised that you would keep an I on me but that was many years ago I was young and a rogue at times for I had no one to play with or hunt with, Jack those days are gone and I can do without your guidance now, so thank you for that.

Then Sir we part on good terms ,no Jack we don`t part it`s just that the estate moves on and you Jack in assessing my physical makeup and fail to see your own as you are coughing a lot and your gait is unstable and not sleeping much.

Jack ,Nelly is getting concerned about your health.

Sir Its spring it changes us all, the birds of all kind come from far lands to set up home here, animals are hopping and jumping in joy many change colour as deer bellow and call for a mate whilst the cunning foxes stay as elusive as ever as magpies tantalise the crows and rooks around their nests high up in the beech trees whilst moles on the ground tunnel and throw up piles of dirt for birds to forage in looking for worms and termites to feed there never ending appetite.

Sir the whole place is alive with activity and nature is calling me to go amongst them and marvel at mother nature and you talk about erecting and repairing fences and walls Sir why do we need to do such things? Our

Deer attempt to jump over them our birds fly over them, and rabbits and foxes go under them.

Jack It's the people who come along and vandalise them, the erection of walls and fences is to keep people out and to determine borders and areas a reference to the enclosure acts and perhaps from the starting point of the Magna Carta.

Sir the church was built before then and so was my cottage and this estate ,so why should you talk of it ?

Jack, please listen to me and to Nelly, take a rest go to your Methodist church and take a sabbatical from this estate and go amongst the people ,they need you much more than what you find to do in and around your cottage.

Jack your church and your spring effected flock will gather and build a new home as they will break down any fences or walls that will obstruct their progress in to a good spiritual life.as they have done at Abbes springs.

Dad took up his challenge for a year when a vicar arrived to take up permanent residence, Dad lived long enough to see his achievement established that of a Methodist church and to see his Grandchildren Will and John , Dad is buried at the church on the estate under his beloved spruce tree of many cones facing the walnut tree and stone steps that witnessed many hurried trials and judgements and a few hangings.

In the cottage near the entrance to the estate we took up the residence to find nothing had changed since I was a child I sat and cried a little as memories flooded back to me as I could see mom baking with flour up to her elbows as Dad would talk of much of what was and not of what would be whilst my brothers fought amongst themselves in chastisement in who is responsible in carrying out various tasks ,the echoes of the past haunted me all day until Albert came home from his workshop with more wooden toys for the children to play with.

Nelly, he shouted its nearly done and the children can walk more and much stronger but will be delighted for I have made a trolly for them to ride about on.

Nelly in the community area they throw lots of stuff out that I can make use of ,3 small wheels I found I think those may have come from factories but I find many things and put them to good us as I deliver furniture to them.

The factory owners want me to build larger wooden sheds whilst brick builders build permanent buildings but Sir Harry is a bit reluctant to let me fell any trees but I`ll talk to Matt for he suggest me not to approach Sir Harry as he really has little to do with things now .

Albert keep away from Sir Harry all, he`s bothered about is the next hunt I don`t know why for he is much too fat to climb on a horse let alone the horse carry him

Albert it's a lovely day let us walk the estate and enjoy a day out together and give the horses a rest, then who is going to push the pram ? both of us but they can walk a little as I can gather some herbs for they are at their best this time of year Nelly many people with ailments come to you rather going to see a qualified doctors, Albert I supply doctors with my many of herbs and remedies as the public pay doctors much more than what they give me that is those who can afford it .

Albert reason there is so much sickness about is because many cannot afford a doctor and were do people bury their dead for its not at the church here on the estate nor at the Methodist church for they don`t have a burial ground ?

Nelly you are like your dad through and through for that is how he would speak but if it`s any consolation they bury them anywhere it suits them like their own back garden in the forest or in open fields but the practise appears to be easing up.

Albert, I don`t wish to dwell on this subject but were does the people who are executed get buried? Nelly it was not long ago that they stayed hung until someone would cut them down yes ``then what`?` Well some were dissembled and fed to the wild life in the forests and some had their heads removed and placed on spikes for crows hawks and rats to feed off.

I asked ``where do they bury their dead``? Come Nelly I will show you and with two play full children we walked happy and merrily along the cart tracks enjoying the sweet scented meadows and buds on trees breaking out into a new life whilst birds of the air coo and twitter and appear to be playing tag as they dart and swoop at many angles as if saying catch me if you can.

A beautiful site as I think that I never see many dead birds in the wild see plenty on dinner tables but not in the wild as I wonder where do they bury their dead yes I know they are eaten by other creatures Nelly bring the boys here for I have found some good herbs.

Albert I never knew of this place its great with herbs look a massive growth of them and some great for aches and pains and facial treatment and that one there is good for colds and sneezes Albert here I have a garden of cures.

We could n t carry much more as we journeyed home in the lovely late spring weather imitating the coocoo and the call of the owls that seemed to have taken up residence here close by the forest away from the church.

My dancing through the meadows with children one on each side of me stopping here and there to pick a few daisies or dandelions and a cowslip or two as Albert struggled carrying our daily medicines

Albert, I shouted with glee ,Will has just said his first word ,what was it ? Coocoo.

Arriving home tired and pleased and with the children asleep I said Albert I am having another baby due in the Autumn he almost hit the low beamed roof with his head in excitement wonderful great oh Nelly you make me so happy and this cottage here is to be called Nellies Lodge.

Albert these herbs are wonderful best I`ve seen for many a year why is that I wonder ? Nelly some say the village`s bury their dead there but I suppose they have to bury them somewhere, but the herbs will give much comfort to the sick and may help to prolong someone`s life.

Albert make me a house sign a large one to append to the giant beech tree saying ``Nellies Lodge`` and one for my herb garden as I`m going to grow my own when you prepare the garden but I will be using manure from our livestock for I like to know and see, what they will be growing on and not inclined to take spade and find out what these we have picked were grown on at the forest clearing.

Nelly have you noticed in the communities there appears not many young men about? Yes I have its because there is little work around here a few factories and farm work so young men don`t want it, so they go and be soldiers as it all looks good in uniform holding a gun and three meals day and that is more than there folks can provide, but they are not told they could be killed as they enter battles and that is the sole purpose of a soldier, but I suppose it is better to die on a full stomach than an empty one.

Albert that accounts for why there are lesser burials here lately.

Chapter 15

The Journey Men

Along the beautiful avenue of beech trees it is becoming a sale place for journey men with many kinds of skills and sale of many artefacts pots pans knives many things that are made from the growth of industries from other towns, a traveling market that brings out the locals in excitement of an inquisitive nature if its only to catch up with news of other areas and of the armies serving the country in the colonies and the Empire either on land or at sea as mothers are anxious to know about their sons.

Many fathers are proud of their sons in uniform were as mothers through their growing strength in women`s leagues and I am one of them who are against the whole issues of war but in fear to argue the point ,as many regiments are organised by ranking officers of much wealth Dukes Lords Barons and title holders who will after victories wear a ribbon coat and dress their estate homes out with trophies and anything else they can carry off whilst the individual may get a medal or mentioned after receiving a bullet.

Albert, we don`t want statues and images or remembrance places of the fallen the answer is to avoid conflict, Nelly are you a pacifist? What` s that?

Nelly keep your views to yourself for what you say you can be arrested, then Albert what my mother believed and died for means nothing is that what you are saying?

Albert, Rose told you about your parents that were cut down as they were on many occasions on the streets with a begging bowl and got caught up in a farmer`s demonstration and who is to blame ?

The state that should be protecting us not engaging in brute force. Nelly you`re wrong my father was shot whilst working on this estate, but I agree could have been involved in many demonstrations.

Nelly you can be caught and arrested talking like that so mind what you say Albert it is what I see and feel for this country is almost self- sufficient as coal is being found contributing well to the economy and of developing steam engines,`` come ask these journey men``.

People are leaving farm work ,for it is hard and tiring work with long hours so they are seeking town work with better pay, Nelly times you have said that so what do you propose, for anyone can say that ,Albert don`t ever doubt me or make fun of me because you men need us, if its only to push you to were you fear to tread.

Albert listen to these journey men who bring news of rioting and breaking up of farm implements as arrest and disturbances are common whilst they are kicked out of their farm cottages with no were to go and its true as the vicar at the Methodist church can verify Albert we are at war as the poor are fighting back as we enter into a period of change and prosperity and the employed want their share and more security, and it`s people like me and the church that is appearing to see things that it never saw before or failed to get involved in but they are now.

Nelly you worry me we have two children to think about now what would happen if you were arrested because of your political views and accused of inciting public disturbances in rioting ? I would expect you to find the answers and fight on but what about the children? We take them with us and let the state take the responsibility.

Nelly you`re talking nonsense, Albert help me to find the answers as it is true what the journey men say and it`s happening here for Matt has told me that Sir Harry is witnessing the same problems.

Albert you know something, Nelly I am sheltering a family of 4 in my workshop as they are helping me , it is the Smith family who Sir Harry kicked out from the cottage near the church and a another family has moved in and that`s the problem there is always someone ready to replace ,my concern is those that are replaced.

Albert you hear me go on as I do, yet you are assisting my thoughts and actions Nelly I wish not for you to know what I am doing as vicar at the church in the village is approaching me for help as he is not pleased with Sir Harry`s actions towards the farm hands ,well what does Matt say. He is talking to Sir Harry with little effect.

Albert these people at your workshop how are they eating ``ah`` yes Nelly they will be eating here tonight

Albert I wish to know more for what is going on with you and your workshop,

Nelly they have been helping me with building workshops for the mill owners as I have housed then in one I have built and it suits them .Nelly the Smith family are one of many farm labourers as others come to me but I am limited in what I can do so Nelly I am going to clear some hedge growth here and do some building and were the hawthorn trees are and employ some at the sale pitch on York road and journey further to other hamlets and crofts with what you and I create your medicine`s and household things are always in demand.

Albert you surprise me I didn't know, Nelly you were not to know for some people are in trouble with the law that's way we call them Smith for I don`t know their names and wish not to as Sir Harry comes enquiring.

Nelly I could be in trouble with the law, so I have to be discreet same with the vicar at the Methodist church as he seeks my help in providing food for the people who are made homeless from working on the farms.

Albert I did n t know you were so active amongst to villages , good I like it that way for I was one once as we seen to be calling then villages as against crofters now ,Nelly listen to me good for I don`t want anyone snooping around here you tell them nothing if anything these people are journey people having some refreshment as many are seeing to the stables and our livestock as some help to make sheds and some if weather stays good are selling and erecting a sales shed up just off Abbes walk.

I pay then upon what they sell and Mr Johnson is supporting my scheme as I am buying timber off him as Sir Harry is annoyed with me in giving aid to labourers he has dismissed, the stupid fat fool Albert ``steady on``

Nelly he is sick with something and you ought to talk to Rose as he has a doctor seeing to him but she thinks he is not receiving the right treatment but of course she is not a doctor and cannot be sure and wishes for you to see him but he says, you are quack.

Albert many say that as I am not a doctor but can recommend herbal treatment and remedies as they come to me were as a doctor treats his patients with his qualifications in medicine but I must be doing something right, as they keep coming for my remedies.

What does Matt think ? He hardly sees Sir Harry as he journeys around the district creating business deals and sales and many other things and only hears of things when it`s too late but is getting concerned.

Albert I must see him as these journeymen bring many stories in what is happening in the outlying areas and I believe them for farm labourers from other areas are calling upon here seeking work but find the same problem`s so crime rises and the problems grow and often than not those in power care little about the causes as they deal out punishments.

Nothing has changed since I was a child but the growth and demand does as young men put on a uniform not to fight for a better life here but to suppress and support the land and gentry in external matters in foreign lands far away as their Mom and Dad`s, here suffer .a constant problem I quote and have difficulty in eliminating as journey men come and go with news of other communities with same problems.

Nelly things can get worse as some are taking to arms and the army can be called in to assist the police to restore order Albert, ``no we will not see that`` Nelly, we will and are seeing it a few miles away at Abbes walk some have been arrested and taken away and Mr Johnson cannot be found as he is wanted for stopping the army and the police from beating and arresting some farm labourers.

Albert, he must be some were as we must help and find him, Nelly he is In the chicken hut awaiting you to take him some different clothes as he intends to change his appearance and Nelly we have 3 journey men who require our assistance too as they have fled from some 6 miles away .

Then Albert we do not wish to know that as we offer help and comfort to journey men at our new inn, we have recently opened so look sharp and get that shed up.

Chapter 16

Going Away

Mr Johnson what`s going on ? Nelly I don`t support the presence tactics that is employed towards the farm labours, my workers I have no trouble yet the police were sent in as workforce wondered what it was all about then police suddenly set about beating people up I interjected them as they turned on me and arrested me for obstruction and the use of violence towards them.

My status as a magistrate had been with- drawn some time ago but I cared little about that as magistrates are looked upon as enemy of the people and disliked and carry far too much authority that is poorly exercised for everything I proposed I was out voted as they feed their fat bellies on pork and whisky so I`m glad to be out of it there are not judges but act as if they are .but little be known to then that is not my purpose in being here.

Along with these here we much appreciate your kindness and like your inn it serves well to the community as we have been here 3 day`s and no one is any the wiser.

Mr Johnson what about your farm?

Oh yes the farm well I am not going back for I fear the hangman, because that Is what they will do to me if caught I am not guilty of any offence that warrants it but magistrates are not my friends anymore particularly that fat lump Sir Harry he ought to be in a mental home.

Nelly come closer I want some dark clothing and an escort to the east from there I go down to the lowlands of Lincolnshire Gainsborough I have property there and grow grain and some root crops it has had its problems but we have settled it and many other farmers are copying our system.

Nelly I want horses and guns for if I encounter any problems ,your horses will be returned along with the guns or I can pay you, Mr Johnson I am a little deaf and not heard what you said ,but Mr Johnson when you are ready to leave here we can see to your safety and at our sales pitch on York road where you may have refreshments and supplies for your journey.

Nelly, I plan to leave early in the morning with 2 men from here but what happened to your horses at Abbes Walk? Call me Tom they are scattered in the forest and the police are waiting for me to go and collect them .

Who will run the farm in your absence, or have you sold it? No but it`s in good hands but Mr Johnson er Tom will you be arrested if you comeback this way, no I will not for soon these troubles will be forgotten as magistrates are losing their powers fast because of public enquiries and various acts being considered ,but for a year at least I will be lost from around here ,but what about your farm ? Oh yes, the farm ,your brother Ben is in charge there I thought you knew.

Mr Johnson be ready for 5 in the morning. and Albert will meet you there.

At the York road sales pitch guns and horses were made available and ready as they made hast to mount and ride towards the east with Ben delighted to say good morning Albert and this is for your trouble £100 ,Ben this is a lot of money not really to Mr Johnson and Albert we have retrieved all horses from the forest and you are to have your pick of 3 no, we only gave him 2 Albert he said 3.

Albert he is a man of great influence in Gainsborough and is going to have an investigation into the farm labours problems when he has sought satisfaction about the behaviour of local authority magistrates here.

Ben welcome home Nelly is overjoyed with your return

Albert, I hear you are in demand for timber yes, but Sir Harry is being awkward from the dead wood I gather Nelly thinks he is sick and requires hospital treatment.

Albert come I will show you what you can have free from me as it is all dead wood and I require that area clearing and there`s enough there to last a long time beech cherry and a few oak trees and further on near the marsh area there are some willow rip it all out for that area is to be drained and new dykes created.

I ,hear you are fairly good at chair making and a set of 4 will do nicely thank you, no hurry but before mid-summer ,Ben what is it with Mr Johnson ? He owns much land, but I knew little about him only that he was a magistrate and a farmer and well liked, does he have any family and a wife?

Yes, and they have been up here a few times but reside in Gainsborough I was told was or is Earl of Leicester and a member of Parliament and chair of the green paper report on the poor due out in the autumn but how true that is I don`t know.

Mr Johnson did not wish to be caught for his cover would have been blown as I think the local authorities here did n` t know who he was that's why they shown force towards the poor and demonstrators I believe he was sent up here to make a report to the inquiry panel and having land and a farm here made it easier.

Well what was this about guns? Well he`s not going all that distance home unarmed, did he not have his own rather than ask me? Yes we have plenty but for you could be in trouble if found in procession and you are being called upon in 2 days and all you have is what you are allowed for if caught in procession you could go to jail and there are some around here would be pleased to see it.

Who are these people? Albert it will not happen as Nelly knows their wives or partners through their women`s league and if their men folk refuses to help them in their cause then trouble may come their way.

Ben what would you do if Nelly were attacked or in trouble? Seek out a gun I have secreted away with some of yours, how do you mean mine ? Mr Johnson gave them to me to stow away and said only if necessary am I to give them back to you.

Ben what`s wrong with Harrogate ? Nothing it`s a wonderful place but Mr Johnson sought me out and made an offer I could not refuse how did he know of you? Because my tutors at Cirencester know of him and send out referrals and here I am, yes and you know all round here and many places others don`t know of, Albert you know of it so tell no one of the secret tunnel below the church, made we think during the early 16th century when Catholics were denounced in England.

When Mr Johnson returns you will see a change in and around here because I know there is a land reformation act taking place and education program being introduced,

One more thing Ben how could the magistrates here vote .him off in being a magistrate ? Albert, I don`t think they did but certainly shown dissent towards him, but Sir Harry may know more so I`m going to ask him.

Ben keep away leave well alone for he will quiz you about the whereabouts of Mr Johnson and Sir Harry is unwell but if you get to know anything keep me informed ,sure will Albert

Nelly your brother helped a lot and we have more horses, so Nelly I am having a staging stop here and for horses to be refreshed and available for replacing as more coaches are cutting across from York road to the Great North road.

Albert the make shift inn is thriving and I thought no one had any money but it's a great talking point and its found work for some crofters who bring me many stories of hardship as it seems only journey men and property holders have money certainly not the farm labourers and crofters.

Nelly your brother has told me many things and the crofters and farm labourer`s positions are under review and some magistrates are to be investigated into their nepotism and the way how they interpret the law and the taking of bribes as Sir Harry is to be investigated.

Albert Sir Harry has done nothing wrong except being an awkward old fool but not against the crofters or anyone else it`s because he is ill I am helping him to get better, good but there is something wrong and I want to know what it is.

Albert it`s not your concern keep clear and concentrate on your workshops stables and livestock here and post more watch over what we have for there is much disturbances and killings in the communities as many crofters are moving out and seeking work elsewhere as developers are moving in causing a drift into the towns from the people here, in the inn I hear many things and somethings I wish I had not heard for much violence and serious threats are made as some come to just ask questions.

Now I am to hold my meetings here the woman`s league as some wish to work the spinning wheel and knit as some wish to do manual tasks like bundle up fire wood or operate the grinding wheel and sharpen up any tools knives and axes an activity of gossip and production for woman only.

Albert you now know why I wanted you to clear more vegetation and make room for further projects, Nelly some people are pleased to just receive a meal for their efforts but financially we are fine with the contracts from the industrialists and demand for furniture and coach building I have to have team leaders to take control and they are doing a good job.

Albert you are asking me in what to do well don`t for I do not wish to be involved it`s your job so pay then a good and fair rate and employ another apprentice for you are becoming successful ,but remember where you came from and remain in that station do not become one of these capitalistic unsocial employers who are trespassing upon the good people here who are becoming enslaved in their environment through no fault of their own than are condemned for it ,so see you remain the man I married for there is nothing wrong with money it is how it is used.

As quickly as I make friends they move on as I give then food to go with it is an exodus of pity and strife as they go on their way to be replaced with new faces as there is no coordination only the effort to survive either by honest means or dishonest means as they journey through life seeking alternative ways to combat depression and poverty in a never ending journey.

Chapter 17

It`s Help Rather than Hinderance

The seasons come and go and with another addition to the family another boy Geoffrey all within 10 years of each other 1874 or is it 1884 I don t now for there`s talk about calendar`s to tell you what day and year it is but what does that matter I don`t care if its Monday or Saturday but I now when its Sunday I go to the Methodist church and talk to my friends who live near the carr and have made a beautiful cradle from willow for Geoffrey.

Now I have a lovely carriage that sometimes I feel very privileged as many acknowledge me riding aloof in a well viewed style with the driver in his black coat and top hat trying to look his best on a Sunday of going to church and meeting people as some try and cover up their problems and pretend all is well but I know different as pain and suffering is never far away as the cure is hard to find like money and the lack of it.

Its problem after problem as wool mills give employment to many and roads and transport increases in demand and highwaymen become more whilst business men travel in their comfortable coaches looking satisfied and dressed in elegant clothing and equipped with lots of luggage that rides high on the roof of their carriage only to be stopped and robbed from people all dressed in black and holding a gun.

Our stopping station at end of Abbes Walk witness many coaches that pull up and in great anxiety scream about their ordeal but we could do little to help only offer refreshment but if asked we do offer armed escorts as many entrepreneurs think it will not happen to them because of their standing in life, I say it is because of that you are robbed.

But no these so called educated men only think of hanging the highway men rather than thinking how to avoid being robbed as they travel in luxury prolificating snuff on their wrists and sniffing it in an independent arrogant manner not knowing the people at my trading stop at Abbes Walk listening to their problems are some who have robbed or arranged the robbery.

After refreshments, many people are offered an escort to safer areas and with kindness and tell the traveller`s to pay them next time they travel this way.

This get rich scheme brought about many hangings whilst travellers secured more escorts Creepy Hollow was a place to avoid as it became known as Dead Hollow and my sales pitch became more of a trading post not in goods but in information as many would pick up a good purse in trading information, it became a time of more money in circulation as crime rose so did people`s pockets

Sir Harry was helpless to do anything except issue penalties to those brought before him as his herbal treatment did him good and enabled him to judge fairly and be more tolerant although much of it was due to Rose his wife to see he follows my medicinal recommendations as prescribed .

Now having 3 sons reminded me about my 3 brothers how playful they were when young as Ben often called on market days as now held down in the crofts, trade had warranted a weekly market from household goods to livestock but Matt from the estate was more interested in expanding the herd of cattle by his prize bull of great size.

The children were great fun on days like that but soon developed into more active roles as they quickly grew out of children`s wear and into what I called adventurous wear for they were ever seeking ever finding and ever suggesting as Albert their dad learnt them many skills at an early age.

I did `n t want them to grow up I was happy as they were but there inquisitive nature brought rewards as heavy foot wear became a fashion amongst the mill workers so John and Will took up some ones shoes that required mending and repaired them and soon after they were in demand as they used their Dads sheds to create a little earner as they didn't fancy cleaning out the pigs or anything else they wanted to be crafts men.

That, was not a problem as we had many eager people to help with the livestock as the boys asked the blacksmith up at Abbes Walk to make them a last for the clogs to fit on whilst they do the repairs but I think Ben had something to do with that, so it was that if not making shoes or repairing them they help their Dad whilst Geoffrey looked on as I have some free time, well I thought I had but like many things thoughts and plans don`t always turn out as you like them too.

I was more busy with woman`s league and herbal remedies and the inn for travellers as news carrier called to say Mr Johnson of Gainsborough has been elected to parliament as a liberal a new face on the scene as political thought is changing as quickly as the landscape and according to the messenger he will be this way later in the year.

Nelly ,can you accompany me to see Sir Harry ? Ben why what`s the problem and why me ? You have your own men take them Nelly I have something to ask him and I want you there, why what is it? I thought your brother handled his affairs he does and you and Albert handle affaires here Ben what we do here is our business so, what is it?

Near the church there was Sir Harry and Rose viewing the old walnut tree as I asked who is it this time ? With laughter and greetings as I could see my herbal remedy has worked as he asked what brings you here?

Sir are you well I asked ? Never felt better, Sir Mr Johnson has been elected to parliament ,good for him as I think he will expose a few wrongs particularly up here were they would have killed him if they could have found him it`s still a mystery how he got away.

Sir he was not too pleased about you Ben I really never knew who he was some thought he was an imposter as I did ,Sir he was dis pleased with you and a few more for you refused to help him ,true I too thought he was an imposter yes and would have hanged him Sir that is way the government have published a white paper on local authorities and the jurisdiction of magistrates.

Sir Mr Johnson was a circuit judge and whilst he was up here, he was compiling evidence to present to the enquiry board and although it was several years ago, he has not forgotten you .

Why what have I done? Nothing Sir that is the problem then what should I have done? Sir Mr Johnson was annoyed how you carried out your duties as magistrate and you are mentioned in his report not by name but by your actions and Sir I am here to see if there is any improvement in your judgement of others Sir it would be better if we talk in private.

As we went into the parlour, I could hear the house staff whispering and Rose looking anxious to know what`s going on for Ben wished for my presence too.

Sir some of your judgements are inconsistent as you have been investigated by the crown courts by recommendations of Sir Richard Johnson, Sir you say? I do and Member of Parliament and chairs a panel responsible for home affairs, now look here I am the magistrate and punish people brought before me here to deter others from breaking the law me not him.

I am not here for you to give reasons ,Ben you are what about 25 and come here to tell me my duties you can clear off or I`ll have you thrown out, Sir this I tell you now is because you have gone through a long illness and your duties as a magistrate was suspended until you were well enough to carry on and because of that this what I tell you was suspended until now.

Sir if you do not listen to me you will be required to present yourself before the law judges of this county ,now have you spoken to Matt ? Yes, I have about the estate and workforce then Sir there is a report being compiled about it and will be out shortly, but I am here because of your position of magistrate.

Ben it`s me you are talking to and address me as Sir, what are you, a messenger boy coming here telling me what to do.

Sir this is final that if you wish not to listen than I am obliged to forward my report about your behaviour and Sir when you address me you call me Sir ,Sir Ben will do fine thank you so having said that I will go come Nelly and thank you for witnessing this incident.

No wait a minute you say Sir yes because amongst other things I am chiefly responsible for drafting the report a royal commission on workers and the law a massive investigation some say next to the Magna Carta but I don't know as I was not involved in drafting that.

Ben how do you think I ought to react to such accusations from someone I don`t know their status ? With respect at all times than, what is it ? That is better, now Sir to cool down we would appreciate refreshment would you like a beer. No Sir as I am a Methodist.

Sir I remember it well when my father came to your help there was a spate of hangings then, how time changes not so many now but more than enough.

Sir Ben you never told me, Nelly I wanted to see how people perform when on equal terms for if they knew of me they would either clamp up or go their way certainly would n` t approach me as if I am an evil or a nasty character seeking ways to bring them to justice and that's not my role I am here to help.

Ben what is it with me? Sir Harry you have made mistakes in tallying on with some nasty people in bowing to blackmail to bribes of which you declared and resulted in many arrests .Sir you sentenced some people on false accusations and your severity of punishment was well over the crime warranted.

Sir you knew of magistrates who deliberately flaunted the law to suit their own ends as innocent people took the blame and you did nothing about it.

On your estate there were many hangings yet you did nothing about it, your estate no one else`s Sir my father helped you a lot in eliminating much of your troubles yet you let other troublemakers into your business as they robbed you, your wife Rose warned you but you like many think women`s views are not to be heard or considered.

Sir, Matt my brother tried to implement these statue orders from the royal enquiry, you refused the compliance of these orders and nothing was done Sir these reports and orders are something you must do over a period of time, that time has expired and you have done nothing and don t blame Matt as he has approached you on many occasions.

Sir I have delivered orally what I have been sent to do and here Sir is a written report from the commission ,

Sir this is a royal commission report and serious consequences could be sought in your non-compliance.

Ben I didn't think it was serious as many said take no notice Sir Harry again you listen to the wrong people Sir I have done what was expected of me that is to see you have got the message, excuses are not for me but for the commission to hear .

Sir you have Matt doing wonders for you and many fear him yes fear him whilst some creep around you and you listen to them and override Matts suggestions, Sir Harry these people want you out as you are not prepared to sell but will before long if you keep listening to these land grabbing gentry, now Sir am I right?

You are right so what can I do? Listen more to Matt and Rose and less to outsiders Nelly what do you think? Sir at my inn I hear many things about you, and they are not good to hear, its true they want your land and Albert knows plenty but well it`s been said you don`t wish to know.

Ben it seems I`ve been a bit of a fool so now what? Sir Ben what can I do ? You could lose your estate, I don`t want that to happen then listen up, this is what we do.

Due to a long sickness I have been unable to give direct instructions regarding the royal commission findings and over looked much mail as now I am compiling with instruction and made a start as my convalescence is now over and my agent is fully aware of what is required.

Sir sign it ,thank you that will do fine now Sir we`ll have a piece of ,that cake that you failed to cut.

Sir off the record may I suggest you have a meet with your trusted staff once a week that is Matt your Rose Bert your coachman and Ken your gamekeeper and Albert for he is a great force of information and a protector of this estate along with Ken,

Ben thank you ,Sir it`s my job as I work to help people not to discredit them.

Now about this Bull you have for I have few cows requiring a companion.

Chapter 18

Leave the Law to Others

Sir Harry after a period of illness appeared a new man approachable and willing to listen ,Albert he said,`` I have been very ill and could have lost everything,`` Sir I replied not with people you have around you for this estate stays as it is for the people to admire as they stroll through it towards the church and cherish the history of old England and that of its manor.

Albert he said, ``how is the workshop these days?`` Sir I am as busy as ever and thinking about opening premises down near the crofters an outlet for sales as here is getting a little over stocked ,then sell more, yes sir that is simple economics but sometimes difficult to apply ,not if you prepare for May day festival right here in the paddock.

You mean, yes I do and Matt and Nelly are organising it as it will be a massive undertaking of exhibitions traders journey men and showmen, of course there will be a site fee so get a site booked as demand will be great, then Sir we hope the weather stays good, yes but we have marques ordered as we intend to hold this function every year Sir you spending money , now, now, Albert.

Sir no doubt you will be showing your fine shire horse I will, but many are attempting to steal them and its upsetting me, and the horses so we are on the lookout, tell Nelly for she may hear some gossip ,but reason I am here is for you to repair some fencing the field near the paddock and a gate requires erecting.

Sir on the show day can some of my boys exhibit their work and the 2 apprentices to show theirs ,Albert I want your 2 to apprentices to stand on the entrance gate to take a small entrance fee for I know they could use some extra money as I know their family good church goers fine people Sir, Matt can see to all that.

Sir it is a good idea to bring the people in, get to know them share each other`s interests and the community will thrive, then Albert you ought to thank Nelly for it`s her idea.

I have come for some candles and not the plain singular ones I want decorative ones that can be affixed to the wall and two that fixes into lanterns and how much? well er, er, what`s that over there ? A garden seat the boys made it along with the apprentices well I want it and another like it .

Albert the two apprentices you have their parents are in need and as I have said they are good people so what I propose to do is award a scholarship each year for apprentices on the estate and that includes your staff and mine ah yes we will include Abbes Walk for the best piece of their own work to be judged by me you and Matt now here is £5 that should cover items here?

As from now the competition is on and this time next year at the annual May day show we will judge the best piece of work from the apprentices and award £5, thank you and good day Albert, as Ken my driver will collect items later .

Nelly, I have heard about May day.

Albert I`ve been robbed of a lot of stock sacks of flour fresh pork and many cooking pans and utensil`s but they were looking for money and desperate because things were strewn all over the place .when was it? about 10 30 his morning there were 3 of them with horses and rode off towards York road 2 were armed and all 3 masked ,customers were in fright for their lives as they kept demanding money but the boys came through with one of your pistols and fired, it missed them but frightened them as they mounted and rode off as Will was reloading the pistol as my thoughts were for them as they protected me as young as they are for John had a long sharp blade that he threw and missed one by inches and rested in the door and that`s it there.

How did they manage with the flour and other things? one took the dray and my horse then we shall ride after them for he will not get far on your horse as it is not a runner but a puller .

Did you recognise anyone? John did from his footwear for he repaired the shoes recently and delivered them, its Jake Black recently released from prison for theft but according to Tom his son and Mom they didn`t want him back ,yes well what about your cash, I refused to tell them where it was so they searched for it but that time of the morning I`m not likely to have taken much as much of it was in a small money bag under my skirt as their frustration grew desperate until Will frightened the life out of them.

Nelly I`ll ride after them on a fresh horse Crisp my fastest, not alone you don`t Albert, let the police do it Nelly the `re not horsemen, then go through the estate and get Matt to help, I will ,Albert I`ll ride with you ,who are you ? A witness to the crime and they have my purse ,yes but who are you ? Call me Captain everyone else does then Captain join me.

In amazement to see him leap on his horse with a gun I had failed to see Captain you could have used that, no it was unloaded but not now and when I catch them it will be used.

I want to call on Matt the estate manger he will be in the Manor that's older than the church itself and Captain you ride well, it`s the horse that runs well, what brings you this way as you seemed to know my name?

Captain this is Matt and Matt Nelly has been robbed and there are 3 of them who rode this way with the horse and dray carrying flour and other things from Nellies inn, Albert then we ask at sales pitch at end of Abbes Walk for if your robbers have come this way then they would have seen them.

At the sales pitch we were directed down Abbes Walk and sure enough there stood 3 men watering the horses laughing in a joyful mood and eating away with Nelly`s home cooking we thought it best to go slowly and pretended not to be interested in them as we dismounted for water .

They were in a joy full mood as Captain too joined their gaiety and asked if flour and kitchen items are for sale as the sale pitch is end of the road they laughed to say they would not let them on their pitch, the Captain roared with laughter with his coat collar well up onto his face that appears fashion, after watering his mount he walked coolly over to one of them laughingly he addressed him then shot him dead. .

With his other gun at ready the other two submitted to his demands of kneeling down whist their hands are tied when it was done, he went to one and smashed his gauntlet hand across his face Matt looked at me in wondering what`s going on as Captain shouted Matt ride on and aware Ben of this and bring him here before I ,well just bring him.

Captain you can`t do that ,Albert what would you do with men who has terrorised the county, murdered, and burnt down thatched cottages in their vial and destructive ways and your property and Sir Harry`s were to be targeted.

Captain how do you know that ? I have been tailing them for some time and they have escaped the hangman at York and come here as they wanted to hide up in the forests ``how do you know that ? Well Jake has family here but they hoped he would never call, Ben will tell you when he arrives but you Albert may take your dray and goods and go home tie the spare horses to the dray and you`ll be fine .

What about these two here? You`ll hear no more from them.

Albert go now as Ben is coming ,Ben these are the men who killed old Joe and his wife and burnt their house down then rode on to steal goods off Nelly and I thought you would like to see justice done.

Captain these are the men but Captain what are you doing so far south? Ben you know I am from the Sheriff`s office from York as I have followed these men to here, yes but not on your own, true as I have men making inquiries elsewhere.

Ben these men are on your domain I thought it best for you to know that we have them but where to bury them, do you think your men can bury them, Captain they are not dead, Ben they soon will be for I`m not taking them back with me .

Captain I have seen them and now we are going to ride away as they are your responsibility ,true and punishment is be served as they have robbed and killed many.

Captain I hear Nelly was lucky as one the boys shot at them Captain anyone threatens our Nelly then they must face the consequences ,Ben what I want is for you to know that they are in my custody as I make my report out for the magistrates office at York.

Captain, a horse and cart will be this way later to fetch some hay and water as we bid you good day, come Matt.

We rode away as 2 shots rang out, and in a distance, we could see Captain disappear onto the York road, Ben he has shot them did you see him ? No of course not, but ,no Matt neither did I as he was going for a magistrate and assistance then who did ? I don`t know do you?

Then Matt I suggest you get to know people before they join us and share their stories, you, did n` t know of Captain, I did and do for he is Captain James Rood of York from the magistrates office ,`` what ,don`t talk daft`` then ask Sir Harry, then why was he on his own? He was not as he has men making enquiries all over the place.

Captain, chased Jake Black all the way from York where he was to hang, but shot him as the Captain thought he was going for his gun the other 2 also wanted dead or alive the Captain preferred them dead, but you say it may not be him no I did not I asked did you see him kill them as we have no proof ,the Captain knows who killed them and I am not going to dispute his claim or actions as he may ask again for my assistance.

What assistance ? What did you do? I told him where he could find Jake Blake you see brother if I am to be a magistrate to my parish it helps to have some good references and dastardly people like those 3 who roam our country side in killing and burning of peoples property deserve the full force of the law,

Ben the Captain shot 2 in cold blood ,Matt how do you know that and what if our Nelly got shot how would you react to that? Brother you are a good estate agent and financier but leave the law to those responsible for it.

Chapter 19

Hang them High

The news travelled fast how Captain acted bravely in appending the wanted 3 men but did nothing to reduce crime as hangings continued whilst towns took on more responsibility with more secure prisons and magistrates had their own court separate from more serious cases but made little difference to the crime rate that doubled in the last year according to local magistrates reports and my name Nelly is constantly mentioned as I wonder why.

I wondered why my inn had become more of a news gathering place as some depressed and suffering families would call for a bowl of soup and a crust of bread as many were in a sorry full and pity full state ,the plight of many was growing as I was tired of having to tell people not to be critical of people in need as our society is becoming infested with people in want.

So rather than condemn them you has Christians or any other faith should endeavour to help like me as I ask for your help that any surplus food and clothing to be dropped off at the Methodist church or the Salvation Army amongst the crofters for this problem is not new, and any small change you have will be appreciated deposited in this collection tin

Nothing changes as this is same as when I was child as the hunger and hangings continue, hanging reduced the population but not the crime rate and the burial sites were not always at the church as it seems nothing changes as except when I was a child we had a travelling hangman now it`s done in towns and cities as if that's an improvement .

What, is an improvement is the women`s league who rally and congregate at the Methodist church to feed the poor, as the poor can only offer a word of appreciation.

No matter what I say it made little impact upon the needy as some worked hard and long hours were others thieved to survive or taken into the work houses that now became a nasty word to use and a place to avoid like the law and police constables who seem to be more in force and think sometimes in calling on me that they could secure a cuppa on the house but no for I viewed them as not helpers but of a fear on legs and the sooner they went on their way conversations restarted without putting a hand to their mouths.

This somehow pleased me as my boys restarted their play games of toy guns pretending to shoot many in sight as it seemed their development and growth called for more serious activities until they said it was what many are thinking as there is lack of trust and faith in peace keepers, something they had heard amongst visiting guests.

I could not believe it as many visitors talk about hangings and bet on how many will hang in one week and mark down the numbers with a piece of charcoal underneath the table they were sat at, as if we didn`t know, so in disgust John my son would alter their count and caused many a fist fight .

The boys were getting wise as they quickly grew and became in self education smart clever and wise as John and Geoffrey helped him to repair shoes and now riding boots and other leather goods as leather tanning became more accessible due to the growth of industries and Will not into one thing but all things that came his way in seeing a situation or object and improve upon it in, how can we make it better? But I had to keep an eye on them as they played soldiers for from where they got idea`s from I never knew but they loved to listen to traveller`s adventurous tales.

Albert their Dad would say, It is that Methodist church that's broadening their knowledge for it is not just spiritual education they receive it is much in English maths and general knowledge as other places of worship do the same and the Methodist movement is greatly involved as Albert would say they are old enough now to be thinking of what to do when they leave their schooling.

John and Will heard us debating their future as Geoffrey looked on, John the thoughtful one said Dad I am not being a farmer and neither am said Will for the hours are too long the work far to laborious and wages insufficient for me to live a progressive life ,then what do you want to do asked their Dad ?

You leave school a 13 so you should be thinking about a career Dad I am going to open a shop in selling furniture John, you could do well as there is great demand and you Will, Dad I`m thinking of staying with you and expand as the demand is growing for due to the influx of labour and growth of housing developments.

Dad, shouted Geoffrey, I want to have a shoe repair shop and sell new shoes too but I maybe a soldier and have my own gun and walk through the villages with pride and pomp wearing my bright red tunic and dark blue trousers and a hat to match and with shining black boots I will walk with pride and dignity in honouring my Queen and country.

There was a moment of silence as Geoffrey took up a broom and quickly came to an attention and slung the broom over his left shoulder and saluted ,we all roared with laughter to his disappointment as he was expecting an applause.

I do I do he repeated in all seriousness as we tried to change subject as their Dad said you 2 meaning John and Will we can work towards your intentions and John a shop in the village would help your intentions so keep focused on that.

A time of change as many education acts were becoming a focal point from government and religion conformist`s voluntary organisations and many public figure`s as well has the National Education Union and Conservative and Anglian movements that helped to bring about the education league and Anglican movements to have an act passed in1870 for the benefit of education policies .

During this spell we had many Irish labours here who fled from their famine of mid 19 century Ireland who contributed well to the local economy particularly on the land but all was not well as news from our navy and land forces engaged in conflict in the colonies of the British Empire as unrest grew during a time of industrial change and Britain was becoming a strong force strong enough to be elf sufficient and supress any dissent from the colonies for news of such happenings was reaching the once uneducated who could now read and argue a point.

My boys so adventures kept well up with local and foreign affairs and talked much about South Africa and its richness in land and mining and of many who sought a new life there and a new world has it seemed a time of a new life far from their troubled hard time here in England.

They are not children for long as I was beginning to look up to them as they grow in independence of self-help and preparing to carry out their objectives after schooling from church authorities as Albert had secured a workshop for Geoffrey but realised not for a young teenager so he sought out old Henry Mann a 70 year old to be in attendance and to tutor Geoffrey into business management.

Henry an Irish immigrant with red rosy cheeks standing well over 6 feet and one time bare fist fighter and flute player and dancer in the ale houses has from what was his regular work that gave him a fair standard of living until hard times found their way into his social and domestic life so he is an entertainer and a keep fit fanatic and only too pleased to keep an eye on a 14 year old and manage the shop.

The time has arrived for them to make their future as their schooling is over and I have not got them listening to the well -dressed gentry who call at the inn whilst it is noticeable that the people in much want and care go to the Methodist church and other voluntary compassionate groups like the Salvation Army who apply help aid and support in their black and red uniforms .

For my boys It is so much different in not having them around as Albert too is pleased to know they are now serious in their objectives and more pleased they have less time to take their friends rabbiting for a few pence and less use of catapults as they scare off ducks moorhens and other birds who frequent the carr.

My boys not yet grown up but expected to work for a living at their age because I was, and their Dad was but makes little sense in what they could contribute to the economy at that age as education policies are strongly argued from fee paying schools to what is now called public schools.

A little too late for my boys ,but thanks to the church education they are almost ready for what lays ahead as storm clouds gather in a time of industrial unrest and trouble in the colonies and rearmament of the services in a time when the commoner is allowed to be educated and to know what is happening around him and because of that the hangings continue as the learned are seeing what they never saw before and dislike it in a period of laze- faire politics.

On the estate nothing seemed to change except the manor that is regularly under repairs to maintain its beauty and historical status as less people trespass or poach due to increased labour and working long hours in industry and the opening of ale houses and other social amenities.

Much of this accounted for the estate to make alterations and progress along with new farm machinery and with less hassle from people committing offences on the estate same for other farming communities also it increased the new developed industrial communities but the punishments was no less severe as the hang man remained gainfully employed.

The influx of labour brought many different customs and habits as the Irish were a joy to listen too with their singing brogue and customs but from the north of England this appeared not so as development brought many customs and habits that appeared difficult to understand and accept from their diet language and methods.

Albert would sometimes say I don`t know what they are saying but pay well when purchasing, so they must be well employed, but for foreign labour was little as they preferred larger towns and cities and disliked rural magistrates who were hard on the farmers and broke up offending families ties for punitive offences.

Any serious offence judgement and penalties never altered as it was, hang them high.

Chapter 20

A Decade of Prosperity

Many new faces many new accents customs and habits all helped to make a thriving community prosper more than ever and my boys were developing fast but more of young men tall and handsome as young women about their age were taking interest in them but the boys just laughed and chastised each other as their popularity grew and the Methodist church membership increased because the girls wanted to be present were ever they went as youth development was taking place.

My market place became more in demand as people seemed to have more money to spend as they hold their children`s hands in perusing amongst many new introduced household items in an atmosphere of gaiety and laughter as women wear new fashion dresses and a parasol to match whilst men wear a suit of a tight fitting trousers and a short cut coat of dark grey or brown and plain grey dull shirt with a starched stiff white collar as its weekend and Saturday market time and certainly best clothes must be available for Sundays.

A noisy scene of hens geese ducks pigs rabbits and an odd horse or two always an interest to the more affluent visitors whilst others found more interest in vegetables bread and cakes but why they were so noisy I never knew for everyone wanted to shout as if everyone is deaf but not the immigrants who were finding their way into our community the Jewish and Indian people and many from the colonies all seemed quiet and reserved with much respect of each another.

It became that my premises are not large enough to meet the demand of people wanting market stalls for I am not inclined to do any more deforesting to make space as what is happening amongst the crofters and near the carr as house building is reshaping the landscape and I am not inclined to contribute to it and have no need to.

Albert is in over demand and his place has served its purpose it`s time to move into more modern and productive premises and John now well established and Geoffrey with Henry Mann commonly known as paddy is prepared to sell off his land adjoining his premises and so it was for John a new manufacture of furniture and show rooms was established of much demand in tables and chairs followed by dressers much on the line of the Welsh dressers.

A period of steam of locomotives and auto mobiles and the growth of families created much interest excitement and pleasure in a period of demand and supply, from shipbuilding and locomotives to raw materials all contributed to a period of happiness to those who kept well clear of breaking the law.

The law, many still never knew what was the law they knew what was right and wrong and the difference between pain and pleasure as it became more clearer as more people could read and write but what is the law many asked?

A realisation took hold as the masses learnt that of criminal law Statue law common law and civil law that dealt with offences within that group that in a way the offender knew or understood what type of crime he or she had committed and more serious crimes will be dealt usually out of one`s locality.

All what changes brought was the system and procedures but not the treatment or reasons or why as the hangman remained unaffected in his duties as prosperity increased and church membership expanded as many nominations were eager to establish themselves within local communities as the Methodist movement and the Salvation Army who became a growing influence but for the Catholic it seemed they had to travel elsewhere for the education acts only considered those of church of England faith.

It was a time of not knowing what is happening as many changes were made as one could experience it when it happens but not knowing previously, like the factory acts a farce in the beginning as factory workers never knew it existed and only 2 maybe a few more men appointed to see to safety of all the country as many accidents happened and not reported as many was in fear of losing their job.

After many years of struggle more and more people began to realise that what their forefathers argued for is to speak as one body and organise representation as a trade union, irrespective of what the state and employers think and because of that employers became angry and negligent in many areas as industrial unrest grew and a period of strife occurred in various pockets of industrial England.

That brought many back to the land and farming as farming was in constant demand for labour and those that were unable to find work found plenty in the rural areas to be had during dark hours or in the forest or setting snares for rabbits as the law came back into play as it did to their forefathers.

Many saw their future in the forces the army was a consent call as communications were now much better as news -papers became popular depicting success of armed forces abroad in protecting the Empire and claiming it to be a good career to any young men who wish to break away from the dull dismal life of a factory worker and see the world.

The reading in the papers of armed forces success after success and glorifying in suppressing the enemy boosted England`s confidence in foreign matters and recruitment of young men to join the ranks but failed to tell them why there are vacancies.

Prosperity in England is all I knew and heard nothing about Ireland as Paddy would often ask or Scotland and Wales as the Boars in South Africa were making news in resisting from losing their lands but it seemed one sided news as the Boars are wrong and England is right as Boars meaning farmers in Dutch so it is Dutch farmers who are resisting, then why are commonwealth soldiers there supporting the British at Rourke`s drift a small farm stead that belong to Mr Rourke ? I cannot make sense of it only to think we are a waring nation.

Here we are seeing less of stage coaches and less activity around the cottage now many have no need to come this way to reach the old Roman road and the York road and the inn is now losing its popularity as we consider in closing it and concentrate on Alberts furniture and my herbal remedies as the boys are now thinking more of themselves as they talk much about foreign matters like South Africa gold mines and what the gold rush brought about up in Alaska or was Canada ? I hear there is much mining here people prospecting for coal as some call it black gold as they claim its worth more than gold for what it can do and provide for as many claim the country will be dependent on it as industry must move on and help to provide a better living for its people as we in the woman`s league will be ready to accept change if it`s an improvement from previous decades.

I don`t know the answer and some-times care less about knowing as I am happy to stand and talk to passes bye on their way to church and forget about world problems as they are widely known through the media that saddens me for I am happier in not knowing ,for at times I pray for good news as it has become a scarcity, people are far too eager to inform me of any disasters arrests and hangings as if I wish to know as I sometimes feel like going indoors and slamming the door behind me.

With industry thriving and farm work having new types of machinery to hurry along harvesting and vegetable crops a period of development was paying off and helped to contribute to the wellbeing of a growing society in a decade of development.

My boys like a good many took advantage of it as Albert and I reorganised the cottage ``Nelly`s Lodge` as it is called by many who pass on and attempt to snatch a rose or two from the overhanging bush.

Some do leave small change on the help yourself table displaying flowers and vegetable`s but seem to get satisfaction from the overhanging rose bush as it pleases them to pick a red rose and pin it on to their girlfriend`s coat we would laugh to see them prick themselves and shout ``ouch`` as they pin the rose to their friends coat as we would laugh as they walk on pleased to think they have something for nothing as Albert would shout ``,if she`s worth taking out ,then she is worth spending money on``.

As many viewed Nelly`s Lodge in passing as a meeting and greeting place as when out and about we would hear people say fine see you at Nelly`s lodge where the flowers and herbs smell lovely amongst the grey chimney smoke from burning pine logs that drifts idly into the atmosphere as we enjoy a decade of growth and prosperity even though a rose or two is on the house.

Chapter 21

There`s Always a Price to Pay

Albert is pleased to see the boys as I call them who are making good but seem restless as if wanting more activity in their lives for when retiring from their daily business or activities the nights are long with little to do as I say go and feed the ducks oh no not for then, more interested in commonwealth affairs as placards display last news of foreign events .

Its either girl friends or latest news as I thought don`t bother us and get on with it and so it was business first and play later but nice when my brother Wilf called to say he had taken up more acquired accommodation near the race course to be near his work as now more of an important role from that of chief hosteler at the race course and planning to marry as he would slip us free tickets to the most important races of the year as I would buy a new outfit of fashion of the day and Albert would get out his old bowler hat and still in good condition and spit on his hands and rub it into his hair to pat it, down,

Every year I get to telling him to use my herbals of lavender water or rose water and many more to choose from but old habits are hard to lose he would say and remind me of developing something to remove walnut stain and mahogany stain off hands rather than having to wear gloves when staining furniture.

It was great fun as we secured Sir Harry and Rose tickets as we would ride in their coach all posh and appealing of rich and famous but not knowing what was rich is, as we`ve never been there but comfortable in what we have as we ride in style in Sir Harry`s coach as small boys would try and hitch a ride at rear of the coach as driver would turn in anger and try and reach out with his whip to deter them from any danger don`t know why we went to the races for I could never choose a winner but it was lovely really as the presence of horse driven coaches gave a pleasant sight of antiquity as against automobiles becoming more and more of a taking point to replace horse power to motor power an innovation that's changing many things in its development.

There is always a price to pay as many wait in excitement to see many auto mobiles on the much improved roads suggests I am right as many things are changing and it appears for the good ,the good of the majority and an improvement from when I was child.

Trouble with me is I am a wonderer in living in a cottage as old as the mansion and older than the church I feel I fit nicely in that category as all round me is changing and I don`t want to change but change I must as cottage industries are becoming unnecessary as now I know when the boys bring their girlfriends they view me as an old un fashioned mother who talks too much about wild life nature and herbal remedies as they look in wonder and I think you have lot to learn my dears.

I could see love in their relationships that I know that the day will come as Albert would say it`ll not be long as love is in the air as we have given them a good start in life the rest is theirs but I wish they would take less notice in what is happening abroad it was all about the Boars in South Africa or whatever they called it as now that seems to have passed over as it seems the battle was fought and that was that.

Soldiers cannot say that for as soldiers they go to the next problems as there always is a another problem for man is a peaceful living animal if left alone but in this changing world he is not left alone as he is in constant need want and demand.

Nelly what on earth are talking about and who to ? Albert I was just thinking about present situations of people seeking power ,power and dominance over others, Nelly you were thinking allowed I could hear you outside even the hens geese and rabbits stopped to listen, no Albert they went quiet because they saw you with that knife in your hand.

Albert I`m pleased to see our family have progressed ,all of them have turned out to be worthy business people it was not their schooling well the church played its part the rest was down to us and I`m proud of them.

Geoffrey he has really surprised me his name is often in the papers talking to dealers and introducing new designs in footwear and winning many orders even the centre of shoe making like Northampton send representatives to his workshops and marvel at his designs now the armed forces are giving him contracts for marching boots now I think it will not long before he`s into top hat and long coat but at least I Bet he would treat me to a pair of his fancy ladies shoes.

Nelly, he would but when have you been a lady?

Nelly you, ``bet`` better not let me catch you gambling Albert a constant joke of mine for no I am not into that as I always will be a true Methodist and a lover of horses as it is paramount to my nature to love all animals.

Albert it is you I worry about, you walking about the garden carrying a knife frightening hens geese and rabbit`s like that, you should go and apologise, and for goodness sake whatever are you doing wearing a rabbit fur hat whilst the rabbits cling to their wire mesh door trembling in fear, do you not have any respect for Gods loving animals now go and apologise?

Nelly I never thought you felt like that as you were talking about family originally ,well now you know ,now if you will excuse me I am busy getting tea ready, good Nelly for I am starving and what is for tea? Rabbit stew ,why is there a problem with that?

Nelly I have been approached if we wanted to sell this lodge as there is some interested parties keen on it if the price is right ,Albert there is a price for everything but not this lodge no Albert not for sale so they can keep away unless they want some buck shot around their feet, Albert this lodge is a piece of old England and it was during the Conquest when this was built so every stone cobble or piece of grit is precious, so these fellas flashing their money around can clear off as I have no time for them.

Albert tell them that but you won` t you are too nice a fella and it will be left to me ,Nelly it`s your lodge not mine, stop it Albert no more discussion for I intend to live my live out here now eat your rabbit stew and change subject.

Nelly were will John and Will live when they get married? I don`t know they have their own premises maybe, can manage there, we shouldn`t be concerned about that as its their life but if they wish for advice and help it would be good for them to know we are around to help but what brought this on? It`s John because it`s getting serious with them and I can hear bells a ringing.

Albert, I seem to forget that the years roll on for John will be soon 20 I remember it goes 20 18 and 17 whooa it seems to have flown by so what year are we in ? Nelly times you ask me that, you work it out as we were married in 1872 well I think so and you said you were 18 then, in 74 John arrived in 77 Will arrived and in79 Geoffrey arrived now John is 20 so it is what? 1894 correct, but Albert how do now that`s correct ? because the papers carry dates ,well where do they get their dates from? Calenders and who makes Calenders? Printers Nelly I think you`re teasing me, I am but not keen on local papers for this trouble in South Africa just doesn't seen, to go away now who wants, to be reading about troubles abroad as we have plenty here?

Another, thing the navy all conquering foreign naval shipping, I don`t believe that, they only print what they want us to believe because it makes good reading and sells, now tell me, when did they print something that defends the rights of man or woman? Albert we must always look and take alternative views and see where we can improve as it`s just not right for young boys going up chimneys or working long hours in industry and falling asleep at a machine as injuries are plenty, and thank God, none of mine have had to, experience any of that.

Nelly, it`s on the farms as well, I know it is great in summer months awful in winter and. whilst the masses do nothing about it nothing will change and it concerns me a lot as some would say it`s alright for you riding` about in Sir Harry coach as I don`t have to as we have one of our own , but to be seen with him people come to their own conclusions and not nice to listen to but know where to come when in need.

Everything has its price and usually it is the poor who suffer in a market economy like ours as they have nothing to offer or barter with as money is the only a means of exchange.

Nelly, to say you had little or no schooling you seem to have made up for it somewhere, Albert time will come when women will rule this country, not yet for some time and maybe not in my life time but it will happen or else you men will be preparing your own meals I ask do you think women should have more say in politics and day to day affaires? For I do.

Nelly thank you for some lovely rabbit stew but for me I have not voted in my life and when I am asked then I shall say what about my wife too now if you have the money you can vote as like everything else if the price is right might and power is right.

Albert, a conception I would like to change.

Chapter 22

Nelly Focus More on Us

Nelly in business all 3 of them are doing fine and it`s good to know that as they often bring their girl- friends for tea you know them all and their families all good people and church goers but I do think you worry too much about them,.

Albert, they are all very close to each other were one goes others follow as if they cannot do anything alone ,so what`s wrong with that? Nothing ,but they must learn to act independently they can`t keep doing what the other does ,why not ?Albert we are not back to questions and answers again ? Whoever they marry will have different ways and thoughts as 2 people must act in concert with each other to have a successful marriage and may wish to move on to different areas to live, our sons cannot keep relying on each other as if they are boys as they broaden their outlook on life.

Nelly its time you focused more on yourself stop thinking about them all the time, concentrate on your woman`s league ,the church and the 2 horses we have for they are getting old and devote more time at home now you have got rid of the inn, and what shall we do with the space that we used for the market ? Nelly you can find plenty to do without wondering what your sons are doing.

Albert, what shall we do with the space ? Open a shop instead of having a couple tables displaying your wares have a covered shop a lock up shop ,then Albert build me one, right Nelly it will be part built of stone and finished in timber as all the interior will be of wood and sufficient shelf room for your herbal remedies and preserves the building will have one large window of panes about 6``square interior will have display storage cub board`s and barrels for flour and grain you also will have a new type of glass bottles and containers has Hiram Codd bottles will soon be a thing of the past.

The interior base I`m not sure but thinking of stone for a fireplace to be fitted now that is only a small part of the area for rest of the land I will have my work shops and that's where the dogs will stay for if any intruder`s than the dogs will be alerted and Sir Harry wants a pup off Beth the German Sheppard I`ll not charge him for he`s been a good friend for many years although at times I felt like well you know Nelly he was a bit of a fool before he met Rose .

Sir Harry will want to pay you for the pup and the kennel for it to shelter in, he will who, says so ? Sir Harry ,and I want to put Collar the dog in part of the hen run until you compound it all off, ah yes nearly forgot Sir, Harry says you can borrow the flat dray to haul timber.

Nelly Is there anything else I should know? Ho ,no Albert I don`t wish for you to think I`m interfering as you should act independently and not in concert with me .

Albert everybody need`s somebody and I need you as you need me Nelly it was you that was showing concern for the family yes because it`s not the girl friends or money or work it`s this interest in world affairs as papers are making much play of things about trouble in the Colonies for I think at times we are better not knowing but no the masses want to know and eager to know.

They will write anything to secure a good circulation of papers and take the focus from problems here right under peoples nose`s Nelly newspapers are in business to sell papers it`s their job and what people believe it`s up to them Albert people around here will believe anything except what we woman shout about to be looked upon as stupid silly and trouble makers and scorn and spit at us of our demands whilst you men folk are supressed and beaten down as rabble and trouble makers and wish to bring down the government as you are hauled before the magistrates .

Albert don`t focus me as an interfering mother but a mother who cares and perhaps too much at times Albert I am aware what is happening abroad I have my sources and true accounts not what papers think for across Europe there is a great movement of people who seek new lands ,these are the people who carry the truth who focus on better and happier times in another country as a lot of them are Christians and of the Jewish faith .

Albert this is a time of great movement of the working classes as people are realising its us and them as its always been, but now`` us ``are more noticeable and argue for change and trying very hard to start with changing some laws as some seek a way out and settle in foreign lands and the Dutch have done great things in setting up new lives elsewhere.

How do I know ? Through the power of God and the church we pray in as we embrace many nationalities in our church and these Godly people are not likely to tell me anything different as I would rather believe what they say than what the daily papers say.

Nelly again you talk about others, it us you who should be thinking about you and me as we adjust to 2 of us as we ought to enjoy ourselves a bit more now we have more time Albert I`m happy as I am but it`s you who is making plans of rebuilding, Nelly you suggested it ,Albert you suggested it not me after you had made plans.

Nelly you had been talking to Sir Harry no I had not ,you did you said you did ,well it was Rose that told me, Nelly is that how you carry on in the women`s league meetings for you confuse me.

Albert we cannot just think of ourselves it`s our nature to go amongst the new intake of workers and crofters parishioners and farmers they all know of us and speak well of us when they mention Nelly`s Lodge an apt name with a kind expression about it as we cannot think too much about ourselves as we are seen to give aid and assistance to many and I am not going to change.

Now you are borrowing Sir Harry`s flat bottom dray but its Matt that`s done that Sir Harry has little to do with running the estate but doesn't mind although you will have it for a couple weeks as you pick up your ordered timber from the canal wharf in Town already cut that's shipped in from Sweden also you are assisting someone to move their household goods into different houses

Albert we are too much in demand to be so selfish in only thinking about ourselves and that's` how I want it ,Nelly I know that what I`m trying to say is we ought to have more time together as we will when I move my workshops here for as I am confident in having 2 good men working for me Tommy and Fred they have been with me since they were boys and served their apprenticeship well as there are good sales men when manning the sales outlet amongst the crofters.

Albert the crofters as you say more like small towns as the crofters are lowly disappearing into large farms as some of their mall cottages are being demolished to make room for larger roads and better built houses to accommodate the new influx of labour .

Then there is a growing market for your business, yes and always will be and many thought I was a magistrate like your brother Ben and surprised to know I am not but like to think I am a defender in promoting people`s rights and of promoting any appeals panel for far too often people`s rights have been eroded through their lack of not knowing.

Not their fault as they aren`t aware of such things, but Nelly they are now and demand greater say in their industrial employment Albert it sounds good but the State doesn't like it your trouble rousing claims are put as trouble makers as they are hauled before the courts .

Nelly I like what you do in the woman`s league but as comfortable as we are I will always support the majority in pursuing a better life, it is not the State that is in question it is the people who regulate it to suit their own purposes of greed and domination for as richer they get the creators and contributors of it fail to share any wealth they have created that`s why we cannot act independently and be selfish as we are part of society time to ourselves and less time for others is not the answer in this greedy capitalistic time we live in.

Albert what`s so wrong in that ? We require capital to invest to promote growth true it is how it is achieved and distributed and because of, my believe that will improve one`s social and domestic life that may enable people like us to have more time for each other.

Then Nelly do you propose I pack up doing what I do, and put people who work for me out of work in order we spend more time together?

No, I would get fed up with you under my feet all day.

Then what do you propose ? I propose that when you have built your workshop and my shop here, we hold our meetings here and Albert I hear from Sir Harry and my brother Ben that you are nominated to become magistrate.

They might change their minds when they hear of my thoughts of the State and how it should be regulated no Albert it`s because of your out –spoken views, particularly those on crime and punishment.

Albert , Sir Harry wants a word and Ben as they wish to see how you would conduct a case before you regarding theft of 2 ducks as it is upon your management and conducting a case that you will be considered to sit in judgement of others as it is upon their recommendations by, a kind of test case.

hen? Now, Nelly I can`t just drop everything and go ,you can for you have good people running your business, or have you no time for people who are breaking the law and the judgement of it ,you so condemn but you want us to have more time together and less time for others .

Nelly where is my coat?

Chapter 23

Sir, I was Hungry

Albert, we want you to take this case and Ben and I will assess and guide you if any problems arise if you handle it satisfactory then our recommendations will be forwarded on to higher authority for their acceptance or refusal. Sir Harry you have given me short notice why could not you tell me sooner ?

When you are ready, we can go in ,I will introduce us to the bench then proceed as you are in control.

The prisoner in the dock you are Stanley Oats and reside at 2 Main Street of this Parish ,the prisoner replies yes Sir ,you are accused of stealing 2 Ducks by 2 of Sir Harry`s game keepers how do you plea? Not guilty sir ,Mr Oates this is your first offence as your records show and that you are married with 2 children both at school ,that is true Sir one moment ,what is it Sir? Albert get on with it or we`ll be here all day the man is guilty, Sir as chairperson I will conduct this case as I wish.

Mr Oats why did you steal 2 ducks? Sir I didn`t steal the Ducks but had intentions to feed my family Sir I am unemployed and have no money to support them, so I have to struggle to survive and any opportunity to secure a meal I take it as the assistance from the support and relief panel refused me any financial help.

Did they tell you why ? Sir ,they said`` haven` t you anything you could sell``, I said no as all we have is a table that we wish to eat off 3 hairs we use to sit on and a few utensil`s and 2 beds to sleep in.

Mr Oats can you not find work as there appears many vacancies in factory work ,true Sir but only available to those they want, and they don`t want me .

One moment please ,what is it Sir why are interrupting me ? What is it? We do not wish to listen to excuses get on with it.

Mr Oates what is your profession? I am an unemployed engineer and an Irish immigrant come to settle here ,at first things were good but since the Irish problems have become news the IRA who are in conflict, and comments from your parliament who the IRA are much saddened to hear, and people like employer`s see people like me as if I am to blame.

The IRA have intensified their activities .it seems that because I am Irish, I am not wanted but do hear Sir that railways are in want of workers as they lay many tracks about the country and could be up here soon at least Sir I hope so as many of my Irish friends work on the railroads.

Mr Oates are you a member of the IRA? I have no affiliation to any organisation except one, what is that ? My Catholic church but, you do not have one here and I feel in neglect of spiritual guidance as I have to struggle to survive.

You are an engineer and out of work Sir I am out of work because I am Irish not of my profession, well what is it, are you a train driver ?

``Oh no Sir`` I am a more of an engine mechanic like an engine assembler and the industry up here are crying out for engineers to keep the engines running to drive the wheels of production.

Sir I am British as you and many more here, yet I am penalised for being Irish and driven to despair so do to me as you must throw my children into a home for wayward children and my wife in a workhouse.

Do as you please for in prison Sir they may provide me with a church and my kind of people who only wish not to go hungry.

Do you know of anyone called Henry Mann? Sir I have known Henry for many years he used to send food around for my children now I hear he is not well God bless him a good man if ever there was one.

Tell me how were you caught? Sir I was apprehended by 2 men who approached me with guns one walked to me and pushed point of a rifle under my chip and said Paddy, I`m going to blow your head off, Sir I had 2 ducks in, a bag they claimed I stole off the estate.

They said they were game keepers for you Sir Harry, yet I was not on the estate and the ducks were running loose not far from Nelly`s Lodge so what am I to do but only catch them ? Sir my life was at stake as I looked down a barrel of a gun ,are you saying your captives threatened you ? Yes, Sir then I was taken into custody as you Sir Harry contacted the local police.

Now let me be clear about this you saw 2 ducks running loose and you caught them and bagged them then where did you get the bag from?

Eric Smith who as passing bye he was going to gather some dead wood.

Did it not occur to you that these ducks belong to someone? No Sir as there are many down by the marshes and I figured these had wondered from their usual areas, what would have happened if you had run off ? Sir they warned me not to, as they would shoot me.

I think I have heard enough good whispered Sir Harry that's it them, well sentence him, oh Sir this far from over as now I wish to question the witnesses ,as I walked slowly nearer to the witnesses I could see Sir Harry in anger.

I addressed the 2 to ask are you the 2 responsible for apprehending the person you see in the dock? Yes Sir, are you 2 responsible for filing the report? Sir Harry wrote it for us, then what is written in your report and what was said is true ,every word Sir.

You are aware to trespass and poaching is a serious offence so before I make judgement upon the accused I want you 2 who apprehended the accused to be absolutely certain in what you said in your report for Sir Harry to put his pen to for you can change it if you are not sure ,Sir it is all true ,good you may step down.

In my summing up ,thank God for that ,Sir Harry I have to re mind you not to comment or interrupt me anymore as I am chairman and will conduct this trial as I see it and as you have a vested interest in this case therefor Sir I ask you to stand down, Sir do not hesitate as if I`m fooling so please leave the court, thank you.

To recap, when you bagged the Ducks you was not on the Estate true Sir, I was on the public footpath yes so it says here in the report but the Ducks could have come from the estate, to that Sir I don`t know.

Sir I had a gun at my throat yes you did it`s all here in their report Stanley you don`t mind if I call you Stanley ,no Sir well Stanley Sir Harry has no Ducks and you were on common ground and no one saw you bag a couple of Ducks as your life was threatened by 2 people who had guns and neither of them authorised to carry guns coked and loaded ready to fire in a public place.

Yes you 2 may look for I had it checked out as you are allowed on the estate to carry guns but you were not on the estate as your evidence suggests and I asked you if you wished to alter anything and you wished not to .

Therefore ,this court allows you Mr Stanley Oates compensation of £4 for false imprisonment and you 2 to pay compensation to Mr Stanley Oats the sum £2 each for threatening behaviour and beheld in custody to attend this court to face charges of that and of carrying loaded guns in a public place and threatening with intent to commit harm.

Business of this court is now terminated.

You are home Albert how did you get on? I found out who got our 2 Ducks its Mr Oats Mr Stanley Oates who is right here come in Stanley, Nelly he is going to fix me up with a powered driven engine for my work shop that right Stanley in fact you can help me to build my new premises too and next time you go hungry come to the front door, and Nelly here will have the hole in the fence mended, Stanley you look troubled what is it ?

So this is Nelly`s Lodge whooa, Stanley this is Nelly and you best be on your way as your family need you so here take this basket with some bread and a few eggs and some chicken breasts for we are out of Duck, come to think of it what happened to them?

Mr and Mrs Lodge thank you ,Henry its Nelly and Albert you just ensure you`re not late in the morning 7 o`clock will be soon enough Stanley, what is it ? Mr Albert I`ve not seen such kindness I feel like crying now I know there is a God for who else would want to help an Irish immigrant family in distress and far from home ,oh thank you ,God please forgive me for at times I doubted you.

Albert, call me Paddy and I have a motor at home I can bring you but its driven by steam, electricity will eventually replace it but until then this will do its job, it is heavy two of us perhaps can manage but we require a flat bottom dray, Paddy we`ll sort it.

Stanley, how old are your children? 12 and 9 and call me Paddy as its not offensive and sounds friendly, then bring your boys tomorrow and they can start to repair the fence as I can find them something to do up to midday at least but I forgot they have to go to school .

No Mr Albert not yet as they are Catholics and there is no Catholic school available yet but maybe in a year, then Paddy they will learn here but not of religion but basics of English and maths and anything they show interest in.

Paddy call me Albert ,and can you ride a horse ? Yes, but looking forward to be, riding in an automobile and that's not too far away but first I must take care of my wife and children to overcome our hunger so thank you for what you have given, and God bless you .

Chapter 24

Magistrates to be Judged

I wonder what the engine, would look like I hope he`s not fooling as it might be something some ones thrown out, so I think I`ll go and have a look .

Sir Harry you`ve just caught me as I was on my way, so what is it ? It`s you and your court fiasco ,what`s the meaning performing as you did in court you made me look a right fool ,no Sir I did not it was done in a correct manner to avoid any embarrassment and you complied with my correct instructions.

Sir, because someone is brought before the courts it does not mean they are guilty as the courts are established to determine ,firstly to see if the law has been broken that is what I did because with-out that procedure we cannot judge then I look to any other factors that can assist the prosecution or defence for the person brought before the courts ,and for what that accused may have suffered from something he was innocent from, and you Sir was part of it for you cannot sit in judgement where you have a vested interest.

The public, why did you not clear the court ? Sir Harry those people were permitted by clerk of the court and given instruction as they are taking notes as they seemed to take much interest Albert. they were watching you of what you did whilst in court.

Now Sir I am pushed for time so is there anything else you wish, to say? Albert Lodge those in the public gallery one was a magistrate and one was a Judge ,they didn`t know of you and you didn`t know of them and they have endorsed your application to become a magistrate and here I have the necessary report and endorsement signed and sealed so as from now you are a magistrate.

As for you making me look a fool that part was arranged and so was my interest in the case as you acted perfectly right and the 2 who bought the accused in ,one does work for me or did and the pair as you recommended are in custody as they thought of gaining favour of me by apprehending someone with 2 ducks at the time I only knew what they told me but I knew I had no Ducks to steal .

Albert Lodge congratulations Sir

Sir Harry are you in any hurry ? No why, could you accompany me for I am about to go and pick up an engine what an automobile ? No just the engine so come.

Paddy are you there, as I shouted from front of his house, ah Sir pleased to see you now come I will show you the engine.

Paddy this is beautiful big but beautiful now Paddy be honest where did you get it from ? Ah begorra Sir I knew you would be asking that, I buy them , Paddy ,Sir I swear I do look Sir have a look at this, what is it ? It is a blueprint of assemble Sir, can you not follow it.

Well Paddy what are doing here, Sir originally, we are from Dunmurry in Ireland then moved to Belfast I then went into the ship building at the engine assembly department, yes but how did you acquire it? Sir you`re being all questions, I worked in the factories here fitting engines to drive the long leather belts I bought them in from the producing factory and assembled them as I carried many spare parts and eventually secured a blue -print.

Paddy that is a skilled profession, to be sure Sir than why are you out of work ? Sir I planted a right hook onto the factory owner`s chin and if he had got up, I was ready with my left destroyer, but the coward stayed down .

Did he press charges? No. he had other methods ,why did you hit him? I would have shot him if I had gun but its, not finished yet .

That rat owes me £245 for supplying and assembling engines.

It was that the IRA were making much sad news in the papers and I am Irish so he started to insult me in front of other people and grin in ignorance and mock me then he thumped me in my chest in mocking me as he picked up an oil can and sprayed oil on me and laughed to say `` it`s not as bad as being tar and feathered.

I hit him with my right fist that lifted him about 2 foot off the ground and that ended my work of suppling and fitting engines to the mill owners.

Paddy why did you not prefer charges ? Sir what mill worker would give witness as they would be in fear of losing their job regardless of their mistreatment, then why did n t you come and see Sir Harry for advice ? Sir I knew not who to trust and Mr Seagrave the mill owner has a few heavies he can call upon as they have threatened my wife and my children here and made fun of them because they speak a bit different from around here.

I think all my troubles comes from Mr Seagrave orders the mill owner as he sends his heavies to me ,this started about 6 or 7 weeks ago as we are slowly being driven out and have no were too go and all my money was tied up in supplying and fitting these engines so, well that's about it

Now let`s get this little baby loaded onto the draw, Paddy are these your boys ? Yes Sir, and this is my wife Mary, pleased to me to you all.

Paddy would you like us to look into it. Sir it would only fuel more problems for he`ll send his mem around and beat us up and smash furniture as they have done before, look we have little furniture now and as sure as God is my judge he will be giving me another call for people around here will tell him that I have been talking to you.

Paddy listen to me I know many people around here and they know of me so stand fast for a moment as I call someone I see over there.

Jimmy ,Jimmy, come here I wish to speak to you ,Sir what is it for if I`m seen with Paddy here I could be in trouble ,Why, because the mill owner says so for I could lose my job and there are others ,Jimmy what has Paddy here done to you ? Nothing Sir I don`t know of him but I do not want any trouble Jimmy I have known you a long time this not like you.

Sir the mill owner holds the power over us we even got a union going but they smashed us with the legality of it then applied their own law and put some out of work, Jimmy I have known you a long time Sir things have changed that's why we have stopped coming to your house to talk in fear of reprisals

Jimmy you are welcome anytime even though I am now a magistrate don`t let that deter you or anyone else but we must go now as we have a lot to do.

Paddy come, jump on and Mary and you boys

At the lodge there stood Nelly admiring the new contraption of an engine as Sir Harry was more interested in what Paddy had to say Albert he said we must talk for we cannot allow this to happen who does the millowner think he is?

Then Sir what do you think we ought to do ? Albert, I like that and what`s that Sir ? You, asking me what to do well we ought to pay the factory owner a visit with our clerk of court Sir Harry I have loads of work to do, and this turns up .

Mr Albert ,I hear you, now tell me what wants doing and I`ll do it .right all this area to be cleared and my workshop to go right here that's the shed in sections ready for assembly and for the engine to go over there.

The other site is for a shop and here is the plan Sir can I start tomorrow, one moment Sir Harry, shall we pay the mill owner a visit tomorrow ? Yes, we talk it over tonight come for 6 ,and bring Paddy with you .

Sir I cannot leave my wife and children for long ,you can Paddy as you are staying the night with me and my wife Nelly for you have nothing to go back to so go inside and have a warm drink as Sir Harry wishes to talk to me.

Albert something seems not right as Paddy here is an intelligent man as I believe there is more to this ,but we`ll see. Sir Harry we talk more about that tonight .

,Albert we magistrates are not has powerful these days but powerful to shut down premises and if not I know some who can but we don`t want to do that and if it`s true that Paddy is owed money than we put pressure on for it to paid to him for I like Paddy ,Albert there are many bye laws that are broken every day and it is difficult to know what they are some we put a blind to and many people don`t know of them but that is no one`s fault of ours.

Albert ,I dislike people exerting their power over others when they do not have the right to do so and I am losing my temper so Albert we must put a stop to it and what do you suggest ?

Sir I suggest we bring Ben in from Abbes Walk and give this mill owner a visit Sir can you send a rider to inform him ? Ben is well up on legal documents and agreements and some factory acts and of trade as we are more of minor issues ,Albert you did n t do so bad as you are the talk of many lawyers and judges as many would like to meet you.

Sir Harry we cannot allow the workers to be held to ransom frightened and harassed ,Albert see you tonight as life is getting remarkably interesting lately as I am intrigued with the engine how do they work ? I think you have to feed some coal into a fire and make steam but I don`t know but know we have plenty of coal as word is they could be drilling for it as we stand on thousands of tons of it.

What drives the drill ? Ahh Sir Harry now that`s a good question ,see you tonight.

Ben good to see you ,Albert congratulations how does it feel to be one of us ? Ben Paddy here is sadly mistreated yes Albert I have the gist of it from Sir Harry and we are not having that kind of problems on our doorstep for if one can get away with it others will follow so I will check his deeds and agreements whilst you check any bye laws he may have broken then as you have told me we have him with threatening behaviour and harassment likely to cause harm.

If he calls witnesses then you Albert can take over questioning as I hear you`re pretty good at that and if it comes to court it will cost him heavily, Sir Harry you as chief magistrate have the powers to check on workplaces within your parish.

Ben he has some horses at back of the factory used for hauling, can you get your brother to check on them, it`s Wilf the chief hosteler or was for he in a much higher status now at the racing stables and if asked he will if we make a complaint about the mill owners stables but that depends on the how other things go, he`ll want paying oh yes the cost will be added to the mill owners fine thank you gentlemen.

Come this way as drinks are served not for me Sir Harry as I a am a Methodist but tea will be fine how about you Paddy ,whisky will be fine ,thank you Sir, as laughter filled the room as Paddies rosy cheeks and fresh complexion and personality filled the room as he played his flute of several popular ballads.

Rose entered the room took Sir Harry`s hand and danced to the music as we all joined in with great merriment until we all were beat.

Chapter 25

You will Comply

It was a miserable morning damp and cold with a drizzle of rain as we called early and waiting at Mr Seagrave`s factory gates as he came and the workforce too as he unlocked the gates for all to enter then Sir Harry`s sent his hostler to take the horses to the rear to where the stables are and to note anything not right about Mr Seagrave`s stables and horses welfare, for if we have to send for Wilf from the race course.

In the office we introduced ourselves to Mr Seagrave at first he tried to ignore us and sharply said he is busy and no time to see us as I addressed him eye to eye to say then we will inspect your premises without you as we have written permission and that allows us in to your factory with or without your permission.

Mr Seagrave you are obliged to cooperate or have you something to hide? No, no, it`s just because I`m busy ,then appoint someone to show us around, well er ,give me a few minutes and I`ll show you around.

I see you are spinning wool, I thought farmers were keeping less sheep round here, true but we are tooling up for change ,yes I see but it`s rather dull in here Mr Seagrave you have no windows in this production room and when we entered the door was locked as no operators could not get out if wanted to ,why is that ? I lock it for they would be running to the toilet every 5 minutes they can be an idle lot if we don`t watch them , we you say, we, who are the others for I don`t see anyone else or do you mean those two men over there with arms folded looking at us?

What if someone is sick or requires the toilet? If they are sick they should stay at home or wait till lunch time to use the toilet, look we don`t want all this hassle as I must keep these people working or they will just get into bad habits and stand about wasting time.

I like this ,is it freshly spun? Yes ,would you like a few bobbins? Well I do not know Sir, here take several there`s enough for all its all good wool.

Mr Seagrave these operators don`t appear to be happy, no it`s because they are concentrating on their work yes, I see is that why they don`t speak? I do not allow it.

What do allow? What do you mean? Well I was looking at these machines not seen anything like these is it a new innovation ? Yes, I invest well to maintain high quality, what if something goes wrong with them and who puts them right? No nothing goes wrong ,but if Its doe`s I stop the cost of repairs from the operator ,for I don`t put up with any fooling about.

What would you do if there was a fire? I don`t allow smoking on the job, that`s not what I asked, then I would unlock the doors and let them out ,what if you had lost the key or you were trapped ? Things like that don`t happen here now this wool is good put that in your bag before you go, and this is the best way out and thank you for calling.

Mr Seagrave you` re so obliging and thank you, then good day gentlemen ,oh no we are not going yet as we have more business with you, look I am really pushed for time, Mr Seagrave it's the engines they really impress me where did you get them from as they drive these long flat belts driven by rotating long shafts wonderful but at a speed they go at are there any accidents?

We have a few nothing serious as they sometimes neglect their work in not paying enough attention in what they do but quickly resume work as I penalise them in time lost ,is there anything serious accidents ?

If anyone is unable to operate through an accident, we send them home ,what about their injuries ? We send someone with them, do you not have a place where they can receive on premises treatment ? No, no time for that.

Mr Seagrave you laugh a lot yes, I try to maintain a happy factory so if that's it I`ll see you on your way and don`t forget your gifts yes, but we have a few more questions ,when we came your main entrance to the factory building was locked then when all was in you locked it again behind us ,why was that? I`m not having workers walking off the job they stay here at their place of work.

Just a few more questions ,I seem to remember a large building stood here a factory doing similar work, yes we converted it into a more productive factory as you can see, good but Sir Harry here is fascinated with your engines driving the belts he requires 2 can you help him?

Well, that can be difficult now as my supplier is no longer around here, but what if an engine breaks down who can service it? I never thought of that , then tell me this, If I wished to buy one how much would it cost me ? Right now, I`m not sure but they don`t come cheap, surly you have receipts of expenditure and income, no don`t bother with things like all I`m bothered about is sales and profit and ,is that why you keep laughing Mr Seagrave ?

Mr Seagrave, we have asked you on several times about these engines and you are not, going to tell us, are you?

May I introduce you to a magistrate from Abbes Walk but you address him as Sir.

Mr Seagrave you have failed to cooperate with our questions we are far from satisfied with what we see and wish to see your accounts of purchases , and deeds of this building and expenditure of these engines and who assembled them for you must carry a certificate of purchase and installation for safety standards.

You are in violation of many factory acts let alone trying to bribe us ,don't talk rubbish, who the hell do you think you are? I`ll send for my guards and have you thrown out you, stupid lot.

Mr Seagrave you are offering violence and insults against magistrates appointed to inspect your factory and the welfare of its employees of which is noted.

Mr Seagrave this is magistrate Sir Harry from this parish Mr Seagrave you rent this building off Mr Dee correct, and you haven't paid him for some time and when he approaches you for rent you threaten him with violence as he is now in fear correct, yes of course it is and those 2 men over there are your security for want of a better name and later we wish to speak to them.

Mr Seagrave you obtained the engines from Stanley Oates a qualified fitter who fitted them and services them but like other people you refused to pay him for them and when approached for payment you threaten him and his family with violence, no that's wrong in threaten, for you apply violence, as he claims you owe him a lot of money .

You bully and mistreat your workers and in violation of many factory acts some recently approved and in force, yes no don't shake your head, you will have plenty of time to do that when in court.

The wool you have is stolen not all of it as the rest requires paying for, the stolen wool is from farms out of this area but identified, don`t squint at me, well these people lie I will send my men to them Mr Seagrave you own nothing here its Mr Dee who owns everything here apart from the engines that Mr Oats fitted.

Mr Seagrave, we have police here as I will call the Sergeant ``come in Sergeant and do your duty`` Mr Seagrave you are under arrest for theft of wool violence and violation of factory acts for now, as other charges are pending this way please.

Mr Dee pleased you kept out of the way now you have your, factory back, thank you Sir as he ruled everything around here with terror, Mr Dee go and tell your workers and get some windows in and keep them doors unlocked .

Albert you did well you got him nervous and on edge and sweating, we knew he was lying you did well, Sir Harry you knew more than I thought you really came out with it ,true Albert and in a short time, but I had a few friends who did some work for me late last night and Mr Oates ``Paddy`` told me lot I like him a good man and his £245 a lot of money is secured ,Sir Harry how did you manage that?

Ask Ben he did it, that right Ben well I too have a few friends and no doubt have found another one in Paddy and pleased to know we paid this factory visit during the night before they realised anything a mis ,what do you mean?

Well Paddy knows his way about this factory here, and late very late last night I wanted to see the factory and to check it out as Paddy had made a complaint, so we took him to the factory we who was we? Me and Sir Harry with the police sergeant who was here but Paddy came home with me true but later told you he had to go to his home and see to something.

We saw in the factory many things that was identified stolen like the wool that had been reported stolen and several other things I asked Paddy to were documents were kept as we found the office and found some office furniture that was stolen from your sons workshops as we had secured a warrant to search the premises, Paddy saw the safe so I made my exit when Paddy came out of the office with all smiles, I don`t know why for I saw nothing to laugh about.

So ,Albert with the authority invested in us and the police we have done well for the people around here and here is Paddy now. But how did you get into a secured factory as the gates would been locked? Paddy had a duplicate key.

Ahh tis a good morning to yourselves now ,Paddy what is it ? Tis Mr Dee he be wanting me to check over the engines for safety purposes as things must be safe for the operators.

Paddy I thought you were going help me with the building of a workshop and a shop for Mrs Lodge , Ah that I was Sir than you`ll not mind that I have left 3 friends and my boys to get on with it and Sir one is a stonemason and one a carpenter seeking work so Sir I have suggested they speaks to you later.

Paddy, is Mrs Lodge alright with what you are doing ? Begorra Sir she is helping and good with her horse ,Sir she is simply great why you ask ? What about your Mary ? Ahh Sir they are to be baking later in the day, Paddy call me Albert and its Nelly ,Nelly`s Lodge, but what are they baking ? Ahh Sir it be pie`s so they tell me , pies what type of pies? Duck pies Sir.

Paddy what kind of money do these people want in helping to build the workshop and food store ? No that be a gift from me for your kindness as the shop to be erected for Nelly is of little problems, but your workshop is a little more complexed as to fit the engine and long leather belt requires a bit of studying but these two belts I have are gifts from Mr Dee and tomorrow we assemble.

Now you want the engine inside or out as it will take some room up, well what do you think ? I think Albert it would be better outside but covered and the belts will run through an opening into the workshop to drive the shaft Albert it will all be clearer when assembled then in a year or 2 they will be electrified driven motors and I want to be ready for it.

Paddy do you and your friends want paying for what you do? Sir I have said It is of your kindness, no Albert, but I will see them right, Paddy would your boys like a job over the weekends ? Doing what, helping in sales at a site we have at Abbes Walk, I have, heard of that , they will not be on their own and will be well cared for.

Is It that the place with a hut there and selling refreshments ? That`s the one ahh you want a better place than that .true we do and you want better place to live in for soon that area where you live is to be demolished then Albert I shall have to spend some money and find some land to build on .

Well get my workshop sorted and the shop and we can see what can be done ,Albert that is no problem its mainly in sections.

Paddy up near Abbes Walk at the sales site I have some good building land, if you are interested you can have a look when we take the boys up at the weekend. Albert that sounds good.

My Mary was impressed with the spinning wheel and that`s some wheel you have ,and worth a lot of money, can your Mary spin wool? Albert she`s is fast as lightening she`ll show you sometime because we are not short of good quality wool.

Thank you, Sir, and good day, no wait ,how did you obtain a key to the factory gates and I hear you have received money owed to you? Ahh Sir you be asking too many questions, but along with engines, I supply, and fit safes and locks so are you to be in wanting some.

Paddy, I wish to know are you still owed money ? Sir Mr Seagrave has not paid me, but I feel more than compensated for my loss.

Chapter 26

Work Shops and Shop Workers

Nelly your shop looks good, and not taken them long ,well it was in sections but true it looks good yes and should serve the public well as the nearest shop is amongst the crofters a fair distance away, and at the back of the shop I have room for the dog so I`m more than pleased and your, workshop not be long as they worked well, what are you paying them ?

Paddy does n t want anything I asked him other day he told me that because we were kind to him, Albert, Paddy said he had no money, true at the time he did` n t but things have changed and he is rather rich now ,how is that? I think and I only think that Mr Seagrave had something to do with it and Nelly all them engines in the mill are on hire from Paddy .

Is ours for it looked like a load of scrap metal when it arrived Nelly not now and hopefully tomorrow it will be operative well how much ? Nothing for he says which I fail to understand it`s compliments of Mr Seagrave but Albert you say, Mr Seagrave could go down for a long time if he dodges the rope, for he was wanted for many crimes and Mr Dee asked Paddy to sort many things out at the factory so he can resume operations in a safe manner as the operators sing in a happier environment.

Paddy has also sorted other people`s stolen wool and goods out and contacted them and everyone is happy with him and they too are wanting engines locks and safes as Paddy laughs and says he will soon be wanting a bigger safe and reason he is not here is that he is still taking stock with Mr Dee of much stolen property to be returned to their right full owner.

Albert in ten minutes tell the workers here to lunch with us for there are a good bunch and work well ,Nelly it will be all finished tomorrow it`s been the brickwork and joinery work that`s taken much time up as I have arranged for the apprentices to bring all the stock from the old site to here.

Nelly where is your horse ? Paddy has borrowed it to ride out and tell sheep farmers that he has secured their wool and come and claim it or Mr Dee will buy it.

Nelly we shall require a sign writer for my works and your shop, yes a sign to say workshops and shopworkers required as we shall require staff and doubt if that will be a problem.as Mary Paddy`s wife is going to help me in the shop while she works the spinning wheel for she`s very good as she tells me he did much in Dublin with her Mother as they had an outlet until they got caught up in some riots and their property got destroyed in the conflict.

Albert with all this work can you not find work full time for the carpenter. Nelly I can as there is some new houses going up and demand is growing but think Paddy will want the stonemason as he is more than interested in the land up near Abbes Walk to build on.

Nelly you are more up to date with things than me as you talk about doing less work when seeking more I`ll never know how your mind works as you confuses me as I am constantly trying to get on with my work but constantly being called upon, Nelly no way could I manage without good staff.

We will never retire or get too old to do anything as we just keep searching for additions to improve upon what we have, but time must come as I see amongst the crofters who have grown old and unable to manage with no income and little to live on in a state I wish not to be in as I see all what one earns is required for that week only ,so what happens to those who cannot work through no fault of their own ? Questions I ask myself as I pity the old and poor.

I cannot erase the thoughts from my mind as I think there must be better ways as many like me are thinking the same but powerless to do something about it and only way they can achieve anything is by banding together in unison to be heard ,as the feeling is growing as liberalism is making inroads into the political scene but it`s not enough.

Time` s I torment myself as people agree with me but we are powerless to alter things and now they have made me a magistrate well I hope they don`t think I am going to just prop up the system as I within the law wish to alter the system as I see it whether it be shopworkers or workshop workers as I prepare my speech regarding election to the magistrates panel .

Albert now what are you doing.

I am pleased with myself in becoming a magistrate but do hope I am not viewed as being a threat as I fear I will for as it is mainly the poor who are brought to court ,Albert there are more of them that is why no ,no .business people are just has guilty but manage to wriggle out of things with bribes it`s true and you take care when weighing out flour sugar or anything that requires weighing for many shops I know try and give short measures I don`t want any of that here .

Albert don`t you lecture me, now something is troubling you what is it ?Nelly how old are our boys? You should know that we`ve spoken before about this 20 18 and 16 why ,I think they are older but how old do they have to be to join the army ? I don`t know ,neither do I, but they keep talking about the troubles abroad more interested in that than what they are doing here, and I am annoyed with it .

I heard then arguing about the troubles in Ireland and their lack of knowledge in it alarmed me like many of crofters they too talk a lot of nonsense but then they only know what they are told.

Albert I`m sure it`s just talk take no notice but I think they are older as John is 22 now yes and not married what`s wrong with them I thought it was serious with them Albert I think you ought to have a rest as you are much concerned about too many things and John plans to marry in about 6 months and others will soon follow.

Yes Geoffrey he contracts for the army in making boots and leather webbing now I wonder if these so called army officers have been bragging about their deeds and exploits to him, you can ask him but they seem happy and comfortable in what they do.

Look here comes Paddy ,thank you Nelly for the horse and all is sorted peace in the valley at last and mind how they have got on with the building it looks good ,Albert we`ll give engine a run tomorrow and then it will be ``hunkadoray``

Albert, I have had a look at the land up at Abbes Walk and can erect a better building for the sales pitch you make the sections and we`ll assemble it but it`s the land that pleases me so give me a price ,Paddy come inside and refresh yourself .Mr Albert what is it as you look bothered about something is it the shop and workshops?

Paddy nothing like that as we are more than pleased but it is the land at Abbes Walk for Paddy I cannot sell if I am in doubt about something and it is you.

Begorra, what have I done? Is it Mary or the boys? Paddy, you have a good woman there, and the boys are fine, so what is it?

Paddy, my sons have been talking a lot about the I R A and what they say I am not pleased with as someone is feeding them false information as it is hard to know what the truth is also there are people arguing the other way so it`s for and against.

Paddy your country has had more than its share of troubles from the victory for William of Orange a Protestant who became king of England in defeating King James 2nd with the Franco Irish Jacobite `s in 1689 –1690 at Battle over the river Boyne known as the battle of Boyne that saw King James flee to France never to return and in 1791 the victorious Irish held their first Protestant Orange Order Parade and still do ,but the troubles are still with them as there is talk about implementing a tariff that could cause much hardship.

The IRA have many legitimate reasons to complain it is how it is done as the Protestant movement and that of the Orange order have because of past problems like the famine political ,social, and religion all contribute to unrest.

You told me you are a Catholic because of that you are denied many things under our present education system, the church on this estate is an all Saints Church ,if it helps you pay it a visit but you`ll be welcomed in the Methodist church too.

The problem is Paddy someone is trying to arouse people minds here into false thinking that is likely to cause unrest or to promote self- interest.

Mr Albert Sir I think it`s the I R A and the stories making their rounds and this is political as some Whig of an MP is making statements and threats aimed at the IRA and they don`t like it so they are hitting back .Paddy what do you think? Ah Sir you be thinking that I be an active member ,Sir it is not what I think or do as I have to recognise the laws of the land I find myself in and this is England and I have no comment to make only to say it is not of my doing but I think I know.

Sir you do well to question the uniform men called soldiers who frequent the crofters in recruiting and your son who supplies leather goods and footwear but Sir you pain me to question me as if I would do such a thing.

Paddy all I have done is ask questions and I believe you, Sir you had doubt, do not ever doubt me but if ever you want to know anything than ask for I believe my Mary and sons have find happiness here amongst some good people,

Paddy tomorrow we draw up sale documents for that land now how much are you prepared to pay? Ah to be sure Sir you know the price of land and so do I.

Sir tomorrow I shall be seeing Henry Mann from the shoe shop he`s a good man and he knows much about things round here and dislikes uniforms, Sir talk to Henry and he is the one that beat up those 2 heavies that worked for Seagrave before you arrested them but Sir you don`t wish to know that do you? A 70 year- old ex Irish champ Sir no one fools with Henry .

Chapter 27

This is No Place for Soldiers

All this turmoil has got me thinking of when we were married for I don`t know when it was I know we were married and that's difficult to know how old my boys are I now there are more like men with growing beards and moustaches as Geoffrey be the youngest as he too has a beard oh I don`t know what to think at times .

Albert our Geoffrey has got hair all over his face he looks like a mop on legs Nelly it`s the fashion long hair and long coats yes Albert coats I hope he`s not thinking of a red one for the army seems to be around here a lot lately with their red coats Albert what`s going on ?

Nelly, I think they are dealing with some problems further north ,then they should be there and not here? Albert, I think they are after someone as I hear the town is full of them Nelly, I don`t now but your brother Wilf may know from the race- course stables as they supply horses for the army.

Well I know who will know and that`s Sir Harry and Rose for they are coming, look over there that`s them on horse -back and racing as if there something wrong ,Sir what is it?

Albert ,on York road there must be about a hundred men with pitch forks, long sticks , and anything they can use has weapons as they march into farms threaten to smash up new machinery they are in riot and some have threatened to set alight many farms ,Sir are they at your place ? no not yet but I ride out to tell other farmers what is happening and to be ready ,no Sir it`s not warning them that's required it is stopping them ,yes Albert I now that's why the army is there firing upon them but they just keep rioting even more no matter how many are shot at they just keep rioting .

Sir who called the army in, I did we can`t have our police force under threat and our community threatened and at risk.

Look we have more riders Ben from Abbes Walk and a few men with him and Matt and Paddy Oats what`s Paddy doing with them ? Matt you come from Abbes Walk thought you would be with Sir Harry I was but he wouldn`t listen to me as I rode to tell Ben ,what do you mean he wouldn`t listen? Well he rode hell for leather through them with his whip he is lucky to be here you clown you yes, you Sir Harry you could have been killed now I suggest you keep well away from here as they are likely to hang you.

They were rioting ,Nelly take him inside and Rose, You Sir Harry keep out of the way do not show your face come men we ride to Sir Harry`s farm for now he is a marked man the fool him , Paddy what are you doing here? I`m here to help you`re not a farmer ,true Sir and all those rioting are not farm labourers as many are crofters being kicked out of their property by greedy land agents.

Also, some are factory workers who are mistreated by being robbed of their wages it was a peaceful demonstration an unlawful demonstration to be sure but how else can they air their views and opinions and to whom would listen? Sir they are angry because the army are instructed to us force like the police and now there is rioting .

Sir I think they may listen to you but you will have to discharge the army and the police and put down their guns as now there could be many a child without a father and many a woman without her husband.

Paddy you seem to now, a lot about what`s going on, Sir these people now of me and trust me as I make my rounds fitting engines and because of that I see a lot and talk a lot Sir there is only one factory around here that's operational and that's Mr Dees and I had something to do with that as now its problems are resolved.

So, Albert what they want to know, what are you going to do about these complaints of mistreatment and bad working conditions ? Sir tis easy to say it`s not your problem as many do and that is an insult to the working classes you must show them that you care for some of these people have nothing to lose.

Albert if you send riders out to Creepy Hollow you will find 2 men hanging their not done by these people in riot but done by travellers who are laying low as they stand back and watch what develops out of these disturbances genially these people in riot have much to shout about but you have people here promoting their own ego nothing new but an old practise as I saw much in Ireland and what you have witnessed here in the past Sir Harry did nothing about it.

Creepy Hollow now is known as the killer corner .

Paddy will you ride with us, Sir Harry you would do to stay out of the way no I go with you then remove those guns ,what if we require them in defence? Sir you don`t require them.

There they are, Sir there must be a hundred or more all settled in the paddock now Sir that appears strange so slow down and dismount you must not appear violent stay calm all of you.

Paddy I think we can manage without you telling us what to do ,Sir then I`ll leave you for I wish not to witness to what may happen ,why what will happen Sir now you listen to me these people are not bothered about you the police or the army and here they are discussing what action may do .

It is of little use as the police stand over there with guns at ready and the army ready with bayonets affixed, for God`s sake man waken up this is not the battle of Boyne for the love of God pull those soldiers out and dismiss the police to a place away from here were they cannot be seen.

Sir if you refuse it will soon be dark maybe in an hour and these people have little to lose and then you will witness a blood bath and you will answer for it, so Sir Harry I bid you good luck in what you do as I leave you to it.

Wait, have you some experience in these matters as you talk as if you have ,Ah Sir you are seeing sense do you want my help or not ? Paddy what do you suggest?

Sir withdraw the army and police send the army away but retain the police and for the police to lay down their shields.

Sir I am going amongst them ,Paddy be careful that I will Sir, Paddy is that a handgun I see under your coat ah Sir you`re not to be seeing that, now stand bye, here I go.

Slowly silently Paddy walked to them as they looked upon him as if he was Jesus ,he stopped to embrace someone and held out his hand to shake many others, a sight to behold as the crowd fell into a silence.

With hands held high standing on a pile of stone he bellowed out as if he were speaking to someone miles away.

People hear me good as I support you and want to help you but you cannot harm the people who should be helping you ,many of you having little or nothing to live on as you are expected to slave all day for meagre returns ,well something has to change.

Now hear me good I thought you had killed someone but with the grace of God you haven`t as you yourselves were attacked and many received injuries, my friends and because of that I am demanding an inquiry about all this and the reasons why ,you may smear and grumble but for those who know me will know I get results.

Men we will repair any farm implements damaged free of charge you cannot condemn new innovations as industry must move forward as in factories it is not just the farmers here it is the whole country.

I want you to divide into 3 groups roughly about 30 a group and appoint 2 leaders from each group to act as representatives for the local area around here and this will be endorsed as legal by our magistrates it will be known as local trades works committee that will meet once a month.

Here amongst you there are men unknown to you so look around you and if you see someone unknown then point him out for these are murderers to those hanging at Creepy Hollow ask them a few questions then treat them as you will.

Now many of you are hungry and as you are in 3 groups that group there you go to Sir Harry`s place wait, he admits what he did was wrong so you go to his place to where there will be soup for all to have your belly full and tomorrow you return to work as magistrate are going to talk to your employers ,the next group goes to Nelly`s Lodge for soup and the other group goes to the Methodist church for soup take your families if you like but remember this you come to me first before you take such an action like this again as you have been led on by those 4 men who you have just sorted out now make your way to the places I have mentioned and the party going to Nelly`s Lodge be prepared for a good rollicking.

Come Albert all of you as you have to feed the multitude as you will not see that again, but keep the soldiers out of things

Paddy who are you ?

Sir`s sorry if I have made some work for you but these are good people that require help not punishment ,Paddy soup at Sir Harry`s soup at Nelly`s soup at the Methodist church how come you could say that ? Begorra Sir Harry I had it arranged did not Rose tell you?

Sir Harry you must make peace with these people the sooner the better you a magistrate, who do you answer to? All of you are viewed with contempt of which you have brought about yourselves as you are equally to blame for what happens here for you are not responsible for the law your job is deal with law breakers so firstly start with yourselves as you break the law every day.

Sir I cannot stand by and watch the public chastised, that drives them to do un except able things.

Who am I ?

Father Stanley Oates

Land reformist minister for the home office

My job is to look at many applications for mainly land for mills and coal mining as much land will be lost to farmers and crofters as their lively hood is at stake and rid this area of fraudulent deals as there are many that you magistrates should be been aware of.

Then I may promote my Catholic believes for under my coat I have my priest hood wear, I showed the crowd and they responded well I thought, Ah Sirs it must be the glory of God as I have many Catholics amongst them who work on the land and have no church around here as the wounds have not healed from the troubles of the 16th Century.

Chapter 28

Soldiers of Fortune

Nelly you should have told me , Albert you listen to me more and you will know more, now Paddy is a mechanic or engine fitter and in the priest hood nothing wrong in that but I now know that Mr Johnson from Peterborough sent for him.

Albert ,Paddy would like to build a Catholic church on York road near Abbes Walk but he cannot it`s not allowed only church of England faith is allowed like in the schools but because of that we must not ignore them as people should always be encouraged to find their faith and to practise it were ever they be.

It is Geoffrey that worries me as he his friends with a lot of these soldiers these red coats who made a mess of things in Canada, Nelly what are you talking about you don`t know that ,well what am I to know? I know they wear red coats when in battle it must be like committing suicide as they should ware camouflage clothing. ``Nelly what is it` ? Them, red coats can you not send them on their way for what are they doing here? They are here to maintain peace ,what would they do if peace were broken?

They did nothing with the demonstrators that was Paddy`s doing , where you ready to turn the army onto the public, is that what our armies are for to kill our own people?

I do not want Geoffrey involved in this matter, so Albert I suggest you have a word ,Nelly I`ll go now.

Geoffrey what are these soldiers doing here on your premises? Dad they are on duty in securing the town ,no they are not we have not requested them so what` s going on? Sir the police sent for us ,then who are you and how many men have you here? I am First officer Jones and I have 6 soldiers Sir ,then first officer Jones get your men together and march out of here, back to your barracks , but where are your barracks? For you were not the soldiers that were here during the troubles as you could not be found.

Can`t do that Sir as I take orders from the army, Geoffrey where is Henry Mann ``Paddy``? Ask the officer as he went under escort to deliver footwear and webbing to their HQ, Officer where is your HQ for I don`t know of your HQ Sir its way up north, Officer do you pay for this equipment and boots ?No Sir not allowed to do that but Mr Mann(Paddy)will come back with a check, good and fine but officer where are your other men? Sir they are employed on standby at the mills or farms , fine officer I`ll leave it to you.

I rode as fast has my horse would go to find Stanley Oats ``Paddy`` who was finishing off my workshop with a glazier Paddy I shouted come quick as I quickly told him what I suspected , Begorra he said`` I will be getting 2 good men to help.

Sir what is it ?Paddy do you know of these soldiers amongst the crofters? Sir they are always about what are they doing? Paddy I don`t know but I think they are not soldiers but renegades, Sir they always seemed flushed in money and lack in duty Paddy, I think they have kidnapped Henry Mann and robing my son as he provides boots and webbing to the armed forces.

Sir I`m a peace officer ,Paddy not if you are under pressure as I saw your gun other day when you went amongst those rioters ,Sir do not call them that they were demonstrators.

Sir we have Joe Flanagan here, Joe leave your rabbits here they`ll be save until we get back and you too Bob can join us as we have a little problem and want your help and what you got there ? Well er, Bob come now you`re not in trouble it is your help we be wanting now leave those birds with Nelly for I want you for an hour, ahh don`t look concerned as Sir here wants your help.

I quickly explained what I thought as Bob said, Sir we thought you knew these are not soldiers at all but demand security money off some mill owners or farmers as they wear army uniforms to try to look threatening but some believe they are of the army nothing to do with those who were here yesterday.

Men will you help me, Begorra Sir of course they will ,Sir if Paddy here wants us to help you than we will but do you want more ? Yes, the more the better, Paddy what are you doing I`m getting 2 more men watch me as Paddy played a tune on his flute a merry happy tune as we waited some 5 minutes as 2 men came from the forest .

Paddy what is it ? I want your help to rid these soldiers from the village Ernie they are not soldiers, we known that Paddy, well they have Paddy Mann then let`s get started Ernie this is Albert a magistrate ,Paddy I know that he brings his horses to our blacksmith works to be shoed, hello Sir how are you and Sir the fields down there are overrun with rabbits then Ernie you will have left some for people like me ,Sir I always drop a couple off for Nelly as she treats me to drop of her warm cherry wine .

Paddy you know the situation Albert these men are aware what I want them to do as you stand back after we know your son Geoffrey is safe ,just watch .

We entered the shoe and boot repair shop as Paddy said to the officer ,Sir good to see you now and when will you be going back to your unit ,and where are you staying ?

Mr this is no concern of yours as this is military business ,Ah do excuse officer but tell me Sir have you been in the forces for long as I see many decorations on your coat you must be very brave.

Yes I fought hard as a hero been in 5 years now as they have sent me here to sort this lot out ,Sir you are armed and I thought that would not be allowed in public areas so Sir you will surrender your weapons to the magistrate here ,Like hell I will as he received a might fist to his chin from Ernie as Paddy relieved him of his weapons.

Sir you are no army officer those ribbons refers to long service and one is of Africa corps and one of an naval award Sir you are a lair ,now Ernie here was trained by Paddy to box so we want to know where is Paddy, another blow to the head as he is held up to receive another then another ,were is he Ernie demanded.

Albert stay outside ,`We`ll deal with it but you are a priest ,He is in the back room and their laid Paddy Mann all tied up ,I untied him.

Paddy you alright now ? I said, sure Albert but go and get the others 4 or 5 of them at the mill edge of town as I have a few things to do here with this creep, then get the police to arrest them, Albert go as you have the authority and you Geoffrey hope you`ve learnt your lesson in playing with your soldiers as I think your father will be wanting to talk to you later.

You clown Geoffrey I`ve heard of soldiers of fortune and these nearly made it, as I kept hold of the consignments for they were planning to move out with it a whole cart full then disappear ,the genuine orders from the ministry are fine as repairs are, but you well I don`t know what your father thinks

Geoffrey your work is first class your business is rubbish now you employ someone who knows what they are doing ,you got to ignoring me and thought these so called tin soldiers were real as I believe you Geoffrey requires further business training.

A week or 2 with my friend Father Paddy Stanley Oates should do you good as they came in time for no money was lost but very nearly was .

Ernie what is it? They are all in custody then you may come back to Nelly`s Lodge and retrieve your reward of a couple of birds and rabbits ,and magistrate Albert is giving you permits to hunt game in season because you are always willing to help as I only need to play my flute.

Father Paddy Stanley Oates will the engine run tomorrow as I would like to cut some timber? Tis not a scaffold you`ll building would be it Sir ?

Paddy I want to know more about you as you are a man of cloth, an engineer ,a crown agent ,a peace maker, and know of many here who will rush to your aid.

Albert Sir they rushed to your aid, as I have no enemy`s for those who think wrong of me don`t hang around for long and when with me Sir please take notice of what I say as that soldier had a handgun and prepared to use it on you, that's why he was smashed about and insulted.

Chapter 29

Geoffrey was Too Young

Nelly ,Geoffrey was too young to go it alone in the shoe re pair and sales shop and if Paddy Mann wasn`t there he would have suffered more luckily no money was lost Albert he is here now with Henry Mann you can call him Paddy he won`t mind I know that Nelly.

Geoffrey what on earth were you thinking about ? Dad I didn't know ,of course you didn't you was not meant to for they were ready to leave you high and dry maybe no money off you but thousand £ `s of stock an whole cart full and would have little problem in selling it all.

I have decided you require lessons in business management and Mr Stanley Oates is going to learn you ,so from tomorrow at 9am you report to him, your shop will be temporally run by a Paddy your brother John and an apprentice for deliveries from here, your studies will be in testified through the day up to 3pm after that time you go to your shop and resume until you close shop at end of the day.

Your banking is unaffected, but you only deal in cash unless we as family endorse it as army contracts are paid differently.

Geoffrey, we thought you were ready but you were a little too young at the time, you`ve grown a lot and a few years ,have as past on but you can only operate with the knowledge you have but when confronted with something you had not seen before you don`t know how to handle it, so you must learn in business dealings to trust no one.

Dad I thought these soldiers were genuine yes soldiers Geoffrey they were waiting until they got enough and ride away after they had killed you both Dad, I thought you had bought me the shop? I have but it`s still in my name until you are 21 thought you knew that.

Geoffrey you were doing well and still are under a careful eye of Henry who lives in the residence part of the house of which he owns but somehow you seemed to want to be friendly with people who you don`t know because they wear an army uniform now tell me what do you know of them?

Dad I don`t know as they left the village at night and back next morning ,they must have been staying somewhere so someone was protecting and feeding them, and Geoffrey how long had they been here ? They were here when you secured Mr Dees factory as they seemed to know much about it ,no Geoffrey they have been here longer than that.

Answer the door its Mr Oats and someone else well let them in .Geoffrey its Father Oates to you ,Paddy welcome come in and hello Ernie , Paddy as you like me to call you ,what is it ? as I viewed him to my surprised to see a towering of a man with much firmness about him as his whole posture was of rebelling to act from his natural self ,I looked at Ernie a much changed man from what I saw earlier today, I quickly realised something is wrong.

What is it I demanded ? Albert the prisoners in custody at local police station broke out and shot at several people as the police have shot and killed 2 but got away.

How did they have guns ? Someone entered the police station armed and shot the guards ,what the police officers too yes all 3 of them, and that person is on the run we think he is laying low around here for we have reason to believe he is wanting to kill Sir Harry and me .

What ,You, why what have you done and who is it? We don`t know but I have lots of men with Sir Harry so at this moment he is safe, Paddy it should be the police, they are there too, who we want had something to do with the soldiers at your son`s place ,Geoffrey is here.

Geoffrey, would you know of such a person? Dad several people came and went ask Henry he was mainly in front of the shop serving as I was in the back repairing

Albert ,Henry is seriously ill found with a bullet in his upper chest

Father Oates and you are father Oates you come here looking much different and you Ernie you both look different Albert they are looking for us so we change our appearances as they might change theirs too, true but were would that be?

Geoffrey, can you remember him? Well there was always someone coming in the shop and talking to the officer, did you see him? No, I was always in the back, did he know that? I doubt it Dad he must be from around here for he knew his way around as he would talk about the estate the crofters and he knew of Abbes Walk and his accent was local.

Dad I never heard him say anything relating to violence it was always about money as if the soldier owed him some and once I heard him say he once lived amongst the crofters Dad I know he said that, I feel sure he said he had been to prison and left his son here who was about 16 at the time but there were no one else with him.

Dad ,think about it how would he now of Sir Harry and want to kill him? It was Roses ex-husband who many thought he was dead, but they say that all the time if sent away by the authorities, and if it was he must be about well into his 6o `s what about Father Stanley here he does not know him and what about Paddy Henry Mann,

Geoffrey not so fast for if it be that man than he does know me. Geoffrey was his name mentioned yes, I remember it was er, er. Bill Hardwick

Albert that was Rose husband presumed drown in Bay of Biscay and I know him as he knows me but who told him I was up here, of course the demonstrations up at Abbes Walk they were there with a few agitators that the crowd dealt with.

After all these years now he is here seeking vengeance from his own doing Father why you? Albert call me Paddy and why me ? Well I married them in Peterborough at the Catholic church there and soon after they moved to here for at Peterborough he was much in drink and began to beat Rose he was very much known there for his vulgarity and violence through drink so they came here to live, at Peterborough I visited them on several times as we as Catholics do not belief in divorces as I tried to help their marriage.

Albert before he left Peterborough he got to fighting and got many beatings and thought it was me arranging it but what he received he deserved there are many other things but we have no time to waste as he is killer a killer on the loose but where did he live?

Ernie yes Albert sorry I beg your pardon Sir no Ernie its fine call me Albert then Albert were do people live this time of year who have no abode? so I suggest you contact magistrate up at Abbes Walk as I think your man is in the forest Ernie that magistrate is Nelly`s brother so be careful in what you say Albert he is a good man for he gives us permission to use the forest from May to September as long has he has our names and not to damage any live foliage and we respect him, well suppose someone gives a wrong name? Well Albert if he refuses all of to use the forest so it is to our own interest to be honest ,then what, well Albert I have known it to happen so we, no Albert you don`t want to know but I know what you are thinking and if its him no other will be involved.

Correct so when you are ready, we ride to Abbe`s Walk and Paddy do you have your flute with you? Oh, yes, I never go far without it .

Albert If it be Hardwick who shot at Paddy Mann and you arrest him can a few of us act as escorts and take him into custody, Ernie we will require escorts and your offer is much appreciated.

For quickness you would be better to go Creepy Hollow way and you Geoffrey you go and inform Sir Harry in what we are doing.

Arriving at Abbes Lodge Paddy turned to me to say Albert he said you are a magistrate so, please you ought not to see what may happen , Paddy you are a priest, true but I think I am nearer to God than you as he will guide me well, than Paddy I`ll stay near the spring.

After about, ten minutes Paddy`s flute was heard as many men came to him I could see at the forest edge as they circled around him don't know what he said but there was a chorus of unity as they hailed him as a savour about thirty of them as they dispersed back into the forest as many have built their home there some in trees and some of bracken on the ground so Ben was telling me as he joined me Albert he said I don`t mind one bit of them living in the forest as they do no harm and serve my purpose well as I know what`s happening as they have their own council rules and laws .

Ben what do you know about Paddy? Albert tomorrow Mr Johnson will be here so, ask him.

Listen here they come, it appears they have someone and so they have all bundled up Albert called Paddy you can arrest him know as he has confessed in front of all these witnesses and if he appears to be bruised he had an accident and admitted of intent to kill Paddy Mann in fact I have it all written down as he has signed it.

Now with your permission some of these men have volunteered as escorts to Sir Harry`s security men who then hand him over to the police.

Men take him away and Albert these men speak well of you and for anyone to hurt Nelly well I pity them for what others may do to them and Nelly is much upset about Paddy Mann and that of the police as some lives are threatened but for him he is responsible for many murders around here.

As you know Albert. I cannot condone violence as that man will no doubt suffer in hell as he was wanted in Peterborough for murder as many thought he was dead died at sea while working as a merchant seaman.

Paddy are you trying to tell me something, Albert at first, he never recognised me but when he did, he went into a fit, but the men soon took control of things.

Ben it is very noble of you to help these people as you do, Paddy they don`t do any harm in the forest in fact I was going to ask Albert here if he could make a large hut to be erected in the forest for these men who seen to have their own organisation and democracy a lot of it is down to the Salvation Army as the request comes from them but it will not be used for aiding people who are wanted by the law and overall responsibility will be done by the Salvation Army as the people there will have their own council yes because Captain Booth of the Salvation Army was a Methodist before organising the S/A

Albert, will you do that for the unfortunate people around here? Ben I will and build it in sections to be erected on site free of any costs but you Ben and the Salvation Army and myself are the executive board to whom their own elected council will report to for us to sanction any ideas that will promote their wellbeing.

Any spiritual connections will be for the Salvation to govern and control.

Chapter 30

The Trial

Nelly what is it ? Albert I`m thinking of Geoffrey and how lucky he was for you to intervein, Nelly we perhaps ought to shoulder some blame for he was too young for his position and never learnt anything the longer he was there and that's a few years ago, we should have educated him in business management first, John and Will are fine it`s just Geoffrey.

Nelly his work is flawless, but his management well it could have been much worse if it had not been for Paddy Mann as he is on the mend and the trial of Hardwick is tomorrow as Mr Johnson is chief prosecutor the judge is Silos Young and the jury has been selected.

I had feelings of there being no trial as the mocking people vented their hate towards him and so did I ,Albert they showed their feelings not hate don`t use the word hate in referring to people as you could become an hate full person yourself and you are not as I hear there will be 3 for trial as I was told they will hang in town not far from the guildhall of which I was disgusted to hear as some people glorify in death.

People here are all too eager to execute the accused before being tried and people like you Albert who have all too often dismissed the penalty before being judged and because of that the trials and judgements become much fairer Nelly he has admitted all charges.

Albert this man if guilty will face the death penalty and some say he is lucky to face a court as many would have liked to hang him at Creepy Hollow but I stopped them I rode there knowing what they would do as I persuaded them to let the courts decide .

They were crazy with their proposed actions as I screamed in anger as I put the noose around my own neck to say you will be just as guilty in hanging me as you will of him, it is for the courts to decide as it will for any of you, Albert I persuaded them not to act outside of the law, yes Nelly I can see that.

Albert you must not pre -judge as we all expect to be treated equally no matter what status one is in.

There will be many witnesses as Geoffrey is willing to be a witness too but I thought he knew little about Hardwick, and Rose who he was married to and some from the crofters so Albert it appears I now more than you .

Nelly what appears and what is are 2 different assumptions as I do not accept of what appears as I have to eliminate any doubt in my search for the truth as I am elected to the prosecution to prepare notes of the trial but thank you for correcting me as I wish not to talk about it anymore.

Albert then what are we to do with Geoffrey? Nothing he has learnt his lesson, if anything we ought to prepare for wedding bells for him and John ,Nelly we care too much about them as they are old enough and hopefully now wiser enough as we have our shop and my workshop to look after and if you do less gossiping in your shop you might sell more Albert doubt if I would sell more but I would have more time to myself as some do come to just gossip, but that's the nature of having a shop as now I am selling papers as the local gossip is now published.

Yes. full of nonsense for us to believe stories of won battles abroad as their news should be questioned but never is as if it be printed that must be the truth.

Albert I grow weary of many things I see and don`t know whether we are going in the right direction as smoke bellows from factory chimneys as many who work there look sick pale and anaemic with a language of their own as I hear of many accidents of young boys falling asleep over operating engines or machines.

Albert things are not the same the smell of smoke drifting all over the valley and people coughing and spitting as they come to me for a medicinal cure as I think many have wool fibre on their chests.

Albert we are doing well yet I am unhappy in what I see, our beautiful trees are disappearing our skies are full of smoke all day ,and our people are sick from industrial life as our farm labourers suffer in silence not always the farm owners to blame as it is the circumstances of hard work what farm work demands.

Nelly you are a champion of their cause as you try and hurry along better working conditions that requires change in technology but many don`t want it but it is coming maybe too fast but it is coming to be accepted as progress as an ongoing system.

Albert, I fear for Rose, as many things will be mentioned in court that could be hurtful to be reminded of as the Judge is Silos Young and very thorough with detail.

I could not sleep much in thinking of Rose as we prepared for court, in arriving at court stood Rose elegant and good looking as her marriage to Sir Harry blossomed as she looked over to me in acknowledgement of my appearance as all took up their placings as the prisoner was bought in heavily escorted and chained then entered the Judge with great pomp he peered over the court to see all were in place then seated.

A moment of silence that appeared a strange silence then the clerk of court read details out to establish who the prisoner is then followed by announcing an whole lot of offences of murder here and at Peterborough with witness after witness followed as he shouted across court I wish I had done more especially, you Judge Silos Young and would have done more if those soldiers had followed my orders as we planned to even many things up around here and not to be governed by yes men.

It appeared he had lost any sense of reasoning as his mind was out of control.

You will be silent in my court and only speak when asked as you plead guilty in all offences and the soldiers or those who pretend to be ,will be dealt with later it is you who is on trial here and you have no defence as the jury have no choice to find you guilty on all accounts.

The Jury have endorsed my recommendations and find you guilty of all offences mentioned and you will hang until you are dead at 9am tomorrow, take him away and keep him in chains.

Albert that was short but fair and a great relief to Rose, Nelly a great relief to many people around here but maybe I shouldn`t think as I do but what drives people to do such things as I only deal with the law and not reasons, Albert an admission you should correct quickly.

Maybe education has something to do with it ,Nelly to that we will see as education becomes more accessible for many but that depends how one intends to use education when educated, than Albert what do you think ? Nelly, I don`t have an answer.

Albert is it a physical answer we seek in reducing crime or an academical or a social one ? Nelly what do you mean ?Well you can reduce crime by sending more people to prison or joining the armed forces but to send people to prison you require more police to arrest people violating the law ,so you think the law ought to be tougher? No, the law should be fairer for there are many who commit crime and never arrested as we do not have enough police to protect the public.

But why do people break the law? Is it lack of education or is it the law is there to be broken, or are there too many of us to control ,and being educated does not stop anyone breaking the law, but we are talking about how to reduce crime and how to implement it.

Albert It is a social problem as people lack security not only from physical institutions but in economic circumstances to ease the power of want in supply and demand as many lack the power of demand so in a nut shell they require some financial support from an improved social system as I would recommend a government cross party to enquire into the whole social system.

Nelly, we have just witnessed a man sentenced to death as some jeered some smiled as we left court as no doubt there will be more before the day is over and our son Geoffrey was nearly involved with dealing with them as Paddy nearly gave his life in protecting him so I think Geoffrey`s works come into my work shop at home for the building he has could be demolished under new town and country planning as there are plans for many houses to be built down there and I want him closer at home as what has happened changes many things.

His, shoe and boot repair business ,deserves a boost as demand is overwhelming as more people flock into new estates and more factories opening up and boots are more in in fashion particularly ladies` boots.

Albert here comes Rose and Sir Harry, Rose you alright? Nelly what an ordeal but now you know what I went through why he came here I`ll never know for there was nothing here for him perhaps he thought I was waiting for him yet many thought, he was dead ,Nelly he was some mixed up man as violence ruled him or beer did, Rose forget it and have a drink of this cherry wine and you Sir what would you like? Nelly I am partial to your rhubarb wine, ah Sir you know the good stuff .

What it is, we are all invited to Abbes Walk tonight 7pm as all the dignitaries will be there and your Ben has put on a banquet and I think hog is on the menu as I can smell the roasting of it drifting all across the fields to here.

Chapter 31

Why Should I Think That ?

It seemed as we get older, problems increase I thought it was other way around as our life is buzzing sometimes I think we have no time to sleep but nice to see Paddy Mann now recovered from his ordeal as he is here.

Albert. I thank you but if it wasn`t for father Oates I would have killed him for he had plans in killing me and don`t put too much blame on Geoffrey as I should have seen it coming but now I see you have more staff there now and ` that's a good think as it is a busy shop.

Paddy what are doing now? Nothing really but I like to be active ,to keep me fit as I`m not a drinker to be stuck in the tavern all day like some do that`s not me as I look for what I can do .

Paddy ,Albert and I have much on with the shop and the furniture making premises here as you can see how we have altered many things around here.

Paddy would you like little job here as I require someone to look after the stable and live- stock and then go over to Alberts works and keep it tidy like sweeping up the saw dust so the operators have an clean area to work in.

I suggest 2 hours feeding the live- stock and 2 hours in the work- shop but if interested the live -stock requires cleaning out and feeding first, Nelly that would suit me fine except Tuesday and weekends for Tuesday I am at the Salvation Army hut you know the one in the forest as I have several taking up boxing and wish for me to train them. men and boys

Good for you but what about equipment ? Ah Nelly and that`s a laugh as we have improvised with straw stuffed in bags and tied with ropes hanging from the ceiling and pummel them ,and any heavy items we throw around to keep fit and intend to make progress as it is a new venture ,Paddy that's great ,yes thank you.

Nelly I have something else too and you can help me because in your womens league you have some ladies who are good at singing and I want to organise a choir as the hut in the forest is good during summer months and during winter the Methodist church would do fine as I plan a mixed choir and Nelly I have heard you and one or two more and you are good and Mrs Annie Evans is interest to be the choir leader,

Nelly what do you think? God bless you Paddy it is a wonderful idea let`s get it on, if we do Paddy what shall we call it? I do not know ,the valley vocals or the new century songsters as it will soon be 1900 or The Salvation Songsters or Annie Evans singers that's it The Annie Evans singers .

They use the hut during summer and the Methodist church in winter but Paddy some may not be of that persuasion, no that doesn't matter if they can sing that is all that matters or care about so Nelly let`s get sorted and see how` it goes ,right Paddy let`s put smiles on people`s faces and fill this valley with song.

Paddy we thought we had lost you ,you might have if Father Oates hadn`t arrived, Father Oates yes Paddy he really smashed that so called soldier about in wanting to know where you were, not enough Nelly as he saved some for me but, he is a priest ,well what could he do with a gun pointing at him and your Albert? If Father had used his judo instead of a fist that soldier in disguise would have been killed as he lethal at judo but I thought it was Eric who hit him true as a priest wouldn`t do such a thing.

Father Oats likes to be called Paddy, Nelly only when he is unknown to people around him that doesn`t make sense and you know plenty about him but not saying, he came to us destitute with his wife and children yet he is a good engineer and has contracts to fit many mills with engines now he cannot do that himself .

We have disturbances whiles Paddy has many friends in the forests and he has accommodation some were else not far from here also he is a very learned man.

Nelly, why don`t you ask Mary or his sons? Paddy, Mary is just as wise as him, and his sons just say ask Mom, well ask Albert to approach him, its Albert who has asked me.

Mary is here now, ask her I don`t like, well I will Mary, my darling Nelly is enquiring your presence around here as she thinks you are someone else .

Nelly sometimes I wish I was ,Nelly what is it ? Well er I don`t know ,Nelly you are in doubt what is it ? Your husband Father Paddy Stanley Oates he is not what he seems , Mary who is he? He is Father Stanley Oates from Peterborough.

Mary I thought Fathers in the holy order never married Nelly come we go inside and you Paddy now settle down and listen carefully as Father Oates work is not finished up here as there is a meeting of many dignitaries up at Abbes Walk later today until then he has something else to sort out so Nelly what I tell you see that you keep it to yourself until this is over.

Nelly Father Oates Is a priest of the highest order a man of many languages and sits on many councils and advisory bodies he drafted much about the factory acts of which there is much more to do he is very political in promoting his liberal views and involved in the town and country acts and this is his purpose up here appointed by chairman Sir Johnson who is here and arrived yesterday.

Nelly Father Oates cover was nearly blown when he sorted the riotous gathering out at Abbas Walk but it passed over and apart from Paddy here only a few know his mission here and we sensed Albert was quiring a few things.

Nelly I am not his wife the children are mine my husband is Sir Tom Johnson so I personally apologise if a little fib was told it was or is for you and others benefit ,but why the secretes surly all this is not necessary.

You even had a house by the crofters and been here some 6 or 7 weeks true but doubt if we spent 2 days there sometimes we let some other`s stay for shelter you ask the Salvation Army who will be converting it to hold their meeting once their planning application is passed might be ready for the winter as the land it stands on is unclaimed land that is the merits of knowing someone being involved in town and country planning.

Mary the trouble from the factory thought the thugs paid you a visit ,true they did Ernie and Bob who are escorts for Father Oates would stay sometimes at the house and have lamp burning but would never answer the door they played their part well we thought but Ernie is of special services Mary what is it all about?

Here comes Father Oates and your husband Albert, Father Oates welcome Nelly it`s over a sad sight to see but it`s done, what`s that ? The executions ,there were 5 and 2 were Catholics ``Albert were you there ?`` Yes, I was allowed in I and hope now we have some peace now, Albert I don`t think it`s over, do you Father Oates?

Father Oates do you have any unfinished business here ? Nelly what is it ? Father I know who Mary is and you are what you say ,Albert Father here is on a mission as Mary here is Sir Johnsons wife and been working undercover with Father here and some people living in the forest are agents for Sir Tom Johnson so what`s going on as you did well in convincing us when you caught the ducks and went to court.

Nelly all is true as now you will be informed when we go to Abbes Walk as you can smell their cooking from here, Father I want to know now for I should hate to think you have been using us as you are a mechanic engine fitter and have business in factories you supply too and a Holy Father and come here to do what ? For what has been done is plenty with murder hangings riotous crowds thieving and poaching and you don`t come all the way from Peterborough for that as that is what is happening all across the country.

Father what is it for it cannot be more serious than what I have said ? Nelly we are supposed to be going to Abbes Walk yes Father we are ready .

Nelly and you Albert listen apart from what you do know about me the people who we are looking for are 2 men in their 30`s who are up here who have stolen many artefacts from the All Saints Church at Peterborough and when caught and if found guilty may hang or expect a long sentence.

Many items are priceless or difficult to replace we thought if I was to mingle amongst people here it may be beneficial, and I have done that with little effect well apart from that stupid man trying to steal a mill as we thought he was involved.

Firstly, I asked why here ? You do not have a Catholic church but have an all saints church same as Peterborough and I have rode about the area as you know ,Nelly I borrowed your horse for mine was at Abbes Walk with Ben and that you didn`t know .

I had men planted in your inn to try and glean any info I had men in the ale houses and helpers in the mills but I feel convinced the items are up here and not just few but many that would fill 2 sacks and worth a lot of money, I know people up here cannot afford such items as if they could they would be in fear of displaying them so I asked myself where do I go from there ?

The problem coincides with my duties here in checking the right full land or property owners as there are many rogue dealers as industrialist are in too much of a hurry to establish a factory there and when operational ignore safety regulations, all that I can manage its these artefacts that trouble me all roads are checked as the York road and the north road all have been watched.

When you are ready, we shall ride to Abbes Walk I wish to go now whilst it is light and Albert a word in private if you please so please excuse us for a few minutes.

Albert St Helena church at Abbes Walk what do you know of it? It`s probably the oldest church around here, did you mention to some one that there is a secret tunnel there made during the early 16th century when bloody Mary was denying faith to any other except Catholic and burning many at stake for practicing it.

Albert who would know that, and be at Peterborough to come back here? Albert our thief will be amongst us at the meeting and Sir Johnson could be in danger.

We are here now so Nelly please take Mary to her husband and tell him what you have heard from me and Albert and I will have a bit of hog and a few vegetables and be with you shortly.

Bernard nice to see you, Holy Father thought you were at Peterborough what are you doing here? Now Bernard you don`t ask priest their business as you should know I am Gods messenger as I should ask you? for what do you do these days?

I ride with Sir Johnson as escort, good man, but you live here and I was told you came here several weeks ago ahead of Sir Johnson true as I am the messenger yes but your abode is here, ah yes someone else would return to Peterborough when Sir goes back ,who would that be? Oh, I don`t now know why? I thought it was Bob Carol who I see over there yes Father now I remember it is him, why father is there something wrong ? Again you ask questions you should not be asking a Holy Father questions as I may think you are troubled from something , but I ask that I may require someone sometime now excuse me for Sir Johnson wishes to talk to me.

Hello Tom, Holy Father how are you and Ernie come join us Tom our thieve is amongst us and Tom here has found the stolen artefacts below the St Helena church in an escape route that was made in the early part of 16 century during the troubles.

So do we eat and do our speeches first or call time on our church thieves, Sir Johnson and you Father we have that's me and Alf have been watching Bernard for a few days and followed him on 2 occasions to the hiding place below the church.

Sirs this is Alf who has be drinking with Bernard on several occasions, thank you Tom Sir, the church stolen property and the man that helped him is over there his name is Bob Carol one of your outriders Sir the stupid man is wearing a chain pendant that was handed to the

Peterborough church by no other than King John prior to signing the Magna Carta who did much hunting there.

Holy Father did you know of this ? No but was thinking on those lines that I had seen that pendant at Peterborough and noticed Carol wearing it here.

Ernie get your men together and get Bernard and Carol, tie them up , and hold until police get here as the police are invited and should be here soon and see everything is accounted for and returned to Peterborough after all being displayed after dinner and speeches, very good Sir.

Now may we eat , ah Mary you played your part well and Nelly at first, I thought some crofters maybe involved or some travellers at your inn now why should I think that?

Chapter 32

You Put Years on Me

The whole issue made many aware to what was happening around them as more land became available for factories mining and housing as years came and went with more local shops opened to meet the demand as mine was no longer viable and not necessary and Albert was running his furniture work shop down as that too was not viable but the sale shop in the village was booming with more modern furniture that more tooled up factories could do.

I time of vast change now John and Will have got themselves married and Geoffrey can`t make his mind up as they are all working together in the business as Albert is happy doing what he loves that being the love of nature in feasting his eyes on the estate as we both seem to be back to meeting public demand in selling our wares from our sale patch and laugh to know we had Mary Sir Johnsons wife working the spinning wheel as we have along with many dignitaries have their photos appended to a display board near our sales pitch at our garden gate as many stand and stare or walk on to the church whispering ``that's Nelly`` and acknowledging many stories that their parents have told them.

Albert much pleased with the furniture outlet and looks over their books and ordering as Geoffrey now after much studying intends to enter the Methodist church and if anyone were to do that, we thought it would be John.

John and his wife Ruth often call with their children and if it`s not them then its Will with his wife Beth and 2 year Harry as we become a kinder garden of much laughter and joy to see motor cars replacing horses and carriage`s and engines being replaced by motors and electricity replacing candles a change so swiftly done that hurried along production and created much employment and wealth.

Like many things a price to pay as we for casted that of the estate and the vicinity in losing much of its appeal as more land is being adopted for industry and international relations are hitting the headlines of trouble across Europe with the South African problems being put to rest with much dissent from the Africana`s and that of the concentration camps that British army devised that accounted for many prisoners dyeing in hunger and neglect as it alarmed many in power.

Now local papers have a much greater audience as many more people are educated through compulsory schooling and hot meals are available in schools introduced by the Liberal government but international relations are under threat again along with the Irish question the IRA are making news with disagreements in how the British Army are discharging their duties as they claim their direction comes from British Government so the killings go on as it appears no headway made since the Battle of Boyne.

Albert reads daily news in his old baggy trousers and clay pipe and rabbit fur hat and hair all over his face and a pair of boots that Geoffrey made some 8 years ago can`t you move with fashion I asked ? Nelly I`m happy as I am as I go through the estate, Albert that's fine in the estate it`s when you go into the village to the furniture shop to do the accounts and books as you are beginning to look out of place now get some decent clothes on begin to look the part, up here is fine but not in the shop in the village.

Nelly, we don`t have a tailor`s shop here then go in town but alter yourself its same in church ,Nelly I am the same it is other people that have changed now they have found more work.

Albert you have some good clothes here start wearing them when not working ,Nelly that's a laugh as I am always working, I have no time to dress up, no, you are not, so smarten yourself up ,Nelly I wouldn't mind one of those automobiles we keep seeing puffing and shunting along the lane in fact I plan to have one before Sir Harry has one.

I thought we would be seeing Father Oates up here as many factories have changed to electricity driven motors Albert it is a company a large company with many employed and Father Oats is something to do with the directorship.

He has done much to improve one`s working environment as now it`s become more noticeable there are less accidents but still too many ,but it's the land nearer the North Road that is being bulldozed over that's attracting much attention what`s that all about ? Coal, they have found large deposits of coal and I am told there could be many around our town many in close proximity of each other.

Albert I feel sad and feel like emigrating for this land of ours is going to give way to horrible slag heaps and the beautiful environment of wild activity will be gone for ever and as we are high up here I will able to see them destroy all in front of me, and that tells me only this estate will remain untouched and that of Abbes Walk as we are high up from the valley below.

Albert I was born here grown up here and live here a much sort after place that will now lose its appeal and value for who wants to face slag heaps and sickening thick black smoke belching out from chimneys high in the sky whilst hooters and sirens fill the valley with noise to frighten our domestic animals whilst the wild life will seek a more pleasant area to be.

We are Methodist and embrace our public with love and care as ale houses will grow in demand and gambling to be more widespread as I fear that the black gold will ruin many a good man as it endeavours to improve their standard of living as it will and take many a man`s life in pursuant of it as well as reducing one`s life expectancy in retirement.

Albert we can expect to see industrial development in a large scale and to witness a changing society in many aspects that we have not seen before and I fear it cannot be part of me as I wish not to change as I must prepare for somethings I cannot alter like constant activity and noise as beauty and stillness of the valley will be gone for ever.

Albert it will put years on me as I retrieve back into my much loved environment with my grey dress on and pudding like white hat on as I will offer my greetings as they ask to where is the church as I expect many dialects habits and customs in this changing world of ours.

With grandchildren now running chasing the hens about just like their dads did when they too were about their age as time seems to flash by but does nothing to reduce the poaching in fact there is more as the population increases and the wild life is more confirmed into smaller woodland areas due to deforestation.

Albert that is better now you look smart but why you`re not walking amongst the villages looking like that? No Nelly all dressed up and looking aloof they will think, well I don`t know what they will think, as I wish not to look a toff like Sir Harry.

Today Nelly I am a magistrate and have some court duty to see too and that is why I have changed only time I dress as I do , ``women I will never understand them`` , Albert I can hear you, yes I know and your woman`s league is growing in strength and that choir has many people standing outside of the building listening to you as there is no room in side.

Albert we have to change whether we like it or not as the people are changing and creating a better society and pleased to come together and share interests as there were a time when they were frowned upon and punished as those sad years have gone.

Nelly you don't change with your herbal remedies and that spinning wheel and your dresswear you are quick to tell me but you don`t alter through the years for, if you don`t know it the Victorian era is over.

It is time you changed as we come to an end of another decade, no Albert I can`t do that, but I do when singing In the choir but would be in fear if you buy an automobile as I am happy in my little world as people speak well of us as we are their history as they make history in developing the coal fields whilst we here will be here when the coal fields are not.

What we can only do is catalogue it preserve it and sometimes cherish it for we have seen many things in our 50 odd years here and perhaps the last decade was the most terrible one for infant mortality rate was very high due to mis- management of government as there was too much of self -interest in industrial growth and not enough interest in social and domestic growth as we had a lazy -fair system.

Wealth and prosperity a wonderful thing as rest of Europe is changing as they race to develop from what they see here as we are the first to be industrialised that has changed the whole concept of how things were, as now it is a power struggle, the power of industry ergonomics and innovation.

Chapter 33

A Changing Society

Our song group improved and increased and so did womens argument for more rights and a greater say in society as now the Salvation Army have their own premises and Methodist church is popular whilst those that go to the All Saints church on the estate find how meaningful and importance of having a Christian faith as many toil hard all week to contribute to a thriving economy then thank God for it.

Particularly at weekend`s when men dress in tight fitting suits and with a flat cap whilst women with new dresses and large decorative hats in enjoying their new found wealth as one knows when its Sunday as one wears their best clothes as it is the only opportunity to do so.

Many shout Nelly at my garden gate never Albert always me as if they are frightened of my dog as many have all kinds of ailments for doctors are few and expensive in relation to ones earnings as my demand never altered from colds fever aches and pains to skin rashes boils cuts and abortions that I refuse as I wish not be responsible for if things went wrong but that's not my field of treatments I like to think I am an herbalists and it stops there as all too often I am approached to act improperly.

Many problems are self -inflicted and many are through neglect and many are through a poor diet as most are from industrial injuries for me to try and hurry their recovery so they can return to work as it is no work no money and if it be an industrial injury they would not put in for a claim in fear of losing their job.

I could only prescribe an herbal remedy as times I thought in just talking to them was a big help, but who I did treat and got well was more than generous as many would ask me of my secrets of any mix I might use as I never would tell them or any herb that would treat various problems as some never knew one plant from another.

The more we became industrialised the more people came with their ailments and create a queue in waiting sometimes I thought many just wanted a chat and note my interior of a cosy lodge as if I have nothing else to do so I had to have a treatment area made.

Rose would come and have a chat which was great and bring some fruit as I would offer a large meat and potato pie as we would catch up on local gossip as she would laugh and say she can`t get her daughter married off as she has too much of a good home but Rose I would say she has two homes yours and mine as she has been housekeeping for me for many years now as she goes about her duties singing as sometime we both sing together.

Nelly ,what it is in town there is a factory making motors as now the demand is enormous from these industrialist and lighting as sometimes I often wonder how we managed with just candles and no street lighting as many feared in going out during dark nights .

Rose now the whole village is lit up as children can play outside in safety and thieving has be reduced but not that of poaching as again its being done in small gangs as game finds its way to the local butchers as we have 3 butchers shops as husband Sir Harry suggest along with Albert they pay them a visit.

Rose, I hear you, Albert, Harry thinks you may ride with him to the butchers he will be here soon that's right Rose drag me in to it ,time and time I have told him and he takes little notice ,Rose I manage the upkeep of the estate and wish not for him to be involved as I know what`s going on and there is a spate of poaching.

That's not main reason why you are here as your whole family are down with a sickness and some workers whilst cows stand un milked and hens and other feathered friends are unfed but you and Harry seem fine Rose there is much flu about and fever but I don`t think that be the case as I need to see more before I can fully diagnose then Albert what do you think ..

Rose is that Harry? Rose, he has a car, well the crafty devil thought I would be first ,Albert jump in Sir you`ve kept that quiet Albert I think some of our game is finding its way to the butchers shops ,Harry if it is, you can`t prove it as all butchers display their game hung up outside of the shop rabbits pheasants ducks from all areas around here for you cannot accuse butchers for why should they ask the seller to where the game comes from.

Sir I hear you have a lot of sickness amongst your workers ,what is it ? Albert, I don`t know as many jobs are not getting done, I don`t know what it is and going to call a doctor in when I`ve dealt with this present business, then drive on as I can`t wait to see this contraption go.

Sir leave it to me .there in the butchers shop stood Fred with a blooded clever in his hand as he eyed me with suspicion in having Sir with me ,Fred I know you are busy but I would like to know to were you get your meat from, Albert what kind of question is that ? You know as it comes from the slaughter -house other side of town why is there a problem? Fred what about your game ? I am supplied by many game keepers from all around this area ,Fred we think some are poached off Sir Harry`s estate ,Albert it could be as I don`t know to where it comes from same with the meat of beef lamb and pork.

Fred there is a rabbit decease making its rounds and can wipe out much of the rabbit population apart from making one ill who consumes cooked rabbit now I am not sure but all the signs appear to be that but, Wilf you know Wilf Nelly`s brother up at the race course is chief vet nary and course superintendent is being sent for.

Now Fred, Sir Harry here has several of his workers off sick by eating rabbit and requires some temporally workers, a milk maid and 3 fieldworkers to lift turnips and, other field work, do you who know anyone seeking work?

Albert I know some out of work but if seeking work I don’t know but I can help you, here take this A board write on it and stand in front of the shop and in next to no time you will have all you require Sir Harry did you hear that ?Albert I can`t do that, why not ? Harry be part of them not aloof as they will appreciate you more.

In little time we had a milk maid and many rushing forward to cut and bag turnips and other tasks as they clambered into to Sir Harry`s car to enjoy the novelty of riding in a car that's becoming more and more noticeable on the roads .

Later we sped off to town to inform Wilf who confirms there is many rabbits affected in the area as he has received many complaints and problems and will come and test to confirm it and if so, medical doctors are to be informed too .

Sir Harry, I thought you might have noticed these things Albert I leave things like that to others as I am not involved much as Matt does most of the financial work Harry, he is not responsible for hiring and firing he does the management of business, now have you not got a farm foreman to take care of every day affairs?

Albert, we have not sorted out who is the poacher true but there is more than one but how do we catch them? Albert when we do, we serve severe penalties to deter others, no we don`t Harry we make the area more secure and introduce a receipt system from butchers who purchase their meat from, no receipts than questions can be asked.

Sir Harry it guns they use now as they are more available yes Albert they ought to be conscription to get these young men in uniform, that will reduce poaching

,Harry there is much talk about conflict abroad and it does not look good but I am not in favour of conscription, Albert if we are involved in war you might change your opinion and what about the Irish question?

Harry you ask about conscription and we don`t have it but wars should always be avoided as it is the common people who will suffer as it was in the past, difference is weapons of war are much different with bombs and bullets and transport and if we were at war we would be employing all the technology we introduced in the last 2 or 3 decades to apply and to destroy the human race whereas it was meant to improve one`s living standards.

Albert I think we are heading for war as the papers are full of Regencies from Belgium making headlines ,papers again I don`t believe all this they print there will not be a war far too costly in manpower and finance as its all idle threats as the industrial revolution is over now countries are trying to see how one stands up under threat, no Sir Harry it would be far too costly to go to war.

This changing society will not allow it as all Europe is racing ahead in technical know -how that's producing great advancements in living standards growth and education as the common people have never witnessed such speedy development in their social and domestic lives.

Albert what you say is true but you once said man is a peaceful living animal if left alone but he is not alone because of that man is a war like animal as his satisfaction is never met and what I read and see I believe we are heading for war a war of great consequences that`s never been seen before.

Sir Harry I think I might be a pacifist as I am a Methodist and pray to God that what you say is wrong for it would pain me so to see young men go to war to kill one another for the sake a political settlement but I must confess that my opinion may change if the enemy were at my door.

Sir Harry you come to me with a sickness problem with rabbits that we can manage, but if you are right about a war then the problem of poaching will decline as conscription increases.

As I pray to God you are wrong in our much changing society.

Albert this is what I know from good sources that we along with France Russia and Ireland have a treaty that if any one country is attacked than others will come to their aid and Germany are allied to Austria and Hungary for the same reasons.

Chapter 34

We are at War

Rumour after rumour as everything else means little as factory workers and land workers muster at weekends debating the topic of the day that being war and talking as if they are too be called upon and would soon put a stop to it as if GB is dictating terms and all- powerful to supress any opposition ,as they can only believe what they read as I remind them that we cannot settle the Irish question as many questions require answering about it, and the Boar war has left many questions to be asked and who would protect us if we were attacked ,but if we were attacked the damage would be done long before any aid came.

These Europe countries are on the mainland Europe as, we are, surrounded by water ,but it seems no matter how I view things the intensity grows stronger of war as, many in town talk about nothing else of the assignation of Archduke Franz Ferdinand of Austria and his pregnant wife Sophie and Franz was nephew of emperor of Franz Josef and heir to the throne of Austria and Hungary.

Now it is inevitable because a group of Serbian terrorists called the Black Hand in the region of the Balkans started it in the city of Sarajevo on June 28 and that being a month ago, that is what Sir Harry was building his premise on.

War is all what people are talking about as posters display the words ``Its War`` and papers are snatched up as quickly as they are displayed as people appear to be jubilant not sad or disappointed but in a keen and a hurried mode to tell everyone as if only they know and have an attitude of we shall show them not knowing the full facts or reasons why as learned people say its caused by militarism alliances imperialism, and nationalism .

Sir Harry you are right? I told you Albert and it will be a long and sad war, as many seem pleased as they know little about world affairs but we are in it now, whilst many think it`ll be over by Christmas as its only July how they come to that conclusion Albert I don`t now as I fear it will be a long war as many here know little about the history of European agreements deals alliances and treaties .

But we in GB are constantly at war a war of want and change whilst education for the masses has been denied until recently.

Sir Harry I don`t follow you as you have altered a lot in these last few years no Albert it's the people who are changing as they are rushed into war and delayed in schooling as if the state controllers only want you to defend the state but not to be advising or interfering with it.

Harry you confuse me this is not you as you a magistrate were for physical punishment to meet the offence ,Albert I have changed as a good marriage can contribute well to ones attitude in life ,then Sir you have a good wife in Rose, true Albert these are the best years of my life ,Sir we are in a world war and you claim these are the best years of your life ,Sir you are confusing me.

Albert, I tell you this the people are so misguided with this war, as it is going to bring much hardship and sorrow as now I see in town people rushing to join up as if it be a bit of fun to go and see beautiful cities of Europe then comeback and talk to their children how lovely Europe looks.

Your country needs you as army personnel are in towns recruiting with much ego and excitement with flags waving in jubilation as many are in ill fit army uniforms feeling proud and encouraging others to join up and defend your country, as mothers wave white handkerchiefs in excitement but not knowing what lays ahead or knowing the enemy for as soldiers you are to act as one, as you carry a rifle to kill or be killed under orders and if you refuse you will more likely than not be shot by the rifles of what your companions carry.

Sir Harry you have changed ,well Albert what do you think about the situation? Sir you know where I stand but I am no coward or traitor or a gutless wonder as people echo the words to those who are against war, for my reasons I have mentioned many times as a Methodist.

Sir Harry, I fear in the next few months we shall see change in opinions as many people in none- essential services will be called to arms , you are right Albert as I see many changes as the war intensifies.

Nelly you`ve just missed Sir Harry yes and no doubt you`ve been talking about the war as I have just come back from town ,the town is alive with activity of soldiers marching through it, were they are going I don`t know some say to the docks to be shipped to France as they sing and wave all in happiness as if the war is over yet I noticed some young men who are from around here who could have not had much training but carrying a rifle.

Albert our Methodist members and the Salvation Army were there too giving support in the recruit`s departure, Albert do you see this lasting ? Nelly, I do as many think different as there has never been a war like this with bombs and bullets, and mobility is more available with different methods of warfare that will be sought to the cost of many, I hope I`m wrong as this country has gone through a boom time of much growth and development to see it ruined because of international relations.

I thought it was a terrorist group that caused it ,true but this is where we are Albert, in our womens group we are against it and will demonstrate our feelings but some of their sons have volunteered so it’s a bit ,well I don`t know as their sons would expect support as their fathers cheer them on that`s creating a mixed feeling in families but we as a group are against war as I have to tell the group that we should support fathers and sons no matter what views we have.

It`s alright me talking as men don`t wish to listen to woman as it’s a man`s world as all too often I see signs of ``men only`` in pubs and bars and voting and various employments ,one smart guy asked why do woman have small feet? He said so they can stand nearer to the oven when cooking ,several laughed so I asked why do men have big foot he looked at me as if I should be laughing and shrugged his shoulders ,as I replied so they can fit into their mouths.

The woman in question I turned to me and said you should be annoyed don`t let men make fun of you as they always will, you are equal in everything except sex for its because of them we are at war we woman don`t cause wars we woman never crucified Jesus yet they can have a Queen who rule them or misrule them as they will take up arms to defend her whilst the most important person to them is their wives or mothers as they go about making fun of woman and attempt to isolate them from equality.

We are not their slaves as now they take us into a war to defend what? Not you or me for when it`s all over we woman will be treated just the same but not if we keep united so wake up and do not let men rule you.

Sometimes I feel depressed and disappointed in my task as apathy is rife as many women are too frightened to argue for equality as this war is now taking effect in not seeing as many young men about the streets.

Albert understands me in my quest in defending woman`s rights ,as grandchildren come to tantalize Gertie the goat that stands docile and unaffected as John and Ruth his wife call and make pleasant talk but now it is all about war as he says Will is serious in joining up for if not he might be conscripted and Mom I think same as our business will not be exempted as it is not of national interest.

John listen to me as I`m shocked to hear it , your Dad will not be pleased either to hear that, Mom our country needs me, no John, Mom Father can run the furniture shop, John you can work the land for Sir Harry or your uncle up at Abbes Walk can find work then you will be exempted.

Mom I have to go and Dad can look after things here ,it will be all over by Christmas and I must do my share and so will brother Will as we gave it a lot of thought now we can be officers or work our way through ranks as we join.

Dad here you are, I was telling Mom of our joining up, I heard you and only hope you know what you are doing, Dad it's the right thing to do as I have to support my country and Will is of the same mind ,John what about your family? Dad they will be fine for a few months, Dad we go next Monday we both are not sure as yet for if we wish to take a commission.

John then you have done it ?Yes Dad and Will, Dad you can manage the company until Christmas when we shall be back 3 month Dad that's all and Geoffrey will be fine as he is much developed from his past experience ,Mon don`t worry be proud as whole GB is rallying around the cause as we are called to arms ,Mom we want the whole community to be proud of us and not to look upon us as draft dodgers.

Now, Dad and Mom do you think we ought to have a commission? John you go with our blessings and yes if it is what you want I can look after things here and you ought to take a commission both of you but ,well we are sad to know but proud of you, thanks Dad you too Mon as Will shall be here later.

Nelly I never thought a day like today would come Albert my heart is sad but there is little alterative as we cannot allow society to view our sons has cowards when other mothers are losing their son`s we are part of it no matter what we think as we strife to improve things in our woman`s group I would not be able to face them if we failed to face our responsibilities .

Nelly that`s not it as we are not responsible for their actions but we can stand proud of what they are doing and you carry on in what you do at the church and woman`s league as you will be called upon more so and so will the Salvation Army for don`t take sides or support individualism but act for where ever there is a need either here or any were else.

Nelly here at our little abode will become an hive of activity again as an information centre as many will come here as if we know all what is going on but Sir Harry was right ,now I wonder where he got his information from.

Albert, as we get older life gets more difficult as I never thought I would see the day that my sons would go off to war for Geoffrey will be next as we have many pockets of unrest in the colonies ,but a world war Nelly

this is different and we don`t know what to expect
that`s the problem.

Chapter 35

Farewell Cheerio and Good Luck

Echo` s of singing of farewell cheerio and good luck as other areas of conscripted men parade through town on their way to the railway station to be shipped off to the docks and over to France all cheerful and happy in serving their country .

If reports are true than they have no reason to be happy but maybe not told the truth as they would be far too busy training and when that is completed its France.

No reports of any casualty but reports of conflict and holding of positions as every day here is military activity in town centres all joyful and happy as I wonder were all come from but then our mobility has always been restricted through long hours of employment and a horse and cart but now its trains and automobiles and more songs introduced to keep moral up the popular one is`` Keep the Home fires Burning``

Nelly you never fail to attend when they come parading through town on their way to the docks singing as they go Albert look there John and Will but I thought they were in different units Nelly I thought they were in the Free Foresters but no as I don`t know what they are in can`t make it out from here.

Albert, I`m deeply concerned as I hear there are many casualties on both sides as Mrs Hardcourt has her son home as he has lost an arm and says its hell on earth as thousands have lost their lives in the first month as you are told to charge with bayonets fixed only to be quickly shot at as many fall under fire like committing suicide as some refused to go and charge ,they are taken out marched away and shot its nothing but humane slaughter on both sides whilst many officers stand back and just give orders and has one wave of troops charge forward they are shot down as the next column move to take their place as the battle field becomes filled with dead and wounded.

This is a disgrace to humanity as life becomes nothing only a tool to be used and quickly cast aside for someone else to take its place.

Mrs Hardcourt says her son says don`t believe what you hear here as its all propaganda as the truth is not told as many papers only publish success stories.

Albert that is not good to hear as I have heard similar stories but what is it all about ?

Nelly Sir Harry has friends in the foreign office and Mr Johnson of Peterborough keeps him informed as he tells him that WW1 is imperialism and nationalism and been fermenting since middle of last century,

Kaiser Wilhelm 2nd was reigning over most of the dynamic powers in Europe and for meting an unnecessary rivalry with his Aunt Victoria`s kingdom by establishing German colonies around the world and building a German navy comparability with ours.

Also tells me that Austria and Hungary and the Otterman Empire were wrestling to hold together against various nationalist movements notably the

Balkans were Russia was pursuing ambitions of gaining influence through what is called ``little cousins``

The Serbs and Italy recently independent had ambitions of advancing along the Adriatic coast known as`` Italia irredenta`.

Nelly I believe him as the storm clouds have been gathering and this is what we have been hearing through the media but I doubt if the conscripts will know that as they take up arms, for a soldier is trained to kill and not to know the reason why as some may say its political and they are right as all things are in seeking power.

Germany has an empire of colonies as does G B as each one seeks power over each other and because of alliances and difference of opinions conflict arises so Nelly in a nutshell that is about it.

Well I don`t like it as more and more news is available and as some of our soldiers are ill equipped let alone trained ,then what when it`s all over, as it will make little difference to the way we live as some will argue that we are free, but free from what ? Albert I doubt if it makes any difference to the way we live only difference will be world power or dominance in the political will and strength as state leaders are never satisfied with what they have as agreements and alliances are broken, as we here should ask why.

Nelly you can theorise and think as you like as it will make no difference as you support your womens league and comfort those who are suffering and focus your mind on our sons and let politicians sort it ,Albert you are right I must do that as a nation we should support our leaders and brave soldiers sailors and airmen but I don`t like it, Nelly none of us do but it has happened and now we must follow it through as we are an allied nation same would apply if we were attacked our friends would come to our aid as there is no other way.

We must accept it and get on with it as we will see more of our grandchildren and after school and weekends they can come here and if any of their mothers wish to go to work I don`t mind if the children come here as they are old enough to go out and play but leave the goat alone.

It is you Albert who will be taking more responsibilities on with the furniture store, can you not find someone to help you? Nelly I will have to for Geoffrey has now signed up or he would have been called up, well I was expecting it as our village has gone silent of men folk except older people like yourself .

Nelly, do you know of anyone who could help me? Albert the call for furniture will decline but the boot and shoe shop will be more called upon it is that you should focus on and suspend sale from the furniture shop temporally and see how the war pans out for they may be home for Christmas, I don`t know what to do may be keep the boot and shoe business alive as there are a couple of good men their and the contract from the army will have created a greater demand.

Nelly I will shut the furniture shop down after orders are met and concentrate on the boot and shoe shop I don`t wish to put anyone out of work so I`ll try and find anyone left some work and if I can`t Sir Harry or at Abbes Walk hopefully will.

Nelly the sad news is that some people are deserting as the war is not what they expected and if refuse orders in the field means death by firing squad, I didn`t want to tell you but I will for the Dutton family their oldest Ray you know of him yes Ray how is he? Nelly, he deserted and found his way back home to here, some say he boarded a ship and got to the east coast then to his home here.

Well Nelly military police came looking for him, unbeknown to me he slept in our old shed that housed the engine, you saw the military police who got to searching for him you thought they were part of recruitment drive not so as they chased him across fields and it was suggested to get the dogs out but Nelly sadly they found him hanging from a tree in Creepy Hollow he had hanged himself rather than go back for those who he spoke to he told them it's a place where humane life means nothing as soldiers are killed by the thousands on a daily basis with no thought whatsoever for the individual as many refuse and taken out from their position and shot.

Then Albert I must go to Mrs Dutton and comfort her as this is terrible , Nelly don't go for we now have 3 sons in uniform and 2 are officers so leave well alone for you don`t know how she will view you.

Albert I must for this is terrible, Nelly you stay were you are until you are sure in how you will be received go to your womens group and ask around, Albert I must go Nelly, I am telling you not to right for there are 2 more deserters running loose as the police have been here checked our outhouses as they think we have something to do with hiding them.

Albert that`s not true, Nelly I know that but they have their job to do, but now they realise we have officers in the army they apologise but the 2 deserters have not been found and many think they could be hiding up in the forest as they did many years ago when they were boys.

Nelly it appears all is not what many think when joining up they were so disillusioned but would they listen, Albert I`m thinking of John and Will and how they are making out, and so am I Nelly as they have to give orders and see that they are carried out and if not what action are they supposed to take, as orders are orders.

Albert, I don`t like the looks of things for if a deserter came to me for assistance what should I do ? Nelly you could be in trouble of assisting a deserter but what if he is hurt and in pain ? Then people ,might call you Mudd , Mudd why.

He was a Doctor or a veterinary surgeon called Mudd who helped John Wilks Booths compatriots in addressing their wounds whilst on the run from assonating President Lincoln as he didn`t know of who they were or could not refuse treatment to their wounds and served many years in gaol for assisting not knowing who they were but gave treatment as he felt it is duty.

Nelly the choice is yours as you will be judged on your action`s.

Chapter 36

Letter for Nelly Lodge

Nelly we have mail two letters and Nelly this is first time I have received a letter well come on open it, it`s from John he is a first officer in charge of supplies to the battle areas and says it can become a little worrying as the Germans are targeting supplies but I am too smart for them as I change times and different routes and sometimes deliver under dark as I quickly return to base and safety.

It gets a bit concerning but I am fine as I hope you are and hope to see you soon God bless.

John-- Kings Own Yorkshire Light Infantry.

Sorry if my writing to you has been neglected as we have been very active under fire as this is no place for anyone as many at home are not told what to expect as this is hell on earth as raw recruits are sent into battle as it is now reported that we have lost at least 19,000 men and about 38,000 wounded in first day of war as the killings continue as thousands of troops arrive daily not knowing what to expect as I could tell them it`s a journey to hell of no return .

I feel lucky in what I do as I drive supplies up to the front as it is now known meaning to where the conflict is in trenches facing mainly the Germans as some appear not Germans but I do feel that neither them or us are aware what it is all about but now after 7 or 8 weeks there appears no let up as shells and bullets rain down onto the trenches of British soldiers who are scuttling about like rats waiting for orders to climb out of their rat holes and charge forward to certain death as the Germans are just waiting with machine guns as I view with horror as orders given are irresponsible as much more thought should be given into the cost of human lives as hear the top brass arguing as the name of Haig being mentioned a lot as he is responsible for tactics.

Mom don`t worry as I am safe but things here are not what people at home are led to believe at home ,so god bless.

John.

Albert there are 2 letters yes. he perhaps some get delayed.

Will`s letter King Own Yorkshire Light Infantry

Hello Mom and, Dad I am fine as I hope you are as this war rages on and forget it being over for Christmas as I fear it will be a long war ,I am an officer in charge of a division of many men as we hold our positions strongly and daily in trenches with little to do and seemingly a save area as some will quietly sing as some will play mouth organs as there is little more to do as my men are lucky for I dare not tell them in what I know.

Some half a mile away in trenches that they dug out to house themselves is continuously being engaged in battle as they attempt to attack and to be machined gunned down as bodies lay shrewd in their hundreds as this is a senseless war as many try to desert or refuse orders only to be taken away not to be seen again.

My position remains safe but don`t believe what you hear at home as this is a disaster of an humane carnage and questions will be asked when this is over as for me an officer will offer evidence upon what I see and hear for John and I did not buy our commissions we sat for them and passed with distinction as some officers buy their positions and not a credit to wear a uniform or represent their country as I am in constant dispute with them as many are not fit to handle men, let alone give orders or lead men and to that it sickens me.

Mom Dad take care as I will here ,for the sooner this is over the better

God bless Will

Albert they don`t give an address for us to write to them or to send food parcels but I don`t like what I read this sounds terrible oh God I hope they are safe Nelly maybe if we write to their regiment they will forward it on or Salvation Army could help us I`ll ask them as I am going that way.

At the Salvation Army building there were many in tears as news filters through as Salvation Army break news to love ones as I made my enquiries of nothing to report but many casualties on both sides are many as the shine of joining up has declined into fear and criticism for after only 2 or 3 months I can see sadness as curtains are closed to many houses that have received sad news.

Many I called upon to be faced with sorrow as mothers sat and wept in holding a letter loosely dangling from their hands confirming their loss as the words are short precise and to the point.

Now everyone is aware of the consequences as the recruiting continues as those who have affected now turn to anger but the recruiting continues with slogans of ``Your country needs you`` and the parades of marching recruits continue as thousands more are drafted in to boost or replace the fallen.

The weeks come and go without any mail or acknowledgement of what we sent as the only news is what the papers say as Christmas comes and goes and grandchildren lose interest in playing with Christmas toys to call for their Dads.

Nelly come quick we have a letter from Geoffrey here read it he is an RSM what`s that? A Regimental Sergeant Major in Reims, where is that ? Nelly just read it well he says its done nothing but rain and many soldiers come and go as he is called upon to move to the battle zone for 2 or 3 days then relieved by others and cannot make friends and acquaintances for no one knows anyone as the scene is constantly changing as sometimes we lay in our dug out`s just waiting hour after hour in silence as we look sky wards to see a sky lark singing or a crow gliding on the wing and many other birds who seem to be hurrying bye except the lark who seems to be exerting its right and freedom of space in the blue sky above in a period of peace and tranquillity.

We here are ok but we are in a war zone and each day brings many different orders and actions as it seems nothing changes in positions as I sometimes think, what are we doing here when we should be advancing.

It is difficult to say anything different as we are cut off from the outside world but have heard John and Will are officers as we all in the same infantry so with love your son Geoffrey

Albert again no address and no good news ,what were you expecting to hear? Albert it would be nice to know how the war was going and are winning and when are they coming home. Nelly it is war with massive casualties on both sides as no one can win for the greatest loss is to humanity time, and time again we debate the issues as the war lingers on it was Christmas then Easter Whit and Spring and summer as we all worry and wanting to know how things are but in fear of receiving a letter as it seems sad news rather than good news .

Nelly I get more news through our boot and shoe shop as the demand for military footwear is enormous good for business as many die with their boots on and look around the village as it is depressed and in sorrow as this war is effecting almost every family and probably same in Germany and their allied countries and when it`s all over it will take years to put right as the memories of it will be remembered for many years as it will not be forgotten.

Nelly I am creating footwear for soldiers to go and kill as at times I feel uncomfortable with it, as some who make bullets and bombs rifles and guns we are all guilty in Gods eyes but I ask does God show us the way? Nelly this war shows no sign of being over as more news filters through and awful to read.

The British 4th Army of volunteers first time in battle have been wiped out, and the unit of friends of the East Lancashire Battalion wiped out as thousands are killed daily on both sides as now when I am in the village I am given unwelcome attitudes as many know our sons are officers and an RSM and must think they are not involved in combat ,and nothing I can do about it as I cannot approach them to explain as I don`t know and that is upsetting as I understand their hurt.

Nelly Sir Harry is here, and Rose hello come on in how nice it is to see you drop of Cherry wine Rose, and you Sir Harry as usual is it?

Nelly, we have a letter for you sent and drafted by Sir Tom Johnson unit commander of Kings Own Yorkshire Light Infantry, great wonderful but what are you doing with it? Are you post man now? Nelly, he wrote to me with some other business and thought best I ought to deliver the letter personally, why what`s the matter ? Nelly its Geoffrey he has been killed in action we are so sorry.

Oh no my God no, Albert hold me, hold me tight.

Will his body be shipped home so we can give him a Christian burial ?

Nelly, I don`t think so, why we can see to things here? Nelly please it cannot be done, you mean, yes, I do please Nelly, it cannot be done.

Rose will stay with you a while as Albert and I go outside

Albert, he was in an explosion and Mr Johnson is so sorry and is writing up a citation and is annoyed with Haig and his command as his decisions lack planning and when it`s over he plans to have him questioned as many top brass would like him replaced.

Why not do it now Harry? Well it may happen as there is no let up as this war can go on for another year or 2 and Haig has achieved nothing as many questions are asked.

What has Sir Tom Johnson got to do with things ? Nelly he was with a moral boosting party lead by the foreign secretary Nelly that does not matter we are here to comfort you and Rose is, only to please to help you ,yes well thank you, but I`ll be alright.

Chapter 37

The War In-testifies

Albert it`s all about war as if nothing else matters as many now approach me with many suggestions about our womens league as we have grown in strength that many are now taking notice of us and men folk talk about unions as they grow in membership.

Nelly I am being approached by Northampton Shoe Company if I want to sell out as now most footwear is in Northampton but it is our pattern and design as we own the copy rights ,now I could be interested but its John and Will to decide and I can`t do much whilst they are serving their country.

Albert would you sell if you could ? Yes, as Northampton will have the monopoly of manufactory for several years to come under the new technology being adopted ,then what ,oh no its not for me as John and Will have the furniture business that is quiet now, but after the war things will really take off again and furniture will become in great demand as people look for change.

Of course, I will not and cannot sell but big money is being mentioned ,as many thinks about future fashions ,what in a time of war ? Nelly some entrepreneurs welcome war as demand in some things increases but that is all talk just now as I know they want the patterns, but we can wait.

Nelly don`t misunderstand me for I have no intentions of doing anything as they will sort it when come back from the war and the sooner the better as I hear combined forces are making good headway although casualties on both sides are heavy but according to reports things look better Albert, that`s paper talk.

Well what can I believe? The war goes on and no end in sight and letters from John and Will have nothing to report about themselves, it`s all war talk as casualties are horrendous and deaths are in their millions.

Albert my shop and your workshop has made a big difference around here as your garden furniture was doing well until the war broke out, Nelly there is no demand so I concentrate more on the estate for Sir Harry, and the wildlife are in abundance now poaching has decreased as thieving is more towards vegetable crops potatoes carrots peas and turnips which are seasonal but catching game is harder with greater penalties if caught as we have 2 cases up tomorrow and I am called to sit in judgement.

I only hope it is professional poaches rather than locals as the reasons are much different as I have to consider reasons and why and, not of the crime committed whilst the circumstances are very much on my mind.

So, Nelly back to my workshop I am suspending production and any small kindling I have the customers coming in to your shop may help themselves to it as you point out to them the Salvation Army collection box as they are doing a fine job here and everywhere else and Nelly if some commodity becomes in short supply because of the war ensure that people with families are catered for more than others.

Albert, I know that and so do my staff you just see to your own concerns and how long will you be in court? Best part of the morning and I might get to know how the war is going for the news around here is not worth listening to.

Is Sir Harry with you ? No, he is not called upon so much now, but Ben up at Abbes Walk is with me and he is good to be with as he is very knowledgeable fair and understanding as he often laughs in saying I hope the accused don`t view me like George Jeffries the hanging judge of Cirencester as he learnt about him when he was studying there as he laughs to say pleased to know I don`t have the power.

In the shop Albert I have to determine who is in the greatest need as some who I have never seen before will be making their rounds to many shops to stock up were as I look after my regular customers fist as many things are either under the counter or in the back.

Many come to bring news and have a chat for the news they bring is never good to listen to as many cry over their purchases as they are now aware of conditions that their love one are dying in that of trenches ankle deep in water as rain lashes down in bitter cold conditions as they feed from mess tins trying to avoid the rain by covering themselves with ground sheets in hurrying to eat a portion of beans or vegetable soup with a piece of bread not knowing if it will be their last meal as many reach for their chain of crucifix and pray.

Each tit bit of news is welcomed, as many have different stories to tell, sad and upsetting as we do our best from the womens league as banners are now ahead of our demonstrations led by me as we sometimes forcefully echo our believes and intentions ,that being rights for women and stop the war.

Many now listen and understand our demands as opinions change as people are much active in thoughts and deeds as they scream and shout ``end the war now`` but no the war rages on as each seasons comes and goes as same old story of It will soon be over as now it`s well into the 2nd year with greater casualties as whole army groups are wiped out as battles rage on at the Somme with reports of 57,000 casulties and 19,000 killed as I was in doubt until now as now they talk in millions.

We hear of deserters and consciences objectivist as they are viewed with contempt and many are here at home whilst many view them as cowards because their sons are out there fighting it out, deserters carry the greatest scorn and branded cowards and fail to be served when entering shops or alehouses as some take to the woods or disappear and change their identity as red caps come calling.

We hear as the war in testifies and courts marshalled are regular as the death penalty is common, because of failure to carry out orders or insubordination or faking illness anything to avoid going to the Somme ,a place of no return and if wounded one is lucky if carried out to safety to find a hospital bed or quick treatment as the battlefields are pure carnage.

Albert how did the court go ,as he dips his hand into the barley sugar jar then look around to see if no one is listening to say ``Nelly it didn`t, it was Mc Donald`s son he threw himself off the railway bridge early this morning and the other accused shot himself dead as both of them were to be triad for theft then returned back to the army to be courts marshalled so sad as we feel helpless in our duty for if only these people would seek advice rather than do as they do.

Nelly last night there were rioting in the village and some shops windows have been smashed and food stolen and the police say no one is talking as they are not prepared to say even if they knew ,its food they took nothing else but food so Nelly we have to take care.

Albert they will after get passed the dogs first and the alarm bells and your field gun ,No Nelly don`t use that not the gun as you will be arrested but you can use minimum force to protect yourself and property,

Albert if I am under threat I`ll use the gun, Nelly you can be arrested for attempted murder or murder ,what, I do nothing and let them take what they like ? I`ll tell you Albert I shall be looked upon as a fool if I was to do that ,and suppose he has a gun and I shoot first ?

Have I not got the right to defend myself ? When his intentions are to rob me ,and my dogs suppose they attack the thieves and injure them will my dogs be put down for being dangerous whilst doing their job?

Well, it all depends on circumstances Albert they should not be attempting to rob me, those are the circumstances as you should consider the victim not the abuser

Our sons are fighting a world war because of circumstances and its cost millions of lives so will the conquering powers be put on trial for using violence ?

Nelly you`re talking daft now as that is war, right Albert I declare war so append me a sign over my shop door explaining that, if any illegal entry is made to these premises the owner will assume you are at war and take any necessary action it chooses to defend itself.

Nelly your womens league are altering in many ways how you women think and making a great impact upon society as Mary Jacobs of the Netherlands did and I know she has been over here and you have met her Albert that was before the war more like back of last century but what a wonderful women and it`s not altogether the politicians who are obstructive in our struggle to change, it`s the general public who laugh and sneer and wonder what it`s all about as our war upon change in testifies.

It will take time but it will come when women will be more appreciated but for now we have a world war to fight as we bring you into this world and there at the end to bury you and Albert if you see ,Sir Harry ask him how things are as it`s been a while since we heard anything.

Nelly, the war is intensifying as I thought it could not get any worse.

Chapter 38

My Broken Heart

Nana when is my Dad coming home? Soon my darling soon as it will be all over Nana can I play with the goat? Yes give her some hay and gather the eggs but keep away from the pigs as they get rough when feeding but you can feed the horse, Nana can I have a ride on him later when I have finished here ?Nana I will be alright on my own as I can ride ,you can ride later after lunch.

It`s good to have them around but they do miss their Dad as we all do Rose, the children grow fast as the years pass us bye Nelly it is because you keep busy and active for you are never still ,I am never ill so my herbs must do something as, I have a remedy for most things and still got some of Hiram Codd bottles that be a much sought after item in a few years.

Nelly are you preserving history? Rose the Victorians will be remembered for many years to come, as we went through a revolution an industrial revolution a period of our history that will live for hundreds of years as the beginning of technical innovations.

Albert you are back early have you no customers? Does no one want any new shoes or boots ? Nelly not truer word spoken as trading is slow and orders for the forces are little as I believe they are using Northampton for supplies as they are more tooled up to meet demand so I will give it a few more weeks and if no improvement well, I will close the shop and bring the business up here with your shop.

We have room and the repair business is little now but we will keep it going for I do not wish for men to be out of work so I will think of something.

Nelly ,who is that coming? Post man they have uniforms now and a bicycle not bad think I could do with a job like that, letter for Mr and Mrs Lodge .

Albert open it Nelly I do not want to for the markings on the envelope concerns me look, Albert ,no Albert oh no please God Albert ,what is it ? Nelly it is bad news Nelly, our boys have been killed in action John and Will on the Somme two days ago, oh my God why ?

Rose can you take the boy home ,what is the matter Nana why are you crying Granddad what is it ? Nelly I will and bring someone to be with you as I am so sorry now, look I see Mrs Thomas I think she is coming to the shop I`ll have a word with her.

Rose see to the boy and I will take care of things here and staff in the shop I will tell them and see to Nelly and Albert are not on their own, Rose now go as the boy is anxious to know what has happened and Rose can you sort it for someone to be with his Mon? Mrs Thomas I will sort it and later come back here with Harry who will notify others.

Ben the post man delivered the letter and Nelly we have had to put her to bed as the doctor has given her a sedative she is sleeping now Albert, if you require help then say so Ben we have 5 people working for us and I do not wish them to lose work so can you organise the grocery shop and the boot and shoe repair shop.

Albert, Sir Harry says Rose will take care of the shop and Isaac knows what to do in the shoe and repair shop, Ben they are now under one umbrella all up here just across the roadway from the house.

Albert I`ll keep an eye on financers and admin side of things Ben I don`t want anyone losing their job as things are difficult as they are all good people but tie up with Isaac in the shoe shop repair as he does not require supervision and I pay them on a Thursday but Isaac is trust worthy as he goes to the bank for me but I hear you have a car now so take him with you as things will be more secure.

Albert do not concern yourself as I will ensure things are done properly you just see to Nelly and take as long as you like, thanks Ben.

I could not sleep as Nelly was heartbroken as we took turns in comforting her as she is weeping a lot and slept a lot and her voice was incoherent and nothing more we could do.

Ben you here again, Albert I want to see shops are all right oh yes thanks ,and I like the engine does it still work ? but I have suspended operations as things are quiet but will pick up again when this war is all over.

Albert when you are feeling better I want 2 covered barns building for I understand you were going into shed building Ben I was into it but like many things the demand fell off it will return when new housing estates are built for I know the plans have been drawn up but again we have to wait until it all these troubles are over.

Well it`s a fine engine Albert, can I borrow it until you want it back, no Ben can`t do that but can get you one off Paddy well his place up at Abbes Walk ,is that Paddy`s place ? Yes as it says so on his placards in the garden and its Father Stanley Oates of Peterborough, I didn`t know that ,you did ,no honest I thought they were 2 different people Ben leave it a few days and I will sort It for you, but what for ? I have a pulping barrel with blades that requires an engine. someone threw it.

Ben, we are having a designated area at the cemetery for all 3 of them that`s all we can do is have a place of remembrance dedicated to all who have given their lives in this parish that will stand and not forgotten a cenotaph of appreciation.

Albert people are laying flowers in your garden and small gifts a token support as your garden is covered with a whole bed of flowers with many appreciated messages attached as no words can replace your loss as we are family and share your sadness.

Ben I know but it`s your sister Nelly who requires much comfort so go to her Ben and sit with her for a while ,I will Albert but, you take as long as you like from your work as I`ll see to things here.

Now Harry is here as I`m going to comfort Nelly for Harry will be asking me about court duties as now I am chief magistrate responsible for many duties and I don`t wish to annoy him as we now give him less complicated cases as the whole system in how the judiciary works is changing and a bit complicating as the Liberal government changed some things then these conservatives regain office only to try and look at things a bit different than this war intervenes as we as magistrates are limited in what we can do but for Harry he is good to have around but he is of the old school of crime and punishment .

Harry thanks for coming, Albert anything we can do then just ask and I hear you`re shutting down the shed and garden furniture works , Harry there`s no demand for furniture of that kind right now maybe later, I`m trying to keep the staff, as we are alright for a week or two but I don`t want to put them out of work Ben is wanting some barns building later but for now ,well we will see.

Albert near the paddocks there are about 6 horse chestnut trees I want them removing ,Why, surly not as they are beautiful ? Albert 2 have a type of fungi and the forest commission have told me they must come down.

I asked about the wood and apparently if all the outer bark is removed and any poor colouring on the inner trunk than the rest maybe salvaged and they are yours if you want them, Harry there is a lot of timber there they will take some felling ,not with two men on a band saw and I know some farmers who want some drays repairing, and fence repairing ,Albert there is a lot of work out there.

Harry I can find use for if stained and well and treated it will last a long time ,Harry what I will do with the kindle and rough cuts I`ll let the villages have and put the apprentices to work on outdoor furniture for the paddock like tables and benches nothing pretty but, useful for when we hold the yearly show ,splendid Albert wonderful idea then Harry do not mention it to others as the apprentices will have to be judged on his work and performance and we don't want anyone copying but what he does for the paddock will not be that he will make for his entry.

Harry I have a circular saw, a British invention but would like a powered chain saw that I hear someone in Sweden has invented very recently and Harry you should make more use of the paddock like country markets or exhibitions and demonstrations and Sales ,good idea Albert but it`s this dam war but I`ll keep it in mind .

Harry I`ll come tomorrow and have a look ,Albert get over this sad moment first, look Albert have a word with your staff and send them to me and I`ll show them what requires doing and no doubt you`ll be wanting to borrow the dray again. sure ,will as my horse be a good puller but thanks Harry.

Now Harry about this car of yours as we want one so where is the best place to go?

Go to them that will give you good business for if they buy off you then you buy off them, and I think I know the very people. Harry not just yet but in a week or two sure Albert I understand .

Harry, Nelly is broken hearted for this will take some getting over as we have lost 3 sons within 2 years in a senseless war, for what is to be achieved as questions of this horrific war will go down in the annuals of British warfare history.

Chapter 39

End of Hostilities

Bad news, all bad news as we in the womens group fight on, as now many cheers us, as attitudes have changed as there appears a new sense of feeling and care towards one another as news arrives that we could soon see an end to the war as many shout it is hopefully the end political dogma as we have suffered for 4 years and what for ? What have we gained whilst General Haig faces many questions, about his strategy?

Nelly you`re not going to let up, are you ? Rose we women don`t make wars and have no say in how things are done, it's a man`s world that I intend to change and before long now hostilities are ceasing as my war will become more noticed ,as it`s a war on womens rights to vote on ``why should we be cast aside?``

We are not slaves to man`s dominance for that is how it appears this is 1918 and peoples love ones are coming home to a country that we women contributed so much to for little award as we raise our banner again whilst the conservative government is facing change in the political world as the working classes are demanding things that they have been denied for far too long.

Nelly the government have much to do to get this country going again ,no they have not Albert ,they have ministers responsible for each department`s and what do I hear ? All I hear is Boner law upsetting the IRA and the industrial work- force arguing for better wages whilst industrialist refuse to budge as their profits increase, Albert I see much industrial unrest as winning a war does nothing to improve the working men`s conditions .

Albert how do your work force view you? Nelly you know that, as I never have any complaints as I let them determine their working conditions production and concerns as I award a bonus on completed orders and meet once a week to discuss any problems or suggestions.

Nelly why do you ask? Albert ,what would you think if a woman applied to work in your workshop ? I have no vacancies; Albert suppose you had? Well, I don`t know as I have never known a woman to make furniture Albert that is because they have never been given the chance.

Men, can do womens work but, women cannot do men`s work ,then are you suggesting I employ woman ? No, I am suggesting women should be equally considered when there are vacancies.

Nelly good point but try telling some employers that and they would laugh at you, Albert I don`t see you laughing, and I have had men helping me out in the shop when I was unwell.

Albert, can you not see my points? I know this, a women can do many jobs that men do as they could be politicians bus drivers train driver magistrates farmers and judges yes you may laugh Albert ,no Nelly not what you say but how you say it ,what do you mean ? I mean you ought to put more forcefulness passion and determination into your arguments and organise petitions to support your claims.

Then, Albert you will support me ,Nelly I will but let things cool off for a short while as people are readjusting from conditions of war.

Not industry Albert, as they are marking the land out again as I think they are looking for coal fields and found some around here as I`m told there are many in close proximity of 2 or3 miles apart and work could start soon Nelly will you be applying for a job?

Albert there are some jobs less suitable for women as there is some jobs less suitable for men, true but men will be prepared to do anything now hostilities are over as many things will have to change as industry will forge ahead in demand and supply as we see here of many acres of land being prepared for building as heavy machinery is ripping the heart out of our country side in drilling for coal as the development is changing the whole spectrum of our country life as habits and customs will be replaced by industrial behaviour that will have its own behaviour in what will be a tight community of coal miners.

Albert ,what will happen to us? Nothing as we are not part of it as I intend not adapt to what new communities do and we are not geographically part of the industrial planning as the new coal field will be in the crofters area and operations from it will lead away from our area here as we remain unaffected.

What I hear from other areas of what benefit coal brings contributes well to the country economy as many miners are unhappy with offer of payments of 6 pence increase to wages that is causing much industrial unrest and some are calling for strike action as now we are faced with industrial hostilities, you say we are we part of it ?

Nelly, strike action effects everybody in the communities and as we`ve seen in the past it can be come hostile, we are not affected yet, but many factors will arise from the coal industry because of the nature of the work.

Albert the garden furniture shop could benefit from the new communities ,it could Nelly I am expecting orders from them for posts and garden fencing and your shop could benefit from it too I can see it now as many call for tobacco ,chewing tobacco of short black sticks of twisted tobacco as they call it and chew on it then spit it out.

Some from here work at a mine some 2 to 3 miles away and call at the shop I can always tell they are miners as even after washing they still have coal dust on their eyes lashes and in ears and nostrils with finger nails filled with coal dirt all looking prominent on a pale white face.

My next customer would be a farmer labourer with a much different complexion with rose red cheeks pearly white teeth matching a bronze like skin and wearing a much battered and worn hat with few holes in it with a wisp of straw nestling and protruding from one hole in his hat, even at weekends miners still have that same appearance were as farm workers speak in a whooow arrrrre fashion.

Nelly you are very observant, I am when school children call at the shop as many have quick hands and deep pockets as the new school is well ahead of the housebuilding project it is not so much of infants as they cannot reach the counter and usually with their Moms but the leaving school pupils oh dear I feel sure they are given lessons in how to obtain things without paying.

Some have asked for cigarettes for their Dads but I am not having any of that as some of their fathers smoke heavily and pass the habit on into new crazes and old practises, but there does appear more money about as many want my cough medicine and other treatments as I could give verbal cure but no its not because of smoking they argue as they cough and splutter all over the place as they quickly defend the cigarette habit.

So, Albert our hostilities remain that of social and domestic differences and struggle to improve upon the status que whilst our league of women are more stronger than ever and being recognised by Parliament as we demand equality in asking ``Why not`` as they are unable to answer Albert, it`s like all things you get nothing if you don`t ask until you realize you ought to demand for what have you to lose as against what you intend to gain.

Nelly what is it you want that you are so strongly fighting for ? Here we have all we want you are happy doing what you do, and I am a magistrate and an employer ,and soon have a car to ride about in what more do you want ?

I want justice for everyone for the common people are denied many things and my station in life has nothing to do with it as I want more people involved in everyday affaires that concerns them and not to be dictated to by wealthy entrepreneurs. I want equal representation and less individualism and less dictatorship over others I want state control in essential services.

Nelly be careful what you say for many would condemn you and would do their best to smear you as politics can be a dangerous game specially if you do not hold an office, I suggest you get more support from people in higher office first .

I have trade union backing who are backing a new party called the Labour Party Nelly whatever ones does either in politics or in their own social circle it should be for the good of the majority.

The wigs of the last century gave way to the conservatives to that I encourage that there be always an alternative and a good opposition as we all strife to improve one`s lot ,it is war that makes governments unpopular as they don`t fight wars its people who fight wars and there`s always a loser.

Nelly there is nothing wrong in change if it promotes the security and wellbeing of its people for a depressed public achieves nothing only disrespect of law and order anger hostilities and unrest.

Chapter 40

I Never Refuse Help

Albert I hear much shooting in the woods ,Nelly there are back its shooting and game season as the woods are alive with game deer`s foxes pheasants partridges ducks rabbits and on the east side of the forest there I saw grass snakes viper`s as I have only seen them on the east side ,why I don`t know and fail to find out but there must have been as many as 40 or 50 hanging on barbed wire I think is was late August or September someone told me they would be shredding their skins and drying out ,but as soon I was noticed them they all dropped into the long grass and disappeared not to be seen the likes of it again and probably never will.

Albert the gun fire ,is there a hunt on ? No ,then you have poachers ,Nelly we sure have and wish I knew who it was as they come in cars now and have lookouts and make quick getaway`s but they know the penalties if caught for they are more severe than they were before the war because it`s deer they want and use high powered guns and fast cars for their escape,

Albert what are you doing about it? Nelly it`s not part of the estate, the forest is Ben is responsibility, now on the estate I have it well covered and we do have deer but we are not being problemed why the forest I wonder ,I`ll have a word with Ben as they travel through the estate to get to the forest.

Nelly I`m going to see Sir Harry first any messages ? No

Sir Harry, Albert it`s Sir now so what is it as you got to calling me Harry ,I want to know what`s going on for there are poaches in the forest, but not so much here on the estate ,Albert I thought it wouldn`t be long before you came running.

Albert the police are all over the place near Creepy Hollow there has been a hanging not suicide but murder and the police are searching for 2 men believed to be still around here as all roads are covered, well I didn`t see anyone on my way here, Albert, police think they are in quarry wood and could lay low until dark.

The police are here now, Sir Harry there is only one place they can be and that is the quarry wood , officer who are these people ?Albert you know one. it`s Walt Blaxton you had him in front of you last week for domestic abuse and the man found hanged was carrying on with Blaxton`s wife ,who is he? Alan Wakefield the insurance man who calls each week for insurance money ,I have heard of him.

Officer what are you doing for it will soon be dark and how do you know it is Blaxton ? He was seen by a couple man and wife out riding their bikes who attempted to cut Wakefield free, but it was too late .

Officer have you got the quarry wood surrounded ? Yes, and if darkness fall`s we shall be here all night ,not if we send the dogs in, Harry you have two good dogs and I should now as they are from my stock .

Right Albert I`ll send for them ,officer if they are in the wood you will have them before nightfall and the area known has Creepy Hollow will have to be altered as its claimed several lives with those over hanging trees will have go and the bend of the road to be widened ,officer those two witnesses have you their details ? Yes, and they live about 4 miles away ,look I have a written statement from them in what they saw.

Here come the dogs . officer do you know where they entered the wood. Yes, just down there, then if you are ready, we let the dogs pick up scent from there and then will Harry let them loose and command them.

With shouts and screams and barking they were soon found arrested and lead away ,Harry I wish we could close that road but it`s not ours and what`s happened here I hope it does not allow the poachers back on the estate.

Albert, not if they hear about the dogs ,Harry I will make some notices in warning poachers of dog patrols and anyone found poaching do so at their own risk and the estate will not take any responsibility against any trespass.

Harry, I don`t know if the warnings signs would stand up in court ,no Harry as I will nail then to a tree but it might deter some from poaching on the estate Albert I`m going home for I feel unwell I`ll take you for the police have finished here.

Rose ,Harry in unwell I`ll help him down from his horse into the house I laid him on the settee as he coughed and spluttered blood and then died as there was no more we could do as Rose took it well Albert she said he had been unwell for some time but he wouldn`t go to a doctor now the doctor will have to come to him.

Perverted ulcer the doctor diagnosed and put it on the death certificate.

It was so noticeable of Nelly comforting Rose at the cemetery with umbrella`s raised all black and in mourning as sadness and sorry overtakes all present as the rains lashes down to match the dull and unpleasant occasion

Rose in the past you have been very supportive of me so anything you want doing just ask, Nelly you are so kind but I have lots around me as Matt your brother will take control of the estate and the hall is up for sale as I am happy in the cottage, I don`t want the hall much too large for me, Rose does Matt know that?

No not yet than, ask him, do you think he will be interested ? Yes, I do but what, will you do? Nothing I just carry on but will rely more on Matt in fact I will leave very thing to Matt ,yes but you what will you do ? Nelly I will carry the banner high and proud for the womens league as some of our claims are being discussed it`s not enough but a start.

Rose will you join our committee to help us to formulate policies for womens rights ? Count me in ,Nelly so far you have done well but you need to widen your call, I suggest you collar MP s` outside parliament and create more influence.

Rose it`s been the mobility but now we have cars and trains vans and buses as it seems all to have happened in such a short time ,Nelly it`s taken about 30 years or more before the common people could afford luxury goods ,Nelly don`t use that phase many years ago yes but not now we are not common I dislike the phase as in the class structure there could be about 12 to 13 different classes and people should never talk themselves down as I would accept working class as we all work whether for financial gain or not .

Rose welcome aboard now I must go, sure you will be alright , Nelly I have many around me, I`ll be fine, back home Albert had a gathering of miners around him who were asking how would they stand regarding the law if there where to go on strike ,I stood back to listen to what he had to say.

I have recently just lost a friend and you come to me for advise you should have been at the funeral as he did a lot for you many things you never knew about ,``what did he do for us.?`` Someone shouted, he gave you an appeals panel he gave you the right of a solicitor he gave you the right to protest in a peaceful manner in this parish, he gave many more things that you will recognise as situations arise, and was working towards a legal aid system to help people is pursuing settlements either in courts or out of courts.

If you men come to me for guidance ,then I suggest the load mouth here to be quiet who only come to annoy me so what is it you require ? Come now as I am in anger if you require my help then ask but firstly shut up the fool you have amongst you.

Right what is it ? Sir if we go on strike what could happen to us ? You now have unions that are not now illegal therefore you have representation and these people should be advising you ,Sir thank you but our unions require legal advice as we are ignorant of industrial law through no fault of our own and we require people who are aware of these things and was thinking you may help.

What is your name? Ray Tool no, I mean your real name come man you have to trust me, Joe Clark and these people have elected me to speak for them ,Sir it has been custom and practise to be warry of people as unions were a dirty name to the employers and it`s taken many years of toil and trouble in achieving union recognition and even today we are looked upon as trouble makers.

Joe I am not a solicitor I am a magistrate and I now your troubles so before I go any further will you please stop that fool from screaming out obscenities ? ,Thank you, Joe do you have a branch committee and chairman ? Yes Sir ,then you come around tonight about 6 with your committee and we will discuss how far you can go without breaking the law which is a farce in some respects as we all break the law every day but tonight we shall have solicitor, but that fool you have is the cause of why you are looked upon as you are

Sir you say we, then you`ll help us, not if you keep calling me Sir my name is Albert ,Nelly what are you doing here ? Been at back listening ,why am I not allowed to be were men talk about their work ?

No ,thought you might have stayed with Rose ,Albert she has many with her but now I am interested in what I hear here for it seems all about wages and conditions Albert it`s good you can advise but thay have their own negotiating body and advisors Nelly I think they were wanting to know how they stand with the law.

After tea we are going to speak to them as its much better to seek advice rather than to cause chaos in not knowing what it can lead to.

Albert why did you query me listening to you? Albert we women have causes too and are entitled to same rights as unionism means just that.

Here they come with large flat caps and heavy shoes or boots and wearing waistcoats all in dark colours as if one should dress as the same as anyone else.

Gentlemen this is Mr, no Albert I am Stan or Stanley from Abbes Walk near Bens place and you all now of him as you poach his land, wait for it ,as I do but don`t tell him for I had a permit but lost it ,any of you found it ?

Now, you have your Trade Union Congress, but I will speak as a solicitor of what the law is, we have criminal law Statue law Civil Law and Common law and what offence one commits will fall into one of those categories.

Now, you don`t make the laws but expected to obey them but at times we find there is good laws and bad laws as people like me ask for reviews of some laws as society changes like you who find yourselves in new housing estates with inside toilets and running water for before you were crofters but all that has gone under new developments that creates changes.

I am neutral and will give my opinion as many notice that working men are coming together to pursue a common purpose which is fine but what you should pursue is securing your industrial rights and wage councils and agreements as you could be faced with stubborn employers, for If such industrial disputes go to court than your representatives will have something to argue with.

If you withdraw your labour you must anticipate the end result in not only in what you may claim or secure but of what problems you may cause as you are not guaranteed success for everyone have differing social and domestic problems to face for the WW1 is history that left much sorrow and hardship and taken time to heal now some 7 or 8 years on because of the massive growth in the coalfields problems are seen and expected.

What I say to you is I can advise you and represent you but be wary of your employer as he will have the law on his side, it is during times of calm and peaceful employment that you negate and transgress for change in securing agreements suitable for all parties ,not easy but secure in a court of law.

I hope I have cleared the air for you, as we all strife to improve one`s lot and don`t let Ben catch you poaching as I represent him but a piece of advice get your names down for the Autumn shoot or pay annually for a permit to shoot.

Now you have new communities create your own social life, form clubs, societies ,associations ,and develop within and promote leaderships that will enhance your development and structure as you will become like me in never refusing help on issues relating the betterment of the employer and the employed.

Firstly you create good relations with your employ for a stubborn employer will never succeed and neither will a trade union who will not be prepared to negotiate in a sensible manner so I say to you people be has wise and clever as your employer not to bring him down but to enhance good ideas to promote good relations as you are there to represent your members in their place of work and to improve working conditions and wages, so study industrial law and organise works councils.

This is beneficial to the employer has he knows to whom he is talking to and like all of us it`s what`s in it for me.

Chapter 41

Bluebells Violets and Lilac

Nelly we don`t see many people about these days we see plenty at weekends as they take a walk down the cinder track looking for bluebells on the forest and wood lands floors in a mass of a beautiful blue a welcomed addition to the days that get lighter and the wild life become alive with activity .

A sense of spring as we all seem to change in attitudes of acknowledging each other as the animal within us is no different to our wildlife when spring arrives.

Those that toil underground for black gold called coal only see half of mother nature for a third of their life in sleeping and a third underground and with their dirty eyes nose and ears usually walk as far as the Lodge pause light a cigarette or pipe or a sniff of snuff and spit then turn around and go home as we have many times viewed their habits and listen to pit sirens wailing away denoting the time or of an accident.

Now all Europe is industrialised and trade is booming as fashions changes to its fancy frills for women and smart stripped suits for men with flashy trilbies and wide ties and coloured shoes and music loud and jazzy a new introduction from ballroom slow and smoothie style as people are keen for excitement and the louder the better so it seems .

Whilst I listen to the radio and read the newspaper of world affairs, then peer across the room to see Albert tapping his clay pipe over the log fire place ,then scratching his head and look across to me to say ``What`` as if I have spoken or waiting for me to put the local paper down as I think to myself you can wait I got it first.

Then suddenly he jumps up from his easy chair in an inpatient manner to go outside to be confronted with 2 ladies with an hand full of violets good morning Sir they said, we were admiring your lilac as it is so beautiful with a fine fragrance ,and would you allow us a few sprigs please .

Albert pulled from his pocket a small knife and cut a few sprigs there you are he said , but not seen you around here before ,no sir we are from London come up by train and where I live is just a concrete jungle no flowers no trees and no gardens but here it is fresh clean and fragrant with a happy atmosphere , not all of it madam as if you look over there you will see coal mines and piles of coal waste creating mountains of slag heaps.

Sir that is there ,not here, madam who are you and what brings you here on this beautiful day as you appear to be somewhat overjoyed in our surroundings?

I am Jane Flowers, and this is Anna Lords and we thought we give you a call ,but how did you get here? We walked through the estate,

Why anything wrong with that?

What is this ,you are all questions for I have known this place a long time,`` but you live in London miles away`` true but what`s that got to do with it? It`s that I haven`t seen you before ,well we haven`t see you before but heard about you.

Nelly, do you know these people? Albert of course I do Anna and Jane come inside Albert is a bit annoyed because I was hogging the newspaper and in not knowing you as he doesn`t always know what we women do .

Albert Anna here is to marry on Saturday to Matt and is going to live in the Hall as Matt has bought it and Jane lives in London and staying up here till after the wedding ,Albert ,Anna lives in York and Jane has property in London, then what do they do?

Anna`s family own a printing company ,what a newspaper company if so I might get a chance to catch up with the news ,Albert it is a wallpaper manufactory business ``,but they live in London`` Albert go and have a walk around the garden and charge your pipe up for if it`s in your mouth than smoke it.

Now Anna it`s all sorted up here as your parents will be taken care of by Rose and I understand you all have cars but you the bride should be married in your own parish.

True Nelly as I was born at Abbes Walk and loved the place when I was 5 we moved to York there I married biggest mistake I ever made he got killed in the war but he was a swine that was about twenty years ago, then I met Matt must be about ten years go now ,and ,well we thought we ought to marry and that's about it ,oh yes the church, I wanted it.

I am going to York my home but decided to visit you first ,hope you don`t mind for Jane here has never seen such greenery as she thought up here is all black smoke pits and factories and people of little class but she`s gob smacked.

In London she is our southern area sales manager and never been this way before so I we thought we would give her some time out and come to my wedding ,hope you don`t mind in us dropping in like this ,not at all glad you have, and Jane if you fail to understand our dialect as there are many around here since the pits opened up please forgive us .

Anna its only Monday and you marry on Saturday, Nelly Jane is an interior designer for our company and in London there is a great demand for her services particularly around Chelsea ,up here she is going to revamp the hall with a team of 4 who live nearby and will be done for Friday lunch time .

Jane, where are you staying? Well I was going to make myself comfortable in the hall as there is facilities there Jane you stay here away from your place of work as we will make you comfortable and you will learn something about the locality as we show you around .

Jane I told you, Anna I didn`t know what to expect Nelly thank you, Albert prepare the spare bedroom as we have a quest but my things are in the car and we have left that at Rose`s place, no worry we`ll run you back.

Well I think Rose was thinking about me staying with her Jane, that is the kind of people you find up here all helpful.

Jane, I know of you Nelly, I know of you too ,is it true Jane you have been over to the Netherlands talking to Anna Schaft the lady with red hair and her sister and a few more like doctor Mary Jacobs who are active in womens league, here Jane we are very active and made great progress but still have a long way to go as it seems a never ending story ,Nelly I have heard of you and would love to meet your members,

Jane tomorrow night 6 30 I`ll come and pick you up.

Now look here with this lilac take it and later I will show you were violets can be found, Nelly it is the herbs here that have taken my attention for you have many, yes a cure for many things as many call who cannot afford a doctor but you have cinnamon and peppermint, yes I get those from local chemist but most remedies are what I gather in the wild and some I will not divulge as they remain a secret.

Jane follow me I`ll show you my wine store Elder Blackberry, Damson ,and Apple cider then vegetable wine like Carrot Parsnip Rhubarb as some think it to be a vegetable and some wines here are twenty year old ,Nelly what about that one ,that is about thirty or forty year old as you see it is in a Codd bottle one of the first I made from elder flower and this is Rose hip syrup great for colds and Rose petals good for hair treatment.

I believe you are more interested in flowers if so then I will show you woodland blue bells violets, tulips, and fields full of daises and the common dandelions, reason they are called that is because their petals look like lions teeth.

Then there are our beautiful trees of all sizes and shapes with many in blossom, then I`ll show you the wildlife of foxes, deer, ducks. waterhens ,pheasant`s partridges and two legged boars ,two legged boars that I would like to see ,you will as some carry guns and thay bore Albert sick.

Now look around you look at the decor has I don`t use wallpaper never have done for with these low black beams I doubt if wallpaper would suit it and every other year we decorate with flour well soaked and plastered on the walls then emulsion over it.

Nelly wallpaper is not cheap but soon will be affordable to most people as new developing methods are introduced and demand is growing.

Jane what I have seen of it its drab plain and of little colour ,Nelly it was, but now we are introducing floral designs that is why I am so interested in your flowers as I am to run some floral trail de signs off, will you help me in arranging a floral design and naming it?

More than glad to so we go for bluebells violets and Lilac and arrange a display that will look good on paper as I photo it .you got a camera? Nelly it`s very important that I do as I study many view`s before deciding what will appeal to customers as fashion is important in his business as your cottage would not complement wall paper as it is lovely as it is.

Chapter 42

Any Questions

I never thought Matt was the marrying kind, but he has a found a lovely person in Anna and now I remember her as sometimes she would exhibit at our trade fares and shows at the paddock.

This time we have posters distributed amongst the new communities that some are keen and interested because they bring with them new ideas from places they have left to come here because work is plentiful now the mines are fully operational.

Amongst the miners whose wife`s are supportive of the womens league and some are very productive with making of rugs dressmaking pottery drawing and painting the list is endless whilst, some miners are lovers of dog racing whippets and greyhounds but what is so beautiful to hear on a good summers day is the miners choir practising in the open air so wonderful to hear as the sounds travel across the open fields,

Many of them are of the salvation Army who too have a chorus as the new communities are alive with laughter and song something I never envisaged and neither did our Methodist church and that of the All Saints church on the estate.

The mining communities are a joy to know as they band together and act in unison in comradery environment of song and music as they even have their own band with wind instruments and a large drum blasting out popular music that is contributing to a society that was once a deprived neglected and depressed area of crofters struggling in want and dying young.

I stand on a rise and look over that was once a valley to see smoke from many chimney pots circling into the skies above but not on Tuesdays as that is washing day as hundreds of house wife`s act as one and attempt to keep the smoking chimneys low whilst hanging washing out to dry.

Their habits and customs are a welcomed addition to our way of life and prosperity is welcomed after years of uncertainty as we know, well Albert does that of world affairs as Russia has had its problems that we were nearly drawn into a war whilst the commonwealth is constantly under discussion as pockets of dissent arises as many argue the wealth is far from common.

Nelly, did you enjoy the wedding ? Albert it was lovely and heart -warming I am so pleased for Matt well, pleased for them both has they will be a great addition to our ,community.

Albert 3 people here want to know about the show at the paddock ,they are miners but have many hobbies and pastimes and would they be welcomed ? Pardon what do you mean ? Well they say some areas around here they are not welcomed ,Nelly everyone is welcomed here so make a pot of tea and we shall talk after I have fed the hens.

Now gentlemen I am Albert Sir this is John and Walt and I am Don and we are miners none of us are from around here we have come from Derbyshire and work in the pit here and we here that you are putting a show on in the paddocks near the church we, now of it as we go to the church and intrigued with the 3 or 4 steps near the walnut tree, gentlemen they carry many stories from long ago.

Don let`s talk about the show which is next week a week on Saturday and we have one in Autumn this one we have 3 places left for sales at a cost of 5 schillings each if interested here is a program in the past we have averaged a gate of 1200 customers this year we expect more.

Sir we shall take the 3 stalls if you please as I am speaking for others who are interested with their arts and crafts, but Sir could you accommodate our miner`s band and songsters and the Salvation Army band and songsters? Gentlemen what we can do is your miners band and songsters 11am to 2pm and the Salvation Army from 2 to 4,30 but you sort that to suit yours as we start to run down about 4,30 and go home for that I ask for nothing as you collect and donations but I expect you when available to come to our Methodist church and that of the All Saints with your songsters and music

Sir reason I ask is I represent the Salvation Army too.

Sir, we hear you have apprentice exhibiting their work for a bursary grant, could we be considered? Not for this year but certainly for followings years but our grants were not for miners, no, Don it will be open to all as now you are very much of the community.

Sir we thank you and thank your wife for the tea ,Don I am a magistrate, yes sir so we are told Don my name is Albert and my wife is called Nelly and when addressing us kindly use our names and cut out this sir.

Albert my exhibition will be hand carved coal I carve many thing`s animals, tools, portraits, as I was a stone mason but being a miner mining has given me more security with good housing and finance.

How do you hand carve coal? Well Albert our allowance of coal comes in large lumps and I have my mason`s tools and cave and chip away.

Can you do me one of my Dog here the German Shepperd to stand about 30 inches high and 18 inches wide or there abouts? Sure, can Albert I shall have it on display with my other things and after that it is yours.

Is this our dog? Yes, she is beautiful, Walt here trains dogs for the police, but you`re a miner true but I do some work for the canine department of the police and your dog looks well trained, she is as she will not move from the sitting position until I command her.

What is it Don ? Can I stroke her? Yes I don`t mind no, no, wait as I don`t mind but ask the dog, ha, ha, funny ok go ahead ,the dog snarled and with its ears pricked up and ready to take his hand as he jumped back .Don never trust others peoples dogs as my dog in here to protect me ,now watch carefully as the dog`s name is`` leader, leader, steady, good steady, as I touched its ears, now Don you may stroke her. go on she`ll not bite you, not now.

Well I never, Don most people are right handed the dog sits to my left always as the dogs nose and mouth are nearest to a right handed person and she would have taken your hand out long before it would have reach me.

Now Don I have spoken you may now make a fuss of her she`ll not bite you .Walt did you see that? Sure, did Don, Sir er Albert would you care to come to some of our training sessions? Walt I would like that ,thank you

Gentlemen it`s all about discipline learning and training.

Walt next year we can have a dog show would you like that ? Wonderful and we can get the police involved with their dogs, splendid Walt.

Albert you are what people say, that is you are good to know and talk to ,and is that work shop yours with that engine yes as I sometimes make furniture garden furniture and other things Albert I was looking at the cut offs that would be good for kindling ,take some no Albert load it on your cart and sell it to the miners as they are crying out for fire wood to assist their coal fire to light.

Don, you sell it, a box full at a time you go out with my cart and horse Albert can John and Walt help? John with me here and Walt with you, we start Saturday morning.

Albert how do you know you can trust us with the money because will have been costed out when it leaves me yes, but we may not return with your money, then I will come looking for you with my dog.

Albert I`m only joking we are honest and I have, a lot of, responsibility amongst the miners come Saturday we`ll sort something out and bring my trumpet as we sound out our customers , that’s good Walt for you will be selling eggs milk and occasional game as well as delivering orders from the shop. Any questions.

Nelly what is it ? Don`t I have a say ? Albert you take orders during the week to be delivered on Saturday and load more up for hawking around the communities like bread cheese all groceries I can prepare orders for delivery from here and use the car if you have to.

Fine, as we started with off cuts now, we are branching out.

Sir er, Albert do we not require a hawker`s licence? I don`t think so but I`ll check it out with my magistrate`s office and if we do then I shall secure it.

Any more questions?

No, we do not give credit only advise.

Chapter 43

Storm Clouds are Gathering

Albert according to the news Hitler has become chancellor of Germany after all the nationalistic views he has be drumming up cross Europe I would have thought the Germans would have seen through him but no as the Nationalistic party are making in road`s into Germanies social and political structure, Albert it is called the National Party a dictatorship as he claims to have full employment soon ,well he is certainly making news with his outspoken rallies and demonstrations it seems they love him.

Nelly ,Germany has had its problems of unemployment inflation and deflation and argue that immigrants are taking their jobs but that is no different from many countries as politicians search for answers in a much industrial world whilst problems come and go.

What people are now learning is that Germany is rearming and recruiting into all its 3 services as many ask why, whilst Germany colonies are dwindling? as they are like UK in having an Empire.

Albert it is now 18 or 19 years when we had a world war surly you are not saying we are to have another war no ,Nelly I am not, but if not why have they been rearming for a number of years and been recruiting well in their armed services.

Nelly forget it as we now have much of the mining communities buying from us as we take groceries to them and firewood as the new styled electric motor soon enables me to cut timber up. by the away which reminds me how paddy is going on, Albert its Father Stanley Oates ,yes I know and his place up at Abbes Walk is very much in demand what such an intelligent man he is ,but could not get a Catholic church here it's a problem as people who worship have their own faith and throughout the ages its created much dissent ,wars riots and evil acts against humanity.

Albert ,that's going back a bit ,well Nelly we only have memories as many talk about war they wouldn`t if they went through what we went through Nelly don`t upset yourself for those times were awful let`s talk about the newlyweds and your brother Matt for the décor inside the hall is beautiful.

I sometimes wonder of the cost in running such a place Albert the estate is wealthy, I`m talking about Matt and his wife Anna, well Matt has always been a frugal type and does a lot of wheeling and dealing and has some property near York, what`s that? A paper mill for the packing industries ``what`` how did he acquire that ? I don`t know ,that's how he met Anna.

Well, several years ago he claimed some land down by the crofters area drained it off and put some cattle on it ,then sold it off for building houses on, the advent of house building provided a bonanza for him then he invested in a paper bag mill near York as brown carrier bags have become fashion amongst shoppers.

Now you are going to tell me that they are going to change to wallpaper manufacture no I`m not as they intent to expand into larger production in packaging cardboard and printing of labels for the canning, bottling and jar industry as they have set up a design centre there.

Albert all around us is changing I can`t keep pace, Nelly we don`t have to as people in passing complement our picturesque cottage and landscape one time I thought of thatching it but like many thoughts I never got around in doing it but the cottage is still appealing all around the year and this is spring and cannot allow anymore lilac to be cut this time but if they go down by the stream there is some Hazel hanging gracefully with its light brown and pale green catkins that make a delightful addition to ones floral in door displays.

I know they could damage the trees but if careful I tend to ignore it ,it`s when they damage the surrounding walls and chastise the cattle and disturb wild life in mating season as some people come and collect birds eggs that some of us are pushing hard to ban the practise.

Albert look here again the papers are talking a lot about Germany as they claim part of north Poland belongs to them and they want it back ,Nelly wars are usually about land or religion as we here have much land in the Empire as we should ask how we obtained it and what to do if the inhabitants reclaimed it as an independent state?

Our forces are constantly engaged in disputes the white and red Russians dispute I`ve mentioned before that we nearly committed ourselves but pulled out of it thank God but we are constantly at war across the

Empire as many fear the Russians but they have never attacked another country un invited no matter what you think about their politics and their revolution, here in England we are trouble free as we are made or coerced to be free but free from what, Nelly that is the question.

Albert you've lost me, no Nelly don`t pretend not to understand for I have heard your rhetoric as your war is internal and you have to fight for it and lives have been lost in pursuing it ,true except it being internal for we are an international womens league and against war.

Nelly only fools and dictator`s favour wars Albert how wrong you are as you have just explained about Russian and they are far from being fools as are countries who are determined not to be coerced in to submission from greater power`s

That is what is happening in Poland as Germany are well armed as if they have been planning such things for years that makes them a great force to be reckoned with as countries who rearm claim it is for defence as they race to keep ahead of other countries an arms race that it appears only Germany took advantage of when other countries were hesitant to do so.

As many countries now recognise Germany is a powerful force demanding back of what they once owned.

Albert it`s all across the papers as if they have nothing else to report ,yes Nelly a medium to coerce the public to believe in what they read ,take no notice of it for they will never be another world war as lessons have been taught.

Albert I am more interested in your deliveries as delivery on wheels has become popular as now we can introduce produce potatoes, cabbage and carrots these can be mainly from the estate in season and some from the wholesale importer`s and take papers with you anything you can carry and sell, and how are Don John and Walt shaping up ?

Nelly they are good as I swap them around and it suits them and they never bring much back on the cart except a sack of coal, what I am to do is make a cover for the cart in a kind of an apex design to have access on both sides of the cart I have the tarpaulin for if the rains come they have shelter and protection of sales.

Nelly people are now asking questions about garden furniture again now that many houses are built and families have moved in so, what are going to do? Nelly we still make sheds although the market was up and down ,I thought you had loaned the engine out to Abbes Walk ,I did that was ages ago since then I have small motors and electricity and many different tools as we must move with the times.

You do as you please but not this cottage external or internal as we are an attraction to all who pass on by, it`s you Nelly in that long grey dress and pudding looking white hat as you tell me when I`m in my boots and shirt of many colours and trousers held up with braces and my rabbit fur hat that's as old as when Adam was a lad.

Albert your cart will be much better covered during inclement weather as the storm clouds gather as we wait and discuss whether it will affect us ,as it damps one`s outlook ,Nelly you talk in riddles.

Don`t talk in riddles as I think it`s serious as many are asking questions ,Albert it pains me after all these years of losing our love ones the problem arises again after twenty years, cannot people of this world learn we don`t want wars , they should search and find peaceful resolutions, Albert it`s you men who want power over others surly God never intended that as we proclaim him not to make mistakes ,Nelly it is not Gods doing for Jesus was put to death by man it is man`s doing ,than man must find the answer, after 1,938 years man has failed us ,how much time does man want ?

Albert I`ve said and heard enough as we should be preparing our garden for sowing and planting and get those runner beans in as you have abundance of willow sticks for their support and I`ll tell you again we have a bird in the loft get rid of it before it makes an home here and that's the one that's making a mess on top of the car.

Rose hello you have just saved me from angry Nelly Albert what is it ? Well she is pained to think there maybe another war, Albert that`s understandable how you suffered from the last one .

Nelly ,Rose come in and what brings you here? The, show tomorrow have you forgotten? No Albert is supposed to be going there soon and mark out the sites for displays Rose ,that's not why you are here so what is it as you look troubled?

Nelly, I am fed up with these property developers they will not leave me alone Matt is concerned too as they approach me with ugly attitudes insults and threats.

Albert yes, I hear and who are these people and what is Matt doing? Well he is going to talk to you, but I thought I would approach you first, hope you don`t mind Rose you are welcomed here any time now these people who are they?

I don`t know never seen them before but could be from town as their accent is local, well what do they say? They keep asking me if I want to sell, I tell them no. but they keep pestering me ,Rose do you think they know of Ben up at Abbes Walk and me here ?

No, they don`t know of anyone around here, when are you likely to see them again? At the show ground then Rose you will point then out to me ,thank you Albert no Rose it will be a few of our mining friends you will have to thank ,just give them a cheese sandwich and a bottle as they will be more than satisfied for these miners are a great bunch just wait till you hear them sing.

Rose here have tea with us and don`t upset yourself Albert will sort it, I think they know I`m vulnerable well to know that Rose they must know you have no husband so they must know something about you so what could that be?

From the trading place near Abbes Walk as it is a good trading place and for chit chat Rose what did they look like? Well I could show you tomorrow, no Rose tell me now ,there were 3 of them one fat with a trilby other 2 look like brothers about 5ft 6" wearing smart looking navy blue suits and black hair.

Rose when you are ready, I will take you home after I`ve had a word with Alan in the workshop wait there I`ll soon be back, Nelly I have been talking about a foreseeable war as storm clouds are gathering, but we`re not having it on this estate either by great armies or from individuals.

Chapter 44

A Show of Unity

They are turning up in their hundreds, carefree and happy on a lovely sunny morning with apprentices on the gate and manning the car park whilst exhibiters display their wares as every year the showground is in great demand but what intrigues me most was Dons wonderful and appealing hand carved piece of coal that of my dog the German Sheppard called Leader.

The whole of exhibiters with livestock hardware food and household gadgets and many more with some under cover and some displayed on the ground as money changed hands, as if it is going out of fashion.

Rose do you see the people here who have been approaching you? That is then all 3 of them, good, well what are you going to do ? Rose what can I do at my age and a magistrate that many think I ought to step down and give way to younger people well Ben thinks so and perhaps he is right.

Albert get on with it, Nelly I will but Rose does not wish to know or see what action I am taking , Nelly here take Rose for an ice cream as I attend to these people .

Don, this carving is a great piece of work Albert I shall let you into a secret as I`m working on other things as that piece of coal was from the first load to be brought to the surface as I ask for some as a piece of remembrance of first out as I am working on some pieces for the coal mining history museum.

Albert how do you want us to handle the problem with these in question ? Your presence and that of your friends to be with me as I approach them so, here we go.

Gentlemen I hear you are interested in purchasing this estate so who are you? Well who are you? Me, well these men here are my friends who act upon the interest of this estate and we hear you are pestering the owner to sell ,so let me make it clear that you do not come here threatening anyone unless you are prepared to take the consequences.

So I advise you not to be seen here again as you will be escorted off this site as it is not for sale ,who the hell are you telling us what to do ,sir if you do not cease from pestering the owner you will be arrested, oh yea by whose army so clear off before I drop you? Sir are you threatening me as I am in my late 70`s surly you wouldn`t hit an old man, I will and knock your teeth down your throat so clear off, sir put that stick down unless you want to us it well clear off then.

These people here are my friends and that one there is a plain clothes sergeant in the police force and I am a magistrate and the sergeant is arresting you for threatening behaviour with intent to cause injury that is just you the rest of you are free to go under caution not to be seen on this estate again as this is a private estate.

Don you was not required, but thank you, now he is being put in the police van as his records will be checked out and if he is brought in front of Ben he will wish he never saw this estate.

A piece of advice my friends always ensure who you are talking to before you commit yourselves, now my friends the refreshment tent is open I will treat you to a drink, what is it Don ? Albert you will do for us, gentlemen I am tea- total but you have a drink on me as later we go and adjudge the apprentice of the year then you will know what to expect for next year

Albert are we on soon with the choir so excuse us for now as we will enjoy your hospitality later .

The choir as a few hundred gathered to hear them as they sang beautifully attracting more until it seemed the whole show had stopped to listen with the colliery band in support, I was amazed has I had seen nothing like it absolutely spell bounding and a show stopper as I felt proud that we have such hard working talent amongst us.

Ben ,Matt I had my doubts about the songsters but what a performance ,Albert we hear you have had a facade with a few strangers ,no not true they had one with me, as one was arrested and other`s escorted of the premises because they had been threatening Rose to sell the estate.

Albert we know the story as they work for a shady property dealer from town and he will face the courts as he is under investigation for several offences one being tax avoidance ,but you with witnesses can lodge a charge ,Matt I have done as no one is going to hurt Rose or anyone else on this estate as we are a family of friends and have made few more friends in the miners.

Matt and you Ben we have to judge the apprentices carpentry work here, so let`s do it now ,a coffee table ,a rocking chair ,a chest of drawers, and a bird table ,are the best of 4 for us to decide the winner and runners up Matt what do you choose Albert they are good as my chose is the coffee table ,and yours Ben, mine is bird table, gentlemen mine is the coffee table so the coffee table is the winner and look at the entry list, gentlemen it is Ernie Wallace of Abbes Walk one of yours Matt.

Next year gentlemen I suggest it be open to many professions as the miners have brought much talent with them and that being separate from our bursary grant for apprentices working on the estate.

Gentlemen every year this is a great socially and financially event and now the miners have approached me to have the paddock in August for their miner`s gala as they have a site chosen for the purpose but not be ready this year.

Albert tell them yes as they will have to provide their own security not only for people but for the property here, how much Matt? Nothing, if they leave the site as they find it as locals can have a sales table at a cost to be decided and our apprentices to marshal the car parking at a cost. but for now Albert you can tell them yes but they must bring those singers with them as they are good, thanks Matt, Albert tell them I have like you have a solid fuel fireplace built in with a side oven.

Albert the paddock throughout the year is booked for many functions so can you ask some of your apprentices to be willing and available for some weekends to help and prepare the site when called upon as we will pay them the rate you pay.

Matt we must provide better facilities as people cannot keep going to peoples cottages to use their toilets Albert I know and it is in my plans of developing the site more suitable for the public and that is the first task on my list as I have some sanitary people to coming to advise me.

Albert, Ben tells me that Nelly has been upset to think there could be another war yes as I told Ben that we may have trouble from these threatening guys but that's sorted, as for any trouble Ben here was ready so Matt we want security guards whenever we have functions here, splendid we will Albert ,but I was asking about Nelly my sister.

Ben it pains her to think of another war as she suffered terribly, Albert we know that and you did, Ben Its Nelly I think about as she is so loved by the community and active in the womens league and her herbal remedies are still in demand, Albert were is she now?

In the refreshment tent than let`s go and be refreshed .

Nelly 3 teas and 3 pieces of that cottage pie if you please Ben that will be 6 schillings please.

Nelly you must not upset yourself about this talk about war, Ben after some 18 years since we had a world war now there is talk of another world war as not many suffered like me as I know what it feels like and don`t wish it on anyone, We women ought to be heard as our international Womens league is ignored with comments of,`` women what do they know ?``

Yet in many beautiful cities across Europe there are massive statues like we have in Britannia holding the reigns of rearing up horses as the women stand in a chariot holding tight on the reigns in guiding and controlling the situation as many tourist stand aghast not knowing what it`s all about .

War, I fear it coming as we women will endeavour to hold on to the reigns and try to guide and lead men of war to a peaceful existence but I fear we will be ignored like many things but expect us there when required as I cannot condemn you as you take to arms as that is what is expected of you.

It is the whole concept of warmongering nations that must come together to avoid conflict as I see time will come when nations will look back in anger to see their mistakes as we women were right all along but what man will be man enough to admit it?

Am I hurt and upset? To sure I am ,as after the events men will look back and ask why did we allow things to happen,, and gentlemen there will be a war probably a war to end all wars as nations will come together after the event as we women will have more say in not letting one nation threaten another with war as there will always be disputes and difference but remember this politicians don`t fight wars its people who fight wars as our young men will be called upon again with grit pride and determination as they enter into the theatre of war.

Nelly we can sympathise with you and agree but we are subjects and ruled by the power of others no matter what we think as we are expected to give support and If it is war than we are expected to take up arms in defence of it ,of course you are, I am not advocating that you do not, I am advocating means of avoiding wars as there are many allied to each other, I am advocating that all countries to be allied as one body.

A show of unity in world affairs.

Nelly you talk well as we all would like to live in peace but it`s not like that, Ben when you were young you were always fighting you clouted a few that mocked me as it is your nature and still is ,you men have inherited fighting from our ancestors until satisfaction is met as I look at things differently to promote a program of re-education in how to avoid conflict.

A task that appears impossible, but I see it coming maybe not in my lifetime but eventually it will happen.

Nelly there will always be wars ,Ben the wars we should be looking at are wars on want, in housing in hunger disease and in equality as it appears this war is an everlasting issue that politicians struggle to address.

Chapter 45

A Minor Problem

Nelly what a success never seen a show like it and sales not many traders had much to take back home with them as people came from many areas to bye and the Salvation Army songsters they were so amazing and the public`s response to them was heart- warming .

Albert, everything went well and the miners they came in their hundreds to join in the sing songs as I know there is some fine men amongst those miners as it seemed to be a low graded occupation with low educated workers but how wrong I was as I walk through their many rows of houses to see some well cultivated gardens and pleasantries from women with neat white aprons on and chatting away inquiring about ones health.

As they acknowledge me with pleasant greetings as I think my long grey dress maybe a bit out of fashion or my view in life maybe different to theirs as I go to the womens meeting in the chapel as I hear comments of that's Nelly from the Lodge and she Is alright and they have a car you know .

My smiling must have been noticed as other women came to join me as I mentioned our league of women and that they are welcome anytime.

I stopped with about 6 women around me all talking together to hear one say ``you ask her`` No you ask as it went on as I eventually stopped looked at them and said ``,whatever it is ask me`` Mrs Lodge is it true you make medicine?

I am Nelly I make herbal remedies I am not a doctor but an herbalist so no more doubt in asking as I am approachable so what is it? Well we women were thinking about forming a group in doing things like that and wonder if you would help us ,and you are, Elsie ,well Elsie do not view me as different to you as I am old now as I have lived here all my life and made many friends when this area was farmed by crofters and left me with many memories as I helped them.

Elsie, I only help people who deserve it and talking to some of your husbands at the show and seeing what they can do and want to do I feel I have met more friends but this time of year many herbs are not ready like fruit but we can discuss it along with many other interests as we welcome new members into our league of women and that`s where I am going now .

Can we come? Elsie follow me, Elsie were you in the Salvation Army Songsters at the paddock? Yes, I thought I recognised you and you are interested In herbal remedies well I can show you and by the time it comes around you will be well versed for its not just using this or that and bottling it you want to know what it treat`s or cures, measurements and doses to be dispensed and if taken orally ,then there are external treatments.

You are not a doctor and take no responsibility after explaining to the patient, Elsie these points are very important ,if you understand that than we can make a start .

I am a Methodist and so are you in that believe and teaching, as I make wine but never touch alcohol, any questions ?

What wine do you do? Many from fruit and vegetables and again that is best done when fruit and veg are at their best in Autumn.

Elsie your Salvation Amy is an international body as is our womens league as I receive much news from the Netherlands Womens League by phone my brother`s phone at the hall ,are you in contact with your European friend`s?

Nelly. our captain keeps us informed ,yes but from whom? I don`t know, he may have a phone ,were does he live? In town I`ll ask him when he is next here but why do you ask ? Elsie there is much talk about war and my Dutch friends are concerned, reason I ask you is if you have heard anything from your European friends?

We know the German International Red Cross are members of the National Party of Germany and that war is imminent ,my Dutch friends think so too as there appears much activity over the border in northern Germany towards Bergen Belson and Hamburg.

Nelly ,we did hear that Poland airfields had been attacked ,but that is the papers, but not heard anything from the wireless .My God I hope not, and what has Poland done to warrant an attack from Germany? Nelly it`s about a small piece of land but I think any excuse will do as they are well prepared.

Nelly ,Germany is nothing like it was 20 odd years ago for war academicals are still talking about it in who was to blame ,this situation is different as a country has been invaded.

Elsie you seem well informed ,Nelly my oldest son works in the foreign office he lives in Middlesex married and has 2 sons and tells me many things as Ted my husband thinks too that there will be a war.

Chapter 46

Believe Me or Not

Albert, many think there will be a war Nelly ,many talk about it and hope there is as to create more income in there relevant industries that supply guns bombs and bullets and many more things but not live amongst it probably live in the Caribbean or some other sun blessed island well away from conflicts.

Albert, you know that's not true maybe an odd one or two as mobility would be limited and curfews would be introduced so don`t take cynical views of people but talk well of them for without industry where would we be? We require entrepreneurs to run industry and if they get rich and famous from it so be it as we all strife to succeed my argument is that those that help to create the wealth ought to have greater rewards.

What, if I were a soldier in succeeding and contributing well to a war, what would I receive? Nelly you would receive peace and happiness, no I will not I would still be pursuing a way in my employment or social life to achieve and some people may be happier to be governed by some other country or powers.

Nelly that is not true and one should always defend their country well so suppose inhabitants are not happy with their present lot ?

The American Indians fought well to defend their country as many died but are much better off later when Americans took control as did the natives of

Australia and New Zealand as they fought against change only to see their living standards improve

We have many countries to thank Romans Danes the Holy Land the list is endless as we realised, they had brought us much rewards at a great loss of lives because we refused change.

Religion, has a massive following yet many have died in pursuing it, so how do we know that if overran by another country that we would suffer as we don`t know of what policies they would adopt as we are only subjects of the State, those that regulate the State will claim to make you free but fee from what?

These are questions we must seek answers to as countries are allied to one another because they wish not for another power to threaten them into change by conflict so if threatened by war that will bring about change perhaps for the better as some people will not accept it and will fight to protect in what they have.

Albert we have a car a Ford ,Henry Ford of America as we helped many to settle there and sent armies to fight for the right with might , but Henry Ford an American who was making cars turn of the century that is making vast difference to our lives, yet he is American and supports chancellor Hitler in his drive for power in threatening Poland by blaming ethic groups for the reason for change.

Albert this is a beautiful world to live in it is people who attempt to spoil it in wars as we should seek answers quickly before man destroys himself but no that will not happen as man always finds a way.

Nelly you are very vocal today, what`s got into you? Albert all the papers are advocating war and I am now convinced, now listen to the wireless.

Poland has been attacked,

We are, officially at war, can we never learn? 1938 20 years since last one as many have not got over that one and this will not be over for Christmas because Germany have been preparing this for the last 10 year Nelly we are in our 8o`s now we have had a good life and should not concern ourselves.

Albert I know but people stop and stare as they pass on bye and admire our story book cottage expecting to see some sort of fairy book character appearing instead they look at me as if I`m a ghost Nelly it`s your long grey dress depicting the Victorian era can you not afford a new modern dress? I have plenty for special occasions you now that ,but I`m happy as I am.

People would stop and stare more so if I had done what I had planned that was to fit fairy lights externally to the cottage, what a wonderful site that would be but no because we will soon be blanketed into darkness.

Albert listen turn the wireless up my God they have entered into the Netherlands now what have Netherlands done to Germany? Nothing ,that man wants world domination Albert it will not be long before bombers will be coming over our heads because whole of Europe is industrialised, and Sheffield will be targeted because of its steel production.

Nelly, I don`t think coalfields will be affected but essential services will, but if so, we must be prepared to help ,Albert what can you do now at your age? Nelly, I expect a lot of Ariel bombings for if the war is to be won it will be in the air, hush listen to the wireless they have moved into France and Belgium.

Nelly in our cottage we could be safe but if bombs drop on the industrial areas like coalmining then the communities are in great danger so I am going to dig out a shelter beyond the garden that will house at least a dozen people as I have some corrugated sheeting for the roof.

Maybe we can make some sort of shelter in the forest as we need to be ready for Germany to have Netherlands France and Belgium means their airfields are nearer to ours ,but first I think they will go for the docklands ,Albert you seem pretty sure of yourself.

Nelly we have an Empire but if UK was to fall then so would the Empire, well that's how I see it and the war is in testifying ,well Albert if he was to so much scratch this cottage I`ll personally go and put his lights out .

Nelly many of his own people would like to see back of him for his life could be in danger and if he lives through this someone some were will assassinate him, all pure speculation from me as some academics and historians may differ I only hope I am around to see my speculations to be right.

Well ,Albert you have said a lot, that I wonder how you obtain your information ,Ben has a radio transmitter and much information reaches us through our judiciary and Ben is also officer in charge of the home front as he is now recruiting from the miners because according to the reports we are expecting air raids they are not sure but have to be ready.

Herr Hitler is not hanging about in his intentions Nelly he has planned this for a long time but if any of them come to hang about here it will be in Creepy Hollow.

Albert we only heard a few days ago about how imminent the war was yet it seems as if it`s be going on for some time ,I think so too as we only know what we are told but it could mean many things to be in short supply as I hear ration books are to be issued, Albert if that be the case you`ll find an increase in poaching ,true and an increase my presence.

What about your workshops? I`m selling it off to someone about 3 mile away, I am clearing it all out everything as I am, well I want some free time I`ve had enough and quite happy as I find myself, and you Nelly ought to slow down.

Albert I can see me being in more demand ,in what way ? The Womens league ,Nelly let others get more involved both of us should be taking it easy it`s not the money nor family responsibilities Albert you are right as always so get your coat on and lets walk again through the estate holding hands and admiring all in front of us as we did many years ago.

Nelly what`s got into you? Come Albert let`s pretend we are young again carefree and happy with little in our pockets but a body and soul full of love for each other as we sit on park seat until it was almost dark as I would rush home to say to mom and dad that we have been working on something which was true as it was our love and devotion for each other and that has never faltered after all these years.

Nelly, I love you as much now as I did then so what`s brought this on? Albert it`s you as I see some days you are less active you are tiring quickly which is understandable and I am pleased you have decided to call it a day s we don`t need it what we need is more time for one another.

Albert as we sit here reminiscing I can see the hazel tree that you would view the branches to see what would make a good walking stick as you would sell them to many walking groups that would pass this way.

I am not going to say they were happy days far from it as we make our own happiness as we used to say ``for what we achieve today is to build upon tomorrow`` Albert, what is it ?

This war, for here our children would play Geoffrey would sit and carve as we would say be careful with the knife as other two would climb trees and chastise each other ,then go into the orchard to steal Sir Harry`s apples they never thought that if they went to his front door he would give them some, as they would say dad they taste better when nicked.

Sniff, sniff, Albert don`t cry ,Nelly it`s this war as many will suffer as there is little they can do only adhere to governments policies and afterwards some maybe given ribbons to affix to their coats as they will tell their grandchildren of their heroics but will fail to tell them they had to kill to achieve a ribbon coat, sniff, sniff, Albert come let`s go home.

Nelly no one in their right minds wants war after securing great advancement in industrial technology and development of new communities the phone wireless new estates schools, communications and production have all contributed to a better standard of living not just here but throughout Europe yet having secured that and many more we are to throw it all away to be confronted with piles of rubble as we search for our dead.

Chapter 47

Sheffield is Burning

Nelly children at schools have been issued with gas masks I for if the Germans can`t shoot us they are to gas and now we are in darkness at nights for no lights to be seen from the outside as enemy aircraft fly above destination Sheffield the steel city.

Nelly all the road signs are removed and shelters are being built for protection from air raids as now the sky is active with bombing aircraft as many fields have search lights to detect German airplanes long before they approach Sheffield, it's a deterrent but not cure as we at night now muster on the rise here and view Sheffield burning from the bombers who have got through, Sheffield some 15 mile away lights up the skies that many can see miles away only to comment that Sheffield is getting to night.

As Sheffield burns it becomes more visual for further attacks as now the skies are fully active with aerial fights from fighter planes ``spitfires`` speedily darting in and out of German aircraft formations and shooting them down in horrific explosions in the air and on the ground whilst searchlights on the ground identify the enemy aircraft in assisting the fighter planes to come out of the dark clouds to attack, as it appears mainly night attacks we see ,as I tell friends they can see it much better and safer from here at the cottage.

I can tell you this my friends the war is intensifying day by day as it has proven me right to say Germany had planned this a long time ago has Hitler claims his National Party to last a thousand years, well he is certainly making impressions as most of British cities are now under attack by German bombers by day and night.

Bombardment after bombardment as we look on an high rise viewing the coal fields and can only watch ,and accept food to be in short supply in rationing as bread is now discoloured and tastes all gritty with much bran mixed in it as we are to accept anything as there is no chose.

The onlookers look sadly on as I comfort Nelly to know we have our own source of meat and a store of plenty as we see problems of war effecting many from rationing of food to worn clothes of patched up appearances.

As now it appears a little quieter and the onlookers can safely return to their homes, as I turn to Nelly to say many things could have be done in improving conditions and the environment but now everything is overseen null and void as the war rages on and Nelly there are massive casualties on both sides as the recruitment drive is on for if one is 18 and not in essential work than they are called upon to fight ,a National Service of conscription as they are rushed into training then whisked to battlefields across Europe as now we are faced with the enemy on the door step.

Albert ,its war as many fight it out whilst many are taken prisoners and brought in land, some around the mining industry here and many being Italians as they are encamped a few miles away under strict security and sometimes come this way maybe here for if any coal mines are damaged then they can clear it up and could be killing their own men,

Nelly they come for exercise in and round the quarry so you be careful in offering then refreshments as you do for with the convey they could drive off to anywhere ,no they cannot Albert for they are under armed security and I ask the captain in charge who allows me with escorts to offer them bits of comfort sometimes pieces of chocolate or an odd scone or two.

Albert sometimes they go further on to the hall what Matt had as the army have taken it over Nelly, I know that what`s your point ? Well its near Creepy Hollow ,Nelly they go there for accountability as prisoners of war, well Albert they seem a happy lot no doubt pleased to be out of combat and nothing to do but wait till the war is over.

Albert, to try and escape would be futile as all of them are dressed in khakis overalls with a large blue patch on the back and not knowing to where they are as they would soon be recaptured, Nelly they are happy here well away from conflict with nothing to do but just sit it out and enjoy your tip bits.

Albert, sometimes the convoy stop along the avenue of beech trees that look so picturesque this time of year and with their Dodge trucks of people carriers all painted in brown and greens of a camouflage pattern giving off a sharp whiff of petrol a smell so foreign to our woodland atmosphere of sweet aroma foliage.

Albert it`s not just here but all around the coal fields as many try to abuse the Italians by throwing objects at them and voicing obscenities that we object to ,but it`s what is to be expected as some mothers here will never see their sons again ,as tempers rise in this hostile world we live in ,that one man has created, no I don`t mean God as I refer to Hitler the opposite to Godliness and how he gained power over millions to take them into a theatre of war that will result in the death of millions that will be talked about for many years to come meanwhile this war will drag on for a number of years for this is only the beginning.

Nelly I feel for the young men as I will lose the apprentices Albert you already have done by selling the business off, no Nelly thay come to me once a week for tutorials and any odd jobs about the area as they don`t get much money to take home so I find them something to do.

I fear for the dark nights as it will be total darkness no street lighting no lights maybe a few hand held torches but the darkness will promote thieving on the estate once more as we can do little to stop it, Albert don`t be so cynical for people will not have the time and those who are unemployed will be too sick to poach and the employed will be too tired as you will have an open market of sales of game.

Albert the unemployed don`t receive much assistance pay and will try many things to achieve a little extra money but if it`s illegal like poaching and get caught they could get their money stopped as they will be found fit to work ,so I don`t see a problem there Nelly perhaps you`re right as I concern myself too much for Matt doesn`t seem bothered nor Ben more bothered about people thieving from crops when ready in the fields as they target potatoes peas and carrots.

But I am concerned about the avenue of Beech trees that must have been planted there many years ago perhaps when this estate was a settlement during the conquest that they are to be bought down to assist the war effort and that saddens me for beauty to give way to progress at a cost of a diminishing estate ,Nelly this once beautiful estate will eventually just become a walk through to the church.

Albert when towns and cities are under threat from enemy bombing like Sheffield that we see burning who cares about an unimportant estate ?

Nelly it hurts as we both know of nothing else, this has been our life together as all around us is changing as more and more land is required for housing as the population increases, Albert this war is going to change many things when it`s over.

Chapter 48

Nelly You Worry Me

Nelly you worry me as you are too involved in local affair`s, let younger people do more as age has caught up with both of us we cannot do it anymore we are now at a state where if we go through the day aches and pain free then we have had a good day and for the first hour in the mornings we cannot do anything as I takes a lengthy time to wake up.

Albert it is comforting to know you care Nelly don`t joke about it for if ever we needed each other now is the time for we only have memories wonderful memories and some not so wonderful, Nelly that's not what I am getting at it is you as I changes in you your gait and your activity is less as you attempt to do things and your diet is little.

Nelly you should go to the doctor for a check -up and stop getting concerned about others Albert its others that come here who are concerned about me ,then you accept that there is a problem ,I did n t say that but if it pleases you I will go and see the doctor.

Albert it`s this age thing that everyone encounters ,no Nelly as many never reach that stage for wars and conflicts trespasses upon their young and active lives as people like us must embrace all around us to know we are the lucky ones who pass on our knowledge of the past before historians distort it as we have no future to cherish or to catalogue .

Nelly stop it as something is ailing you and I want to know what it is; Nelly is it theses Italians encamped on our doorstep as prisoners of war? Good lord, I am pleased for them, as they are far away from any conflict my thoughts are about the miners who are threatening to strike for more money, but politicians are bullying them not to strike.

Nelly we should not take sides but assist those in need as it is unfair to comment or condemn but people strike from work because of reasons and parliament of elected bodies are elected to govern for the best of the majority and many arguments will arise for or against the miners problem as we have an coalition government.

Albert no matter I cannot change as some will come here in desperation and I will assist as I have always done as you yourself will ignore trespass.

Nelly all this maybe so but it is you I`m concerned about as you seem more concern about other people as it is an ongoing system in your nature of things that's way the churches and other institutions are always available the Salvation Army the International Red Cross your Womens League and many more are called upon for if there was no cause for them then we would be living in an utopia society as that will never be so.

Our strife and struggle will continue maybe not in the form we see today as there will always be competition it is what it causes that we must be ready to offer a hand up to those who have fallen.

Nelly I say we as I should say others as I feel we have done what we can its good on a sunny day and from spring to autumn to welcome our walkers and church goers with pleasantries as we offer refreshment and sale from our much presented sale tables of much choice anything beyond that we should refrain from and reduce our involvement in village concerns.

Nelly who is this coming with a fancy car now there are more cars than horses and people say there is no money about, now just feast your eyes on that, well who is it?

It`s Matt ,Nelly hiya Matt what brings you here? Nelly Rose has died late last night she had a stroke during the day, she visited Sir Harry`s grave laid a few flowers then took ill her last words were`` please God help our boys``

Matt were you there ? Yes. as I am always there, no I mean at the cemetery ?No her house staff came and told me ,the doctor was called and she died soon after and done well for her age 97 and never found happiness until she found Sir Harry as his life was nearly ruined as Rose came to the rescue.

Albert you`re quiet Nelly and you Matt ,I have her to thank as she saved me from being sent into an orphanage and cared for me as my parents ,well that I wish not to talk about as Rose was like mother to me.

A real fine women who helped to save this estate on many occasions that's why we rallied around her at the show and warned off any unwanted quests, and the mining communities will be sadden too as she played her part in womens rights and had many friends in London doing the same thing.

A sad day put pleased to know that her contribution here will not go unnoticed as we write another chapter in the book of remembrance .

Matt what will happen now? Why what do you mean? The estate ,well her daughter Alice who married Seth Moorhouse from Selby was planning to come here to live as they have bought the cottage at the entrance on the east of the estate.

I know Rose has left a Will as I am the Lasting Power of at Attorney I cannot say what it contains, no I will not say until after the funeral but assure you that the estate is well protected.

Albert she had a good innings and found true love in Sir Harry who had his moments before she amended his ways Matt it`s not that it`s my memories as I was only a lad and she could have been my sister but was more like a Mom as she would say ``I`m baking to day and if I had ,some apples I would make a pie `` I got the message and would go and come back with a shirt full as in those days it was a common practise to stuff anything down ones shirt.

Matt, thank you for calling as feel tired and wish to lay down Albert you are doing too much, Matt time and time again, I keep telling him to slowdown but no he keeps creating work for himself, Nelly I must go and I`ll keep you informed.

Albert it was only a while ago as you said I worry you it`s about time you started to look at yourself no Nelly you come first always have and always will as I promised to cherish you and always will as you women are the inspiration of mankind as you fight on to secure equality only to be denied by un grateful people in important roles in society ,as you must ask who put them their as you will be there at the beginning and at the end.

Albert go to sleeps you will feel much better later, Nelly she was like a mother to me as she loved me as if I was one of her own as our education was none we had to use intelligence to secure an education and now look what education has bought about 2 worlds wars in our life time for they cannot blame intelligence.

Nelly give me a drop off that rosehip syrup as I feel a cold coming on its of standing outside at night watching Sheffield burn as those German bombers are relentless in attempting to destroy our whole infrastructure as we are only ,well not a year into war Nelly we have lived through some evil times not of our making as we pursued good times that was of our making.

Albert, do you want a Doctor? No Nelly I`ve caught a cold that`s all but you are right I ought step back and enjoy life a bit more but that sounds selfish as the whole country is in desperation not knowing what to expect as those Italians are better off than us for they know what to expect.

Nelly times like this I think of John Will and Geoff all those years ago and it`s come back to haunt me ,what more does society want from us? Now they destroy towns and cities.

God never made man to do such things in destroying each other as some think this world belongs to them it belongs to every living thing in it as it has a right to a life as anyone else as this is not our world as we are only part of it as we go about killing each other in serving our apprenticeship of time.

Nelly at times I feel as if I have had enough ,Albert don`t talk like that, come take this rosehip syrup and try to sleep .

Nelly, Rose was a, women of true grit and determination as she could stand up to any man as her husband was horrible in drink, but Rose dealt with him as she was not going to be bullied or mistreated.

Now I will sleep awhile as this cold lingers on but leave the curtains open for if the bomber come back I can see Sheffield burning , Albert go to sleep ,Nelly here I am with a cold as it was me who was worrying about you and telling you not to be so involved and slow down, as we will for tomorrow we walk along the lime stone road way until we reach the old workshop that was there and talk about the times we shared together .

Nelly those were lovely moments of a young couple so much in a lasting love that not even a 2 worlds wars could interfere with.

Albert that was lovely to hear

Yes ,Nellie as I worry about you, Nelly don`t cry .

Chapter 49

It`s No Longer A Minor Problem

The miners have returned to work under duress as they are far from happy as there are so many private mines s it is difficult to get a consensus of opinion as the problem is still with them and not a lot will happen whilst the war rages on as many think the needs of the county must come first as coal is of paramount of importance to the country`s economy and survival.

Albert you only know that of what passers bye say for there are many opinions but I do know Matt is annoyed with the situation for the wallpaper shops that his wife have opened in and around the valley she has had to close for supplies for paper materials and inks have stopped as much is required for the war effort.

They have some contracts for the ministry for some publicity posters and some other things, but wallpaper manufactory has finished for now Nelly they have lots of other things to print like ration books lots of small things as I hear it's not effected the work force.

Nelly I`m feeling much better now and Roses funeral is tomorrow as I would have hated to miss it, Alice her daughter is seeing to things regarding a wake and they are now in doubt what to do in buying the cottage for she could move into what was her mom`s property but I think Matt will take it.

Albert I can see the hall being occupied by the army for the duration of the war so that is out of the question but I know Matt keeps a constant eye on it as he was annoyed with a captain there because their lorries had ripped up some turf that was not necessary I was told, Matt was furious and gave the captain a good rollicking and demanded that the turf be replaced and army personal to use litter bins.

Also, he said ,``If I see any prisoners, mis- treated like I saw the other day then your command will hear of it` and I expect the hall to be respected for the rent does not cover damages ,any incurred damages you are expected to make good.

Up at Abbes Walk were Matt was staying he took up the residence that Rose had and Alice is happy in having the annex so that`s sorted but I thought you said he had bought the cottage ,he has , but why? I don`t know but he will have his reasons as I too thought he would have problems but no they are only minor problems .

Nelly last night Sheffield suffered heavily from German bombing as the sky was lit from late last night to early hours of this morning as these foundations shuddered but it may have been from gun fire as the German planes came in from the east and returned by same route and that appears why some were shot down and I saw two pilots bale out and could be in the estate as I am expecting a search party anytime.

Albert ,did you see them drop? They are in the forest it was difficult to see but they are in there ,well Albert eat up as we can join the search what will they do to then when caught .probably interrogate them and then send them to a prison camp.

Nelly the searches are here now some army personal and a few minors ,Sir may we join you ? Are you Albert Lodge ? Yes, then you may join us ,Captain they will be in that areas laying low till darkness but they`ll not know to where they are not even having a compass

Albert you know this terrain so we follow you ,no you don`t Captain as they could be armed, and I am not but you are, so I guide you.

Captain some men over there, and some on the left and rest go forward as I think they are in front of us as everyone stay quiet and still as they could be 2 hundred yards away so stay still and quiet.

Albert you seem sure of yourself ,how do you know they could be over there? Officer the pilots don`t know we are here but the wild life do, firstly it was the birds who took to the flight then the animals sensed our presence as their smell is much greater than ours as they ran in the opposite direction that's how I know.

Captain be careful as they may shoot it out as they are directly in front of us ,Captain may I attempt to bring them out to avoid any bloodshed ,Albert no one would care if we shot them I would and so would a court of justice as you are not here to shoot them but to apprehend them ,well what if they run or fire at us Captain what if, what if, what if, we are discussing that now standby .

Astung ,Astung, ik spraken outslander comest hier maken de snell, Captain I spoke German well I think I did it sounded good whether pronounced good I don`t know . Albert hush , here they come 2 of them.

With hands up and quickly searched and disarmed and escorted to a waiting vehicle ,Captain I said see they are treated as P O W as I went to the, prisoners and offered a cold drink to the surprise of the Captain, Captain next time you come to me it would be comforting if you would introduce yourself for I know who you were but you did n t know that so always introduce yourselves.

You are Terry Mrs Moore son and you once was an apprentice to me Mr Lodge Sir I know that but wished not for the army searches to know ,Why ? Because they fear this estate of being the suicide estate and that the church and grounds to be haunted ,nonsense ,well many believe it ,that a grey lady all dressed in a long grey gown and a pudding shaped hat haunts all round here, good lord Captain that's Nelly my wife and still very much alive.

Terry how are your folks ? Fine thank you Sir, we now live other side of town as Dad still works for cooperative retail industry then give them my regards ,Sir no call me Albert ,Albert when I served with you I won a bursary grant and was given a £5 note I was a winner of best piece of work entered Albert I still have the £5 note as memento of achievement as you presented it to me.

Captain I am pleased to see my guidance and instruction has rewarded you well, now you take care and treat your prisoners according to the Geneva Convention. But what are you doing here Home Guard do these Jobs?

I have brought some Italian prisoners to the hall they were captured as their boat was going down off Whitby coast there were some Germans who we have left at the prison camp near Hull the ship they were on was a troop carrier as many questions are being asked on why was a German troop carrier near our coast line.

Captain I must go so take care.

Albert, we have a funeral to go to Nelly we have lots of time well I want some time to talk to people as there will be people there who we have not seen for a long time ,Nelly don't fuss so as we have lots of time Albert get a move on get out of those rags and into your suit and here have your rosehip syrup.

You drive Nelly a I am still trying to put my tie on and go Creepy Hollow way as they still call it that as now people tip their household rubbish in it ,it`s not them Albert, its building contractors rather than take it to the council tip and pay as they would have charged the householder to take it away as many try and blame the travellers` but we know who it is as the fines are high if caught.

Albert look there are many from the mining community and my womens league members are here to and some Salvationists, come we can go in now for the service.

The vicar has done and presented a lovely tribute to a woman who will be long remembered not just by her family but by many who had the pleasure in meeting her as many families from the crofters of past to new housing estates of today.

At the wake many showed what real people are as I now cling to Alberts arm and with the other hand, I have my walking stick a hazel stick cut and carved for me some 60 odd years ago.

Nelly, as many surprised me in calling as they noticed me and came and loved me as we all in meeting each other cried a little, Albert these are my kind of people as I have never pretended to be what I am not and many of these people present today I have helped in a time of need and how wonderful I feel in doing so

Nelly what is it Albert I don t know but take me home as I cannot hold my tears back as I am in my past my mind is flooded with memories sweet wonderful memories as these people here today remind me of.

Albert will you from us have a large remembrance stone erected at the head of their place of rest saying what such a person she was ,Nelly don`t cry as the mining community have already approached me for such a thing as it will be done.

Yes, Albert the miners I would have never thought that from the hard and harsh life the crofters had that a mining community would emerge of something we had never seen before and not knowing what to expect only to find such a community of fellowship unity and full of song and music for they really touched me when they sang so beautiful at the show ground and then their sounds of brass filled air for miles around.

Albert its times like those that linger in my mind for ever as they are a social class that this country thrives upon ,no matter what industrial problems they may have they are my kind of people as they have brought much wealth and community spirit to a place that was going no were.

Nelly say cheerio as we must go now for I think you are tired Albert ,I am take me home as I have said it before but I keep seeing people who remind me of so many things ,now I am in an habit of saying to younger girls who sometimes help me when I am out shopping. not to grow old as they smile to say ``I will try not to ``as I think of what a troubled world ,we live in.

Albert its night after night with these bombers I can`t sleep for the noise and that's at Sheffield as the whole sky lights up as we see German planes being shot at as search lights situated in the fields nearby focus on them to be shot at and hit for us to see their air craft explode or spin out of control.

No one passes comment and say poor devil or God be with you, no it`s not like that as onlookers cheer in celebrations to see the result of combat as another enemy plane is destroyed.

Many think it`s safer down the pits as they don`t know what is happening above not knowing if they have a home to go to or not at the end of their shift as there is little they can do.

Chapter 50

What It Means to Me?

Nelly, we have the wireless on nearly all day and its bad news as Germany have a stranglehold on Europe as we are beaten only a miracle can save us but save us from what? A dictatorship well I have been dictated to all my life ,Nationalism, well what does that mean? Everything to be of national interests O K I `m fine with that, not to have a royalty well what difference would that mean to me? Not to have an Empire again how would that affect me? All questions but the Otterman had an Empire China had an Empire Germany Italy and Spain all had Empires even in religion as the Roman Catholics was an Empire as so was Spain of Empire of Spanish Catholics,

So, what would it mean to us? The Vikings the Romans and scores of lesser forces have had their time here but we beat them all in being industrialised first and have a royalty these are my observations but more learned men then me will no doubt put a different perspective to it as Russia does not bow to anyone as they are and always will be a force not to mess about with and I see Germany in fear of them.

This war is a senseless war as there will be no winners but a magnitude of losers as man cannot live in harmony as he is constantly at war as historians will look to reasons as futurists will look at greater weaponry to maintain power over others .

Albert this country is on its knees as our forces have put up a great fight, but Germany were well prepared as their subs are ripping our supply line to bits with their torpedoes and the land forces other side of the channel are struggling to get back to England.

As they do they will find London burning along with Sheffield and many more cities, Nelly England well I say England meaning UK has taken a heavy beating within one year by standing back in watching them rearm they were warned and not just about rearming but about treatment of ethnic groups as many industrialist across Europe pulled out and transferred much of their capital to America, Philips electrical group of Holland are an example as they escaped to Americas they are Jews who are persecuted .

Nelly according to ,no Matt has told me as he is in contact with someone who feeds him news and it seems that Hitler is going for ethnic groups to rid them from Europe, Albert you know some stuff, Nelly much of it is on the radio and America are being requested to help out .

Albert I can`t somehow get interested in tactics of this and that I am interested in the suffering of people and what is happening around me like what am I going to do with the German parachutes you retrieved ,why don`t you want them? Of course, I do I`m debating what to with them make a frock ,dress, boiler suit , or overalls.

Nelly how you feeling now as you were not too good at the wake ? Albert I`m tiring much sooner now it`s this age thing so I am slowing down nothing to jump out of bed for in the morning as now we have got rid of much of the live- stock we don`t need it Nelly we don`t need many things now ,time has come for not to be interested in many things yes and that spinning wheel I am giving to Alice Roses daughter as she loved it Nelly she is not a child she is 60 odd year old Albert she will love it and cherish it Nelly you`re not planning in going anywhere are you? No Albert but I would be happy to know it`s got a good home anyway I doubt if anyone will have me.

Nelly don`t fool about ,Albert we have no family to pass our things onto and what we have is no longer required Nelly stop it as we should not be discussing of what may be and if your brothers heard you they would be none too pleased ,so cheer up and pass the blackberry jam.

Albert who are these people who keep prodding about these, ash covered path`s? Nelly there are 2 paths that are man- made and maybe about a hundred year ago predominately through the Victorian ere as everything was thrown away and buried glass bottles stone jars earthenware ladies make up pots and many different types of stone pots beer and soft drink bottles and decorative pot lids all are much sought after items that realise a good price.

There has been some good finds of the Victorian period whilst many research historically periods from the Conquest through to the Magna Carter and through the centuries as many battles were fought as we know about a mile away there is Oliver`s Mount ,as Cromwell passed this way Nelly all round us is steeped in history and if I was a lad again I would search for it whilst the miners bring out fossils of hundreds if not thousands of years old.

Many churches in a ten mile radius of here date back to the 12 Century of lime stone built and still looking good and I still don`t know what those 3 or 4 stone steps with a flat stone top under the walnut tree near the church were for ,as many have their own ideas.

Nelly that should tell you something as this cottage could be standing on much history and if so than we have been good keepers of the past.

Albert it is my family who have preserved the past as this cottage has been in the family since it was built around about 1180 when the church was built.

Nelly you constantly remind me as you tell people who walk by or stop awhile and ponder over your tales of the past and share a cuppa with you ,yes and I am in delight to associate with them as these communities have no history and it is recognisable to see this estate losing much of its appeal not that of the beautiful trees pasture land or wild life and limestone walls that have embraced its enclosure.

Nelly why are we reminiscing? We should be amongst it as the sky is quiet and still after many days of aerial combat ,something has happened it appears Sheffield is taking a rest bite Albert there is something wrong the skies are clear, put the wireless on Albert I think the cells want recharging, listen to the news ,We are fighting back as the spitfires have done their job and caused the Hun many losses ,Albert after 2 years

Germany have failed to trespass upon our country as we had to withdraw many troops from tragedy from the French coastline but now it is back to attack for America have joined the allies forces as the fight now will be taken to them.

It is a crying shame as many ribbon`s medals and decorative coats will once again be proudly worn but sadly not by everyone as cemeteries across Europe will testify as it does for the 1st WW

Albert our memories torment use as we should be out walking but I think the planes are coming back as I hear sirens, air raid is imminent so with helmet`s on and run for cover ,Albert it`s not an air raid it`s an accident at the coal mine.

Come Albert as some may require help ,we go in the car, Albert ,look many women weeping and in a delirious state ,this is awful the pit yard is full of women weeping and screaming as the cage brings more miners out as rescue workers carry stretcher`s of the dead as silence falls momently to suddenly change to howling screams of sadness and disappointments.

Another cage will bring out some alive as love one`s rush forward to ensure their husbands are in good hands whilst horrors of what happened filter through that of a fall a massive fall resulting to many dead.

The howling of the pit sire blast out as all in the valley are alerted as a community of human fellowship band together to share a time of sorrow. Albert this is what I see and what will be remembered as these people will not be forgotten.

Albert all this will not be forgotten Nelly what`s that ? This ,in what you see here what`s the matter with you? These people are the backbone of industrial requirements `` black gold`` and give their lives in achieving it for they cannot give more.

Albert come lets go home .Albert you should have not have come here as you are in flu you should be in bed , Nelly you do fuss ,Albert you will not be told ,you look ill you should be in bed, it`s only an cold.

Why are you stopping here ? Creepy Hollow now just look there a one- time beautiful spring that brought much pleasure to many in fact it was a life saver and took many lives as many would fight and kill over it and that tree there if it could only speak now we are faced with household rubbish strewn all over it .

Nelly I am annoyed with the public spoiling a once impressive estate as its going through difficult times but it will bounced back as it has done for centuries whilst all around it changes and Nelly I never did get you a fox fur wrap that was fashion at the time as now much wild life seems to lay low in the forests as the sound of planes and gun fire frightens them but not the crows who come back to the tall trees at entrance to the estate ,strange that as they seem scarce during winter only to return in spring,

Nelly what amuses me most is the minors who talk of seeing the ghost of ,the grey lady and they visualise you in your grey dress standing at the gate of the lodge on misty or foggy days as they see your figure then you disappear into the Lodge as these miners find many things to talk about as they frequent their working men`s club and love a bit of mystery.

Nelly, Father Paddy Stanley Oates wanted to build a Catholic Church here and after all these years St Helena at Abbes Walk has opened its doors to Catholic followers, pity he never lived to see it ,now there was a man if I ever admired one but sometimes I failed to understand him as he was a man of much talent and influence as once I said ``you are a Roman Catholic`` he looked at me with those piercing eyes and replied I am a Catholic.

I called him, a man of presence as he would laugh with that roar of laughter that passers- by would stop and listen as his presence was always noticed and welcomed as those at Abbes Walk will never forget and if one rests a while at the old sales pitch that now houses a shop they will see in a small part of the garden a displayed plague of him denoting him to be the developer of the site.

Nelly all these things mean a lot to me .

Chapter 51

My God I have Tried

Albert you are attempting things that you should not be bothered about go sit in the garden and talk to passer`s by as there appears more people about today as much of enemy aircraft is not so often now ,but the Italians are still here, yes and getting a lot of abuse as many shout at them but that is expected when some may have lost their sons as we have said it all before and some villages thought they were stopping in the hall in luxury how wrong they are a they are camped in Nissen huts a rough shelter of corrugated tin roofs in fields about mile away.

I do wish people would stop making stores up for its bad enough listening to lord Haw ,Haw on the wireless the Irishman broadcasting German propaganda and people believe him as they believe anything as we suffer in in thick fog not knowing who is who when out in a period of frightening days and nights of darkness.

Albert stop it as you are full of comments and tales of the past just take this mug of tea and sit out there and talk to the animals and do not go by the rabbits with that knife in your hand Nelly I want the knife for my apple look Albert old Fred is coming.

Thanks that is all I need for he is full of wind and water Albert ,alright mate? See Kharkov has been retaken as the Germans are suffering great losses in the harsh winter there,

Fred victories will be celebrated as losses are ignored and stories of valour will echo through the ranks of military engagements as young men are influenced by such deeds not knowing what price they have to pay and sorrow it brings home to their kin folk .

Albert what`s wrong with that? Man has always had to fight for what is expected of him for there is no alternative for he cannot stand aside at the mercy of some crazed fool with weapons to destroy mankind it`s alright saying talk and talk but not if you are attacked this man attacked Poland and march his forces into it .

Then the low countries to whom we were or are allied to so what are you saying ? Are you saying we should not defend our allied friends ?

Fred no I am not as I have this argument many times, we should be aware of countries arming for such purposes.

Fred we have no say as arguments will linger on and on so here have some apple with me as Nelly is bringing a pot of tea for you, Fred I hear the losses were many in the pit disaster, 52 killed Albert a terrible accident ,Fred that was no accident as accidents mean no reasons and there are always reasons why things happen.

Albert, I don`t know as I had little schooling Fred, that`s a laugh for I stole mine ,what do you mean you stole it ? Just that, Albert education is free ,no it is not as everything has to be paid for, the education system we see today that you relate is paid for out of taxes.

Fee paying schools were or are paid for over and above the tax system I pinched mine by learning off others.

Albert you confuse me, Fred the state regulators love you to say that as you should be prepared to argue points with them and less you know the better for them, Fred never accept the position you find yourself in always try and in prove upon it ,in other words what you do today learn and improve on it for tomorrow.

Albert thanks for the tea

I watched him walk away as he failed to see squirrels scampering up the trees and going on the blind side and the fox crouching down whilst Fred walked on and I doubt if he noticed anything around him how blind some villages can be as all around us is filled with nature and if I don`t feed the fox he will be back tonight to feed himself ,and God knows what they think of all these firework`s we have been having as the whole land shook to the delight of roof tilers who are gainfully employed.

Nelly any of that rose hip syrup left ?Albert it is a doctor you want as syrup is good for you but the doctor is the first person to see he is the one to diagnose your problems Albert you have no colour and if you have flu you could give me it Nelly I don`t know as I just feel uninterested in things and tired and should be sleeping more as I am not, so have you got anything to help my sleeping?

Albert you should be in bed but no you get up start doing things then soon tired again ,Nelly I`ll be alright now it`s quieter on a night and less noise and this fog doesn't help ,well Fred didn't seem bothered about it no he wouldn`t Nelly as he goes for a few cabbages from that 12 acre field he`ll be selling them tonight in the ,miners arms, or working men`s club I saw his bag as he will make several trips and if Matt knows he would let the dogs out as crime rate has risen sharply since the outbreak of war.

Now the law society is suggesting that offenders are put to work in the community as some are wanting to go to prison rather than go to war another way of dodging conscription but magistrates are aware of it and disappoint many minor law breakers by giving them a warning as then they are quickly put into uniform as punishment is wavered whilst in custody or go down the pits .

Many falsely claim to be sick, but doctors are wise to it as many are sent for a medical, so they are left with little chose either work in essential services like the pits or wear a uniform.

In Fred case as he is too old for either service so he will be sent down to work in prison on something that will contribute to the war effort as no matter how they try they cannot beat the system for when this war is over there will be questions asked from local level to national level ass all will be judged.

If that be the case I pity anyone who may be judged by Ben`s son Edward as he is now a Judge a circuit Judge mainly sitting at Sheffield and Nelly you knew that last night, Albert you were sleeping and this morning well you were coughing and spluttering all over the place well Nelly I can tell you he has a murder case coming up.

Nelly is that lavendulan ? Albert never thought you would know that as it is usually called Lavender and you will find some on your pillow tonight as it is good to assist sleeping.

Its them bombs and another thing there are people around here that I have not seen before, now who are these people? Albert they are people who call at the hall in respect of the prisoners some civil service people as Matt meets them regarding prisoner`s safety and welfare and some prisoners require a judging about their conduct the army deals with it but any civil offences then magistrates deal with it.

Albert our wood burning logs are low, Nelly I`ll see to it tomorrow not now ,for we shall soon be going to bed not yet albert its only 8 o clock I want to listen to the news and Victor Silvester orchestra and Vera Lynn singing ,well I ought to close the curtain s and light a few candles or the air raid wardens will come knocking Albert they will be here at 8 30 for their Damson wine.

Nelly I`m sick of this war as now they are going to cut down the Beech trees all 4 of them that stand across the path- way one has our notice on that says Nelly`s Lodge and I wish they were doing it tomorrow as they could cut me a few logs for our fire as that would help the war effort ,Albert how could that help the war effort? I wouldn`t be in conflict with you.

Nelly the whole estate is changing and I cannot stop it my ,God I have tried were many have failed for Sir Harry had lost control until your Dad came to his rescue and I have been there when required and has a magistrate I have had to put right many of his misjudgements and I feel in fairness I won the support of the people that contributed so much to our popularity.

Chapter 52

In Time of War

Nelly turn the wireless up its Vera Lynn singing. and we are making much ground in France as Parish is retaken and Russians are in Poland and making a push for Germany as Americans are pushing north through Italy.

Albert you take great interest what`s happening in the war as I look ahead that when the war is over we will still be rationed with many things in short supply as many things will take time to be marketed again as our industrial cities took a powdering and there will have to be an housings program as many service men return home.

Nelly we have come through 2 WWs and for us it makes little difference Albert we are not through this one yet, no but everything is going well ,Nelly nothing will be the same again as industry will look for new innovations and ergonomics as will farming whilst labour will have to adopt to change.

Change in industry and its work force that will demand better working conditions health and safety will play a greater part as the employed will demand a lesser working week too and I say demand as they will be more united in their grievances and cannot be ignored as they contributed well towards the war effort.

I believe there will great social and economic changes as lessons have been learnt and working men will secure and play their part in everyday politics as unification will embrace itself into new and enlarged communities and similar will happen in politics to ensure that man does not destroys himself.

Albert, the war is not over .Nelly it could go on for 2 more years perhaps longer as Germany has lost the war and should surrender and save many German lives as Herr Hitler demands his armies to fight to the end and not to surrender as many high ranging German officers tell him that they cannot fight on.

With several attempts on his life and losing respect of his ,high ranking advisors he is turning on his General Staff and executing them in trying to find a way out of a fiasco theatre of war.

Nelly the wireless gives out news and it appears allied forces are closing in as Germany will be surround and will have no alternative but to surrender but it will take time.

The newspapers are having a bonanza of sales as its all good news ,Albert what difference would it make to us as we are now in our nineties although you talk as if we are still active as you should have stopped being involved in things long ago but no as you sit their tapping your old clay pipe across the fireplace making predictions of what things may be as you would do well to smarten yourself up move with the times put some boot polish on those boots for we have 3 tins untouched.

Nelly I have no reason to be different and those 3 tins of boot polish about twenty 24 year old and will remain untouched and so will the boot laces in memory of

Geoffrey and his boot and shoe repair shop so don`t lecture me as you go about frightening the public in your long grey dress and pudding flat hat as you will be remembered if only by your ghost whilst I will have long be forgotten except in name of that being Lodge.

No Nelly I am still unwell as I should not be here poking the fire embers as I have not been able to get any logs for the fire as its raining fast.

Albert, I see a boy sheltering under the beech trees I`ll shout to him to come inside .boy its dangerous to shelter under trees when there is thunder and lightning about come inside, here dry yourself down.

Have this warm drink and run home as mister is not well, he has flu and must go to bed .now the rain has let up so go quickly.

Frank. he died during the night as my Mum sat with Nelly until her brothers were informed.

Nelly died 3 months later as she could not live without Albert her only love ,here brothers were at her bed side all in their late 8o`s and 90`s.

Nelly held in one hand a photo of Albert and in the other hand a photo of John and Will and a tin of boot polish .

Sadly Frank all what remains now, of the cottage is just overgrowth has the cottage has long gone as people feel an uneasy presence in passing to be confronted with the thoughts of Nelly the grey lady and when they sight the church again they have an strange feeling but in entering the church many claim to have a most comforting feeling of a welcoming embrace.

For what Albert predicted many were adopted all in a late time of a 2nd WW and soon after.

Frank only thing he did not predict was the end of the coal mining industry as many miners lost their lives in a time of need and in most places where a pit was proudly stands tributes to their labour and devotion.

You and I Frank when telling of it ,people will view us in doubt as we know different and that is all that matters.

The End

Printed in Poland
by Amazon Fulfillment
Poland Sp. z o.o., Wrocław

59757901R00228